Tribune's Oath

Clay Warrior Stories
Book #17

J. Clifton Slater

Tribune's Oath is a work of fiction. Any resemblance to persons living or dead is purely coincidental. I am not an historian although, I do extensive research. This book is about the levied, seasonal Legion of the mid-Republic and not the fulltime Imperial Legion. There are huge differences.

The large events in this tale are taken from history, while the dialogue and close action sequences are my inventions. Some of the elements in the story are from reverse engineering mid-Republic era techniques and procedures. No matter how many sources I consult, history always has holes between events. Hopefully, you will see the logic in my methods of filling in the blanks.

The manuscript for *Tribune's Oath* has been scrutinized, analyzed, and marked up by the eagle-eyed Hollis Jones. With each note and observation, she has removed extra verbiage and tweaked the story. Her editing notes are the reason the tale makes sense and flows. For her work and guidance, I am grateful.

If you have comments, please e-mail me.

E-mail: GalacticCouncilRealm@gmail.com

To get the latest information about my books, visit my website. There you can sign up for my newsletter and read blogs about ancient history.

Website: www.JCliftonSlater.com

Thank you for being a part of Alerio's stories.

Euge! Bravo!

Tribune's Oath

Act 1

Although a successful operation, the invasion of the Punic Coast was also a cluster of escalating problems. By inserting four Legions and leaving them there, the Republic claimed an achievement if not a victory. The real problem started when Proconsul Marcus Regulus fought his way to within a day's march of the defensive walls of the Empire's Capital.

The location left twelve hundred cavalrymen and fourteen thousand Legionaries over eight hundred miles from Rome and reinforcements. When the Senate recalled the fleet, the Legions were stranded on enemy ground. Nearing the end of his Consulship, Marcus Regulus, the expedition's General should have been relieved. Yet, the Senate failed to send a replacement. All these difficulties amounted to troubling times, but they weren't insurmountable.

Meanwhile, four thousand cavalrymen from allies of the Empire and twelve thousand mercenary infantrymen arrived at the Punic capital. Adding to the weight of the forces aligned against the Legions were one hundred African war elephants. However, none of these elements presented the real dilemma for the Legions.

For General Regulus and the Republic, the problem was dressed in a scarlet cloak and wore a Greek helmet with a red and yellow crest that cascaded from the top to the back of his helmet. Once hired as the commander for the Qart Hadasht army, the visible cloak and ornate helmet were everywhere. From the war elephant teams to the horsemen, the companies of mercenaries, and the tribal warriors, he arrived, rallied the forces, and delivered explicit directions in a curt manner. And so, the most dangerous element of the Empire's defense took to the battlefield in the person of a Spartan General.

Welcome to 255 B.C.

Chapter 1 – Thirty-Five Miles

Corporal Philetus added his shield to the wall by crowding in between two Legionaries. He paused for a heartbeat, listening to the war cries from across the combat line. When he isolated a specific roaring voice, he exploded over the top of the shields. Bellowing in reply to a huge mercenary, Philetus' arm and gladius snapped out and cut the side of the big warrior's neck. Blood spurted from the wound and coated men on both sides of the combat line. The Tesserarius landed on his feet, stepped back, and moved out of the shield wall.

"You bled that one good," a servant for Sixth Century noted when the big warrior crumpled to the ground. After handing the Corporal a waterskin, he pointed to the medic who was treating two Legionaries injured by the giant. "That beast was about to force his way through."

"If only he had," Philetus remarked, "I could have killed him before he did the damage."

After visually checking for any new instructions from Centurion Aeneas, the Corporal addressed his squads, "Merchants of Mayhem, tighten your shields. Don't make me come up there and correct your stance."

His words filtered through the squad leaders and the pivot men until all thirty Legionaries of his section heard his words. Men on the three lines chuckled at the idea of stopping in the middle of a fight to receive instructions. They laughed because Philetus, if he thought it would help, was the type of NCO to make those corrections in the middle of a battle. The Corporal returned to prowling behind the three lines seeking another danger to his section.

Aeneas, the combat officer of the Sixth Century, divided his attention between Tesserarius Philetus, Optio Kalem, the three lines of Legionaries to his front, and his maniple's Tribune. His head on a swivel, Centurion Aeneas watched for three things: Threats to his Century's formation; instructions from the staff officer; and the state of his Legionaries.

"First rank, stand by to rotate," Aeneas called. His warning order filtered through the eighty infantrymen. "Second rank, rotate forward, first rank, step back, step back."

The Legionaries at the front felt shields slide in between their scuta. While the fresh arms and legs moved into position, the front rank stepped to the rear of the formation. Servants rushed to the sweating Legionaries. They handed out water and wineskins to the exhausted infantrymen and examined them for injuries requiring medical attention.

Every rotation caused bulges and gaps, even if temporarily, between shields. Aware of the danger while the Legionaries settled into their positions, the NCOs and Centurions issued instructions to reestablish the line. Once their line was straight, they called for alignment with the Centuries on either side.

Behind the Centurions and NCOs, the half maniple's Tribune studied the distribution of his Legionaries to be sure his six Centuries presented a uniformed front. Additionally, the staff officer scanned over his combat line searching the rear of the enemy's ranks for unique threats. Between observing his line and the enemy beyond, he checked for directions from command. Usually delivered as a message by a Junior Tribune or a signal flag, any changes would come from the flank officer for all three maniples, Senior Tribune Emerens.

The senior staff officer coordinated his half of the Legion under directions from the Battle Commander.

"Colonel Sisera, we should push forward," Emerens suggested. "Put the mercenaries on their heels and rout them."

Alerio Sisera let his eyes brush over his first maniple. Although hard pressed, the inexperienced Centuries were managing the Qart Hadasht soldiers. However, moving forward seemed reasonable based only on the fighting at the center of the assault line.

On the left end, Tribune Rapti Galba and the cavalry were engaged in a fight with a less than sure outcome. And farther along the Legion line, in Colonel Ferenc's command, the cavalry from Legion East, was as hard pressed at Alerio's North.

Shifting to the opposite side of his Legion, Alerio watched Centurion Grear Keoki and his skirmishers. They had formed ranks against slashing attacks by mounted horsemen of the Empire.

"I appreciate your confidence in our maniple, Emerens. But I think if we move off our line," Alerio said, "we'll quickly outrun our endcap defenses."

"Yes, Battle Commander," Senior Tribune Emerens agreed in a less than enthusiastic manner.

The junior staff officers, and Alerio's right flank commander, Senior Tribune Cancellus, made their silent protests obvious by the set of their shoulders. None of them liked the remain-in-place order. But holding back the staff from rash decisions was Colonel Sisera's job.

Leadership, Alerio discovered when the Legions moved through the mountain pass, consisted of a balancing act. A Battle Commander needed to be bold enough to garner the respect of the toughest Legionaries while protecting the infantrymen from circumstances that would hurt and demoralize them. He understood that squatting behind their shields was safe but not satisfying.

"Senior Tribunes Emerens and Cancellus. I want the second maniple moved up," Alerio instructed. "And split the third. Send the halves to the ends of our formation. Ask the veterans to cut a dead zone between us and the Empire horsemen."

"Are we relieving the first maniple, sir?" Cancellus inquired.

Rather than answer, Alerio asked, "Have either of you ever seen a waterwheel?"

The Senior Tribunes for the Legion looked at their Battle Commander with puzzled expressions.

"I have, Colonel," a young nobleman spoke up. "In Ostia, they have a grain mill powered by water. I spent an afternoon watching the machine work."

"If you laid on your belly and studied the workings of the waterwheel," Alerio proposed. "Tell me why I asked about it?"

The Junior Tribune bit his lower lip as he pondered the question. Using one hand, he made circular patterns while visualizing the motion of the wheel. Then he added his other hand and, as if stirring a bowl of batter, he allowed his arms to go around and around until a smile crossed his face.

"You're going to rotate first and second maniples," the teen affirmed. Then he recalled. "But Colonel, you said we weren't moving forward."

"Exactly. Like the waterwheel that spins but doesn't travel, we'll rotate the first and second maniples," Alerio described. "Each maniple will advance twice before falling back behind the other formation. Twice up then back. We'll chew on the soldiers like wolves gnawing on bones. Objections?"

"No, sir," Emerens assured him.

"The veterans will be happy to get into the fight," Cancellus stated.

"May the Goddess Victoria fight with us," Alerio prayed. "Execute the plan."

As if a column of scythes hacking grain stalks, the first maniple advanced twice. Their shields bashed and the uniformed stabs cut into the opposing forces. Behind them, the second maniple waited their turn.

Although Qart Hadasht soldiers died, the initial movement delighted their commander.

***

Empire General Hamilcar had rushed five thousand soldiers and fifteen hundred horsemen through the valley beneath Mount Boukornine. Hoping to catch the Republic forces unprepared, Hamilcar started his mercenaries moving before dawn.

In the rays of the rising sun, his cavalry and infantry left the valley and advanced across an open plain. Two miles west of the town of Béni Khalled and just shy of the Legion marching camps, triple lines of big shields appeared across the landscape.

"If we don't break their line, we'll be here for a week pounding and pounding without progress," the General grumbled.

"It's their shields," the Major of Infantry responded. "We need them to come forward. Then we'll locate a weak spot and pour through it. Make this a man-to-man fight, and we'll slaughter the invaders."

"That's all-wishful thinking Major. Now tell me, how do you propose to breach the shield wall when it's static?"

Shifting the blame to the cavalry, the infantry commander said, "If the horsemen had gotten behind the lines, we would be there now, General."

The top cavalry officer snorted in disgust.

"Your hesitation to engage at the start is the reason we're stuck," the Captain of Horse protested. "My riders could have circled behind them but what good would we have done? Your soldiers weren't ready to attack."

"They had to drop their extra equipment," the Major responded.

"Enough," Hamilcar scolded. He smiled when the Legion lines moved. "While you bicker, the enemy hands us an opportunity. Move your reserves forward. Find that weak spot and let's bring this invasion to an end."

***

The first maniple stabbed on the second advance then stepped back and back again. From behind the Empire forces, a wave of fresh soldiers charged forward to join the battle.

Pushed from behind, the warriors at the front were shoved towards the retreating Legion maniple.

The initial push of the first maniple allowed a narrow gap to open on the flanks. A few Empire horsemen galloped through, believing they could disrupt the Legionaries' formation from behind.

At the center of the battle line, the charging soldiers ran into the thrusts of the second maniple's shields, and they tasted the steel of the experience infantrymen's gladii. Meanwhile, the horsemen who managed to get behind the lines ran into a wall of muscle and sinew, hardened by years of warfare. The veterans of the third maniple quickly put an end to the mounted marauders.

The advances and rotations of the maniples chewed up Empire soldiers. After the fourth switch, the Qart Hadasht Major ordered a retreat.

"Do we pursue them, Battle Commander?" Senior Tribune Emerens inquired.

Alerio reached for his gladius but stilled his hand. He was mounted and surrounded by Junior Tribunes. Flipping his blade while thinking through the situation seemed unprofessional. His quandary ended when a Junior Tribune from Legion East trotted to his command staff.

"Sir, General Regulus would like you to join him at his command tent," the messenger stated.

"Right away," Alerio acknowledged. To his staff, he instructed. "Hold your positions until I return. Senior Centurion Agoston, get me a report on injuries."

Orders were passed down and Legion North halted. But they remained on guard in case the Qart Hadasht army turned back. During the standdown, the Legion's senior combat officer rode the maniples congratulating the Legionaries and officers while gathering casualty reports.

As Colonel Sisera rode away from Regulus Legion North, First Centurion Palle and a troop of bodyguards fell into a formation around their Battle Commander. Alerio and the group headed for a tent erected to the rear of Regulus Legion East.

***

"Colonel Sisera," Marcus Regulus greeted Alerio when he entered the General's tent. "Your Legion did a good job of stopping their advance."

"Thank you, sir," Alerio replied.

"I know you took the brunt of the attack," Regulus acknowledged, "but I went you to chase them down and keep pressure on the Empire."

"Sir, according to my planning and strategies officer, we are thirty-five miles from Kelibia and thirty-five miles from the defensive walls of Qart Hadasht," Alerio portrayed the situation by tracing the distances on a map. "It's a good place to build a backup location. Once we build a fort, we'll have a secure rear position."

"Sisera, I've sent letters to the Senate asking to be relieved," Regulus informed Alerio. "So far, I've received no response. I feel like a piece of land abandoned by its farmworkers and left alone to go to seed. Well, I will not rest in Punic territory and let grass grow under my feet."

"I understand sir, but I have wounded who need tending," Alerio protested. "At least give me a few days to rest my Legion."

Marcus Regulus slammed a hand down on his temporary map table. The top flipped off the stand and crashed to the dirt floor scattering parchment maps across the ground. Alerio flinched. Not from Marcus' outburst, but from the abuse to the maps. Some of which, Alerio had drawn himself.

"The Ides of March was two weeks ago," Marcus Regulus sneered. "My term as Consul is up. I should be home with my family and sitting in my seat as a Senator. Not here, not as a Proconsul in charge of this expedition, and not at this point in my life. I want this campaign done with."

"General, I sympathize," Alerio stated. "But we need a fallback location. And halfway between where we landed and where we're going makes good sense."

"Eleven years ago, the first time I was elected Consul," Regulus reminded Alerio, "you were a boy just learning to ride. So, follow my orders."

"Sir. When you were first elected Consul," Alerio corrected the General, "I was a Legion Raider. And I have been at war ever since. Please recognize my military expertise and reconsider your order."

"We have them on their knees, and I will not pass up this opportunity," Regulus asserted. "Colonel Sisera, your Legion has been assigned the valley route. Set your maniples and pursue the enemy."

"As you wish, General," Alerio replied.

Outside the command tent, he leaped onto Phobos' back and kneed the stallion, heading it towards his Legion.

At Legion North, cavalrymen rubbed down their mounts on the right flank and skirmishers on the left sat on the ground sharpening their spears. Massed in the center were rows of heavy infantrymen fixing straps and honing gladii. But, no element of the Legion unpacked utensils or took off their war gear. The small tasks occupied their time while waiting for General Regulus' decision and Battle Commander Sisera's orders.

Chapter 2 – A Space for Victory

The Legionaries assigned to rear security, had yet to reach the entrance to the valley. In front of them, the baggage train for North Legion had entered the basin and formed a long procession. Four hundred and ten mules with an equal number of servants, forty wagons of supplies and grain, sixty spare cavalry mounts, and craftsmen and their carts filed into the narrow valley. On each side of the route, Velites climbed the hills searching for Empire warriors waiting in ambush. Although the Legionaries who went first had already checked for possible ambush sites, the light infantrymen made sure no soldiers slipped over the rolling hills or around the mountain during the Legion's transit.

Just ahead of the baggage train and only two miles into the valley, Centuries of the third maniple walked four abreast. In front of the veterans, Colonel Sisera and his command staff rode their mounts.

"I don't like it, sir," Griffinus Agoston grumbled.

"What's the matter Senior Centurion?" Alerio inquired. "Too quiet for you?"

The Legion's senior combat officer gazed up at the top of Mount Boukornine on one side, shifted to the other side, and peered at the foothills. Then he spit as if disgusted.

"Colonel, if I wanted to slow us down," Agoston replied. "I'd place archers on those hills with two Centuries of heavy infantrymen and dare you to leave that threat in your wake."

"I take it you have a point," Alerio questioned.

"Only a quandary, Battle Commander," the top combat officer stated. "Why does the Empire want up to move so fast?"

"Because they're running," Tribune Invisum submitted.

While the head of planning and strategies provided Alerio information such as the location of the Legion and data from scouting reports, the staff officer lacked combat experience.

"Run to where? Qart Hadasht is twenty-five miles ahead and their army is the only thing standing between us and the city's defensive walls," Alerio pointed out. He thought for a moment before asking. "In a bore hunt, you chase the beast to your hunters. What's the last thing you want?"

"For the bore to realize it's being rushed into a kill zone," Agoston offered.

Colonel Sisera kicked Phobos and yelled over his shoulder.

"Come on Griffinus," he invited the Senior Centurion. "Let's go see what kill zone we're being driven into."

Alerio and Griffinus Agoston raced around the twelve Centuries of the first maniple. A half mile later, the Battle Commander, the Legion's top combat officer, and a detachment from First Century rode alongside the second maniple.

"Who has the lead?" Agoston questioned a Centurion.

"Centurion Keoki is upfront with his skirmishers," the combat officer replied.

"As I'd expect from my light infantry commander," Senior Centurion Agoston responded. Then louder, he exclaimed. "He's leading from the front, as I'd expect from every combat officer of Legion North."

The Senior Centurion had expressed an expectation for his officers. His Centurions and Legionaries heard and Alerio approved of the overt messaging.

***

The cluster of horses trotted ahead of the heavy infantrymen. Across a short break in the ranks, they caught up with units of skirmishers.

"Where's Centurion Keoki?" Agoston asked.

Two squads of Velites pointed farther up the valley. Sweating and breathing hard, the skirmishers were too exhausted to speak. The reason, on the hills to either side, other light infantrymen took their turn combing the landscape. Rough terrain made searching for hidden soldiers and possible ambush sites hard duty.

A short while later, the staff riders caught up with Grear Keoki near the front of his skirmishers' formation.

"Anything of interest?" Alerio inquired.

"Nothing is the interesting thing, Battle Commander," Keoki remarked. "Nothing. Not a scrap of discarded gear, nor old campfires litter this valley. It's as spotless as a Temple of Hygieia."

"Marching Legionaries always leave gear or other signs of their passing," Alerio commented. "Especially if they're in a forced retreat. What does a clean valley suggest?"

"The Empire troops weren't panicked when they came back through here," Agoston remarked. "I don't like the idea of a preplanned retreat, sir."

"Neither do I, Senior Centurion," Alerio confirmed. "Let's get ahead of our point element and see what the Empire has planned for us."

"Sir, Centurion Palle won't like you going out front," an NCO from First Century stated.

"I don't plan on a one-man charge into the ranks of the enemy," Alerio told him. "But if it'll keep you in good graces with the Rabbit, give me two men who can climb and one to hold our horses."

Alerio, Griffinus Agoston, Grear Keoki, and three members of First Century galloped forward. They passed the scouts for the light infantrymen and pulled up when they could see the end of the valley.

***

Alerio and the pair of combat officers scrambled up the backside of the slope, reached the top, and poked their heads above the crest.

"Gentlemen, I believe we have our answer," Alerio commented while looking at the flatland beyond the valley.

"Apollo bless me," Grear Keoki prayed. His call to the God of Flocks, Herds, and Boxing wasn't lost on Alerio or the Senior Centurion.

"When we engage at the mouth of the valley," Agoston projected, "our Legionaries will take casualties. We'll kill hundreds and not move one foot. The dead well need to be removed before we can fight our way forward."

Beyond the last hill, thousands of Empire warriors waited. To reach them, North Legion needed to squeeze through a narrow gap of five hundred feet before forming their assault lines.

"Two hundred shields across," Agoston growled about the pass at the valley. "Not even room for a half maniple."

"And if the Legionaries manage to advance, the warriors will flood the ends of our lines," Alerio noted. "We'll lose the two hundred. Then what, I waste another two, then another, hoping the Empire gets tired of killing our men?"

"It's worse than I thought," Grear Keoki uttered.

"What could be worse than that?" Agoston questioned.

"Their front elements are tribal warriors," the Centurion of Light Infantry described. "Look deeper in the hoard and to either side. They have Companies of soldiers hidden in the crowd."

"When we advance against the warriors, and there's no doubt we can," Senior Centurion Agoston picked up the narrative. "The infantry will close in. Our forward squads will be slaughtered in the pincer movement."

"So, the Empire Commander's plan is a trap, camouflaged in a trap," Alerio summarized. "Forget the impediment to our progress for now. What is our immediate goal?"

"To get the Legion out of the valley," Keoki responded.

"Find room to form the maniples into battle lines," Agoston stated another goal.

"Both are worthy objectives," Alerio agreed.

He squinted at the Qart Hadasht army trying to think of a way to fulfill both goals. No idea came to Battle Commander Sisera.

"Sir, if I might," an infantryman from the First Century offered. "Our first goal is to push them back. Until we uncap the valley, we can't do anything."

Alerio rolled over on his back, stared at the sky, and smiled.

"I once knew a Senior Centurion who refused to wear an undergarment," Alerio reminisced. "When I lay on my back during stressful situations, I hope to see him standing over my head giving me a nasty view of his manhood, and a hard time for laying down on the job."

"Sir, what does that have to do with this?" Keoki asked.

"I was in command of the Messina Militia when we faced off against the Syracuse army," Alerio said. "After a morning of defending against their phalanx formations, I was exhausted and my pirates, turned infantrymen, were beaten. After a duel with some Hoplites, I fell on my back expecting the next one I met to send me to the Goddess Nenia."

"What happened, Colonel?" Agoston inquired.

"The Legion arrived, set their battle lines, and saved the day," Alerio said. "But facing phalanxes let me know the power of a concentrated force."

"Sir, we don't drill for the phalanx," Agoston reminded Alerio. "Not since the Samnite wars and that was years ago."

"Senior Centurion, we don't, but we do practice the tortoise," Alerio asserted. "And although we aren't approaching a fortified position, the men are accustomed to the Testudo. I think they can handle using it as an assault formation."

"You want the Centuries to form the tortoise shell and push into the warriors," Agoston guessed.

"Yes and no," Alerio proposed. He sat up, located a stick, and began drawing in the dirt. "This is what we're going to do."

***

Corporal Philetus pulled two squads from the side of the trail.

"Form a box, five men to a side," he directed. After some shuffling, the Legionaries stood in a square measuring thirteen feet by thirteen feet. "Shields up. Interlock them."

From a loose collection of men and shields, at the command, the box formed by the twenty Legionaries shrunk to a solid ten by ten with an empty center. Philetus walked around, stopping to throw a shoulder into each of the shields. Once satisfied with the formation's integrity, he shouted to the light infantry area. "Give me fourteen Skirmishers."

From an empty husk, the square of Legionaries filled with bodies. After setting up the modified Testudo, Philetus raised an arm.

"Ready, sir," he shouted to the Centurion of the Sixth Century.

Aeneas waited for the last of his four mini-Testudos to get ready before calling to Agoston.

"Senior Centurion, the Merchants of Mayhem are ready," Aeneas declared. His description brought shouts of 'Rah' from the men of the Sixth Century. "Let's get this war over with."

More cheering rose from the four small formations. Picking up on the bravado, the other forty-four squares added their voices.

"Sir, the first maniple is prepared," Agoston reported.

"Are my snapping tortoises ready?" Alerio questioned.

A unified 'Rah' came from the men clustered in the squares.

"Remember, don't stop to fight, just push and push hard," Alerio shouted. "May the Goddess Bia, Jupiter's winged enforcer, lend you bodily strength and the will to succeed. First maniple, forward."

Six abreast, the small tortoise formations fast walked from the staging area. As they rounded the final hills of the valley, they slowed for better footing, and split, stacking three testudos to a side. The following formations left the valley and marched straight forward. As if splayed fingers sinking into bread dough, the forty-eight squares shoved into the mass of Empire warriors.

***

"Step, step, push, push, hold it together," Philetus called out in a loud but calm voice. "How many steps to Qart Hadasht?"

"Too many," a Legionary responded.

"How many steps to Qart Hadasht?" the Corporal insisted.

"Nothing the first maniple can't handle," another answered.

"What is the road paved with?" Philetus inquired.

"The souls and hides of our foes," his group of Legionaries replied.

"Push, push, step together," Philetus instructed. "How many steps to Qart Hadasht?"

"Not too many, Corporal," the formation roared back as the forward shields met a wall of spears, armor, flesh, and muscles.

Far behind them, Battle Commander Sisera addressed the second maniple.

"You are my experienced Legionaries. I call on you to save your little brothers who have gone into harm's way to open space for your assault line," he shouted. "Unlike Bia's blessing, I pray to her brother, the God Kratos, to grant you might and the power to rule the day. Centuries of the second maniple, forward."

Without the need to hold a tight formation, the Centurions called the beat for a Legion jog.

"Left, stomp, left, stomp," the combat officers bellowed. "Left, stomp…"

They learned in training to show pride and the familiar cadence brought up the Legionaries heads. By the time they reached the narrow exit from the valley, their right feet slammed down with authority and their hearts pumped with vigor.

"Second maniple, draw," the most senior combat officer ordered as they threaded through the narrow gap.

"Rah!" came back to him in a roar.

"Centurions, form the maniple," he instructed.

From columns jogging along the trail from the valley, the Legionaries dispersed. The Twenty-First Century snapped into the far-left position and shuffled into a three-line formation. Next, the Twenty-Second joined them, and then the Twenty-Third bolted into place. Quickly the rest fell in until the Twenty-Sixth Century anchored the end on the far right.

The eight hundred feet of shields, steel, and muscles paused for a beat. They understood the extra three hundred feet beyond the mouth of the valley, a space for victory, was carved by the sacrifices of the first maniple. The Legionaries gritted their teeth and adjusted their hands to secure grips for the work ahead.

"Second maniple, forward."

As if an armored centipede, the nine hundred and sixty Legionaries moved to engage the warriors of the Empire.

***

The square formed by first and second squads, Sixth Century, distorted when they came up against the warriors.

"Lock your shields and push," Philetus instructed. "Maintain your shape and push."

"How many steps to Qart Hadasht, Tesserarius?" a panting Legionary asked.

"Not too far," Philetus answered. "Nothing we can't handle."

The squads mashed into the bodies of warriors who slashed and bashed at the big shields. As the Legionaries had learned while training, the heavy infantry scutum could be used as a weapon, or as a personal barrier. But when locked together and held by men with heart, they formed an impenetrable wall of wood.

Squeezing into the massed warriors, the squares created holes. Then, the displaced fighters flowed back into place, surrounding the first maniple formations. Because they were excited for the battle, the Empire warriors bashed at all sides of the squares. While striking the big shields, the warriors left their front line to pursue the enemy close at hand.

All the commotion in the crowded hoard drew their attention away from the mouth of the valley. In the confusion, most of the Empire warriors missed the arrival of the combat lines.

"Second maniple, standby," Senior Tribunes Emerens and Cancellus barked. "Advance, advance, advance."

Three hundred and twenty scuta, as if shot from slings, slammed into the off balanced warriors. Before they could recover, the shields retreated, and an equal number of steel blades jabbed out. The line stepped into the gap and the infantry shields punched again.

For the wounded mercenaries on the ground, their last sight was the bottom of a falling hobnailed boot.

"Left, stomp, left, stomp…"

***

Between the valley and the plain were a pair of hills with steep sides. Inclined just enough, they allowed Rapti Galba to scrape through on his mount. Seeing their Tribune attempting a solo cavalry charge, the Legion horsemen kicked their mounts into motion. After following him through the gap, Legion North's cavalry emerged on the plain and joined the battle.

By the third set of advances from the second maniple, the Legion cavalry began carving on the sides of the Empire's forces. With horses as the signal, the surviving men of first maniple began fighting their way out of the hoard.

Lost in the battle was a cry far to the rear of the Qart Hadasht army.

"How did the Legion get so deep into your formation, Major?" General Hamilcar bellowed. "We had them pinned in the valley. Now, they've broken out. Sound the retreat before I lose my infantry Companies."

"Yes, General," the Major confirmed.

Inside, the infantry officer bristled against the cautious decision. The soldiers of the infantry, the Qart Hadasht General wanted to save, were the troops needed in the fight to defeat the Legion.

But the Punic nobleman had given an order and the Major complied. Because, he didn't fancy dying on a cross.

Chapter 3 – The Threshing Board

"Hold this and don't let off the pressure," Hektor Nicanor instructed. He placed an infantryman's hands on a soaked bandage and pressed down. Under the weight, the wounded man moaned and attempted to push the hands and the bandage away. During the struggle, the youthful medic added. "No matter how much he begs, don't let go. I'll be back."

The harsh reality was Hektor needed to wait before treating the man. No matter the depth of the wounds, unless the blade cut something major, survival depended on the will of the injured man. As Doctor Allocco taught, 'you can only save patients with the will to live.' The youth grabbed his medic's bag and dashed to another injured Legionary. After lifting several rags, Hektor examined the wounds, replaced the bandages, and unpacked a needle and thread. This man had the blessing of Zelos, the God of Zeal, and had lived long enough to demonstrate his willingness to fight for his life.

Around Hektor, the bodies of Empire mercenaries and Republic Legionaries lay dead or wounded. Cries of alarm sounded as the infantrymen made sure the warriors of the Qart Hadasht army wouldn't require the medic's time or use up Legion supplies.

***

"Colonel, it's a great victory," Griffinus Agoston boated. "Congratulations."

"Sixty-six wounded and thirty dead so far," Alerio replied. He motioned to the scattered clusters of infantrymen gathered around the injured or the deceased. "I don't think they believe it was such a great victory."

"You have less wounded than if we'd fought for a week to break through, sir," Tribune Palle stated. He pointed at the killing of enemy wounded and whined. "It's a shame we can't take prisoners."

"We have no way of sending them to Rome," Alerio reminded the commander of First Century. "Without the fleet, we can't even go ourselves."

The command staff of Regulus Legion North rode through the battlefield saluting and acknowledging Legionaries, Centurions, and NCOs who weren't too exhausted to look up. On the far side of the carnage, they halted at an abandoned farmhouse. Cultivated fields stretched for miles beyond the house. In the northeast direction, the flat landscape allowed Alerio to see the rear elements of the Qart Hadasht army.

"We should chase them down and maintain contact," Tribune Invisum recommended. "Keep them off balance and prevent them from setting more traps."

"I agree with you," Alerio told the head of planning and strategies. "Once we get our wounded off to Kelibia, our dead buried, and the walking wounded sorted, we'll go after them."

"There's no sign of Legion East, West, or South," Rapti Galba observed. The Tribune of Horse pointed northward and asked. "Should I send patrols to find them?"

To the north, the mountain descended into low hills before the land flattened. There was no sign of any of the Legions that took the coastal route.

"I don't want to send men wandering off with no clear objective. We'll discuss it later when we set up for the night," Alerio replied. Shifting his focus to the nearby farm, he noted. "This is good land. I imagine it yields a healthy crop."

"I can confirm that, sir," Centurion Lecti Gratian agreed. "When we were scavenging, we noticed the Qart Hadasht farmers had to mechanize the harvest to handle the grain."

"Really? Why wasn't I aware of that?" Alerio asked the supply officer.

"You've been busy, Battle Commander," Gratian submitted. He kneed his horse froward to a shed beside the farmhouse. Reining in, the officer lifted a foot and rested it on a wooden form leaning against the outbuilding. "This is a threshing board."

Heavily constructed, the wooden structure measured four feet by six feet. Affixed to one edge was a set of iron rings.

"It looks like a reinforced door for a defensive wall," Alerio guessed. "Nothing about that resembles a farming tool."

Centurion Gratian kicked the board. It fell flat on the ground, exposing the hidden side. Razor-like metal blades covered the backside of the threshing board.

"They harness a horse to the iron rings and a man sits on the board," Gratian explained. "He guides the horse and the board over freshly cut stalks. The blades rip the husks from the grain. You have to admit, sir, it's more efficient than threshing by hand."

"No question about it," Alerio confirmed. "I just wouldn't want to fall under those blades when the threshing board is in motion."

"Or any other time for that matter," Tribune Invisum counseled.

Far to their rear, the wagon train came from the mouth of the valley. As the Centuries had done before the battle, the mules and handlers formed three ranks. The squads' supplies were in order by first, second, and third maniple.

"Tell them not to unload," Alerio instructed when he noted the formation of pack animals.

Senior Tribunes Emerens and Cancellus sent Junior Tribunes to deliver the message. As the young noblemen rode away, a trio of riders galloped from the valley.

"Must be word from General Regulus," Grear Keoki guessed.

"This time he won't get an argument from me," Alerio replied to the light infantry commander. "I want vengeance as much as the Proconsul wants to win the war and go home."

The couriers slowed and guided their mounts around the wounded and the dead. All three were slumped and their horses lathered with sweat when they reached Alerio.

"Colonel Sisera, greetings from General Regulus," one courier stated before handing a scroll to Alerio.

After unrolling it, the Battle Commander read the message.

"The other Legions are delayed on the coastal route," Alerio told his staff.

"What's the hold up, sir?" Centurion Palle inquired.

"According to General Regulus, they've encountered massive resistance," Alerio responded. He rolled the scroll and ordered. "Find Centurion Lophos and have him lay out our marching camp. First and second are staying here for the night. Third maniple and half our cavalry are marching north to help the Legions breakout."

"Who is commanding, sir?" Senior Tribune Cancellus inquired.

"Seeing as you asked, you are," Alerio told him.

"Thank you, Colonel," the flank commander responded.

Griffinus Agoston looked around at the cost of victory and scoffed, "Colonel, if we hadn't broken through, who would be available to help the other Legions?"

Heads snapped around and eyes locked on the Legion's Senior Centurion. The insinuation buried in his comment bordered on insubordination.

"I think what you mean, Senior Centurion," Alerio corrected, "it's sad the Empire army is getting away. But not to worry, I can assure you, we'll get another chance at them."

"Yes, sir, that's exactly what I meant," Agoston confirmed.

The Legion's top combat officer meant nothing of the kind. He was angry that his Legion had taken the initiative and punched through the enemy blockade. But now, his veterans were being sent off to do what a better Battle Commander would have already accomplished.

"Permission to accompany the third maniple, sir," he requested.

"No Griffinus. I need you here to put my maniples back together," Alerio replied. Then he clarified. "And to help me organize the next segment of the invasion."

"Yes, sir," Agoston acknowledged. "I better get…"

Before the Senior Centurion had a chance to finish, Centurion Aeneas ran up and grabbed the reins of the horse. The line officer blew out a lungful of air then inhaled trying to catch his breath.

"I have a man missing," the combat officer for the Sixth Century uttered.

"Who's missing?" Alerio asked.

"I've searched the living, the dead, and the wounded," Aeneas reported. "And sir, Corporal Philetus is gone."

***

The mercenary soldiers, untouched by the battle, marched with energy. Surrounding their formations, exhausted warriors put one foot in front of the other and thanked their

Gods for sparing them. Beyond the main body of Hamilcar's army, horsemen rode to the rear and on the flanks watching for Republic forces.

"Move your legs," an Empire cavalryman threatened, "or I'll gut you right here and save myself the trouble of guarding you."

To reinforce his warning, the horseman jerked the rope and the Legionary tied to the other end fell to his knees. If the infantryman had fallen onto his back, he would have been pulled along hopelessly. As it happened, he dropped chest down on the rope. Nuzzling the hemp line with his neck, the prisoner maintained his forward position. In a few staggering steps, he stumbled to his feet and jogged along with the horse.

"You should kill me now," Corporal Philetus said. "I'll tell you nothing."

"Oh, but you will talk to my Captain," the horseman assured the Legion NCO.

"You misunderstand me," Philetus corrected. "I can't tell you anything because I don't know anything."

"Not my problem," the rider stated. He jerked the rope forcing Philetus to sprint for several steps. "That's between you and the captain."

***

Hektor Nicanor shifted to a more comfortable position and pulled the blanket up to his neck trying to block the light.

"You should go into another tent," Alerio recommended.

"Do you need anything Battle Commander?" the youth asked.

"Other than sleep, what could I want?" Alerio questioned.

There were two pitchers of wine and mugs on the map table. On a side stand, slices of beef and pieces of fruit filled a couple of bowls, and there was a stack of flat bread.

Several strategically placed candles cast light on a couple of maps. The rest of the command tent, and the survivors of Battle Commander Sisera's marathon planning session, were illuminated by braziers.

"I'll be here if you need anything," Hektor said.

"He's a good lad," Senior Centurion Agoston remarked. "He sewed up a lot of Legionaries today. The other medics were talking about identifying his patients by the neat stitching."

"Don't say that out loud, he might get too full of himself to be my valet," Alerio teased. "Let's get back to Tunis. Once over the Medjerda River we'll be four miles from the town."

"But the land narrows after the forest," Invisum pointed out. "It drops to two miles of solid footing before the final approach. Our left flank will be exposed when we move out of the woods after the pinch point."

While the physically stronger men were fading, the head of planning and strategies grew more alert and sharper the longer the session lasted.

"And that's where the Empire will harden their defense," Rapti Galba said. "I can flood the left with cavalry, but you'll need another solution on the right flank."

"We'll be swinging around the shoreline of Lake Tunis," Invisum informed the group. "Unless the Empire has barges to deliver troops, our right flank should be secured by the water."

Alerio rested a hand on a map and traced the drawing from that one to another piece of parchment where the map continued. He would prefer it if two or even three Legions could attack Tunis at the same time. But the wet shorelines to either side of the narrow land prevented it. Only one Legion could pass through at a time.

"If we get the go ahead from General Regulus, what's our order of march?" Alerio asked.

"My Velites along the water and out front," Centurion Grear Keoki described. "We'll envelop the infantry and be in a position to warn about threats."

"Second maniple will be the lead unit, behind the skirmishers," Senior Centurion Agoston replied. "They'll pivot around staying close to Lake Tunis to prevent the Empire from snaking in on that side."

"Followed by my cavalry," Tribune Rapti Galba expounded on the plan. "That will allow us to charge into the open after the narrows and protect your flank."

"First maniple will roll left, following the horsemen. They'll extend your attack line," Senior Tribune Emerens depicted the movement of his infantrymen. He used a hand to sweep left in an arc on the map and ended the motion with his palm over the town of Tunis. "Unless delayed by resistance, the first will use the end of the second maniple as a fulcrum to swing around. All things being equal, the maneuver will be completed before you reach the walls of Tunis."

"What about the wagon train and the mules?" Alerio asked.

No one said anything. They had been so focused on the attack, they forgot about logistics.

"Leave them with the following Legion," Centurion Gratian proposed. "Give each Legionary two days rations and an extra waterskin."

"And if we get bogged down and need to resupply?" Emerens challenged. "What then?"

"The Legion goes hungry for a day," Invisum answered. "The most efficient and swiftest course of action is a Legion sized combat patrol. It's what we described before the Colonel brought up the wagons and mules."

"It's a bad plan to leave our supplies behind," Emerens proclaimed.

"The man who has planned badly, if fortune is on his side, may have had a stroke of luck; but his plan was a bad one, nonetheless," Alerio quoted. "Herodotus said that some two hundred and twenty-five years ago."

"Then we'll travel with our wagon train?" Agoston inquired.

"The historian also boasted, great deeds are usually wrought at great risks," Alerio responded. "We'll leave our train with the following Legion. Now, go get some rest. We break camp at sunrise."

***

While Alerio planned for an attack on the town of Tunis, miles away from the Legion camp, General Hamilcar gathered information.

"You are a Republic officer?" Hamilcar questioned.

"No sir," Philetus admitted. His armor, helmet, and boots had been stripped away, leaving the NCO in a red tunic. "I'm the Corporal of Sixth Century, Regulus Legion North."

He swayed from exhaustion and a beating earlier. Thinking he was moving towards the General, two bodyguards hammered Philetus to his knees.

"Enough. Give him a chance to explain," the Punic nobleman directed. "You told my Captain of Horse that you were a Tesserarius. What are your duties?"

"Sir, I maintain the pay records for my Century, write reports to the command staff, and keep the burial funds and punishment list," Philetus explained. "And I help with training and I'm in charge of a section of the assault line."

"So, you are an officer," Hamilcar decided. "You keep records and handle funds. Those are tasks for officers."

"If you say so, General," Philetus agreed.

He began to topple over. One of the bodyguard's dropped a hand on his shoulder to stabilize the NCO.

"Tell me, Republic Officer, who is in command of your Legion?"

"General Marcus Regulus, sir," Philetus told him. "The Proconsul is in command of the expedition."

"And he personally orchestrated the breakout from the valley?"

"No, sir, that would be Colonel Sisera. He's a disciple of Nenia the Goddess of Death," Philetus bragged. "Plus, he's a sorcerer and a scary staff officer."

"Because he treats you badly?"

"No, sir. He treats his Legionaries fine," Philetus said with a smile. "He is scary because the Battle Commander, while he is killing your soldiers, prays for his Goddess to take their souls."

The club impacted behind Corporal Philetus' ear, and he dropped, loose limbed, and unconscious to the floor of the tent.

"Send him to the capital as a slave. One of many to come," Hamilcar directed. Then he stood and paced the floor. "Scribe, put out a notice. I am personally offering a reward of twenty silver coins for the man who brings me Colonel Sisera or his dead body."

Act 2

Chapter 4 – March on Tunis

Shortly after Legion North crossed the Medjerda River and set up camp, several things occurred. Alerio's veterans and Senior Tribune Cancellus, his right flank commander, returned. They hiked through the gates of the marching camp full of combat stories and good cheer. Behind his veterans, the other three Legions arrived and set up stockades of their own.

Despite the visibility of four full Legion stockades, the Qart Hadasht army was nowhere to be seen. Not a probe of Legion lines nor any patrols were reported.

The next morning, Alerio left the camp to meet with the General and the other Battle Commanders. During the daylong conference, one more thing occurred. General Marcus Regulus agreed to Sisera's battle plan and granted Legion North the honor of attacking Tunis.

The sun hung low in the western sky when Alerio rode away from the General's command tent. He and a troop from First Century were outside the stockade of Legion East when a rider caught up with them. Alerio reined in and waited for the senior staff officer. The two took a moment to admire the majesty of the setting sun.

"Legion East will protect your wagons and mules," Senior Tribune Triticeus promised Alerio. "Although, I wish my maniples were attacking Tunis."

"This campaign is far from over," Alerio pointed out. "You'll have plenty of chances for glory."

"So far the Empire has broken contact as soon as it got rough," Triticeus noted. "On the coastal road, your third maniple hit their flank and like a boxer punched in the ribs, the soldiers folded and backed away. Colonel Sisera, do you think it'll be any different when we reach the walls of Qart Hadasht?"

"People behave differently when defending their homes," Alerio counseled. "Plus, Tunis is only ten miles from Qart Hadasht. A great deal can happen for your benefit or against you between the town and the city."

"I'll make an offering to Mars for your Legion, Battle Commander," Triticeus assured him, "and for you as well."

"I'll take all the help I can get," Alerio agreed as he tightened the reins on Phobos. "Having the God of War watching over my staff can't hurt."

The two officers exchanged salutes and trotted off in opposite directions. Triticeus rode back into the Legion East camp, and Alerio galloped towards his command.

***

When pink streaks jutted across the sky, Legion North disassembled its marching camp. Boards and posts were stacked in wagons, squad tents rolled and secured on the backs of mules, and hundreds of items were packed and loaded. And lastly, extra grain and waterskins got distributed to individual Legionaries. By sunrise, the wagon train, mules, extra horses, and tradesmen headed southeast.

"Men of Regulus Legion North, the God Mars requires your services," Alerio called out. "Centurion Keoki, show us the way to war."

"Rah," the Velites responded at the mention of their commander.

Keoki lifted an arm and pointed his hand at the Legion's Fiftieth Century. In response to the motion, Centurion Scoedia saluted and turned to his eighty pathfinders. Each scout came from the mountain tribes of Umbria and were capable trackers of man and beast. Dressed in lightweight leather armor, they carried a small shield, a spear, and a sica as a side arm. Their equipment matched their mission to move swiftly and patrol ahead of the Legion.

"Optio Conti, clear the trail," Scoedia directed his Sergeant.

"Sir," Conti responded.

The NCO waved half his pathfinders to the left and the other half to the right. He jogged after the four squads heading to the left side of the route. Once the Fiftieth Century began moving, Centurion Keoki addressed his remaining light infantrymen.

"You heard the Colonel," Keoki roared. "How many steps to Qart Hadasht?"

"To many?" the light infantrymen shouted.

"How many steps to Qart Hadasht?" Keoki insisted.

"Not too many for Legion North, sir," the light infantrymen answered.

After the exchange, Keoki saluted the Legions' top combat officer. At the signal that the advanced units were prepared, the Senior Centurion bellowed.

"Centurions of Regulus Legion North, march us out."

Line officers for the skirmishers signaled their nine Centuries forward. As if to match the wolf pelts they sported, the NCOs howled. Just as vocal, but not as gaudy as their NCOs, the light infantrymen settled for smooth boiled leather armor. Their shields were slightly larger than the scouts' and each veles carried a javelin, a spear, and on their hips, a gladius and a sica. Their gear allowed them rapid movement around a battlefield. War cries answered the howls of their NCOs as they moved forward.

The second maniple followed. Covered in waterproof skins, the scuta identified them as heavy infantrymen. In addition to the big shields and heavy armor, they all lugged three javelins and a single spear along with their gladius and Legion dagger. Their equipment allowed them to form an assault line and their training taught them to control the center of any battlefield.

Centurions of the cavalry issued instructions and the horses stepped off. Not far behind the mounted Legionaries, the first maniple fell into the march. Last to leave the previous night's bivouac were the veterans of third maniple.

"I'll see you at the walls of Tunis," Alerio commented to Keoki.

"It's a date, Colonel," the Centurion acknowledged.

The Centurion of Light Infantry snapped the reins and he and his horse trotted away, heading northwest. Alerio looked at his advancing elements, then to the wagon train heading in the other direction. Last, he turned his attention to his large staff.

"I have gone into battle by myself, in the company of a handful of associates, and with maniples of every grade," he stated. "But traveling with a crowd still feels strange. Enough talking, on to Tunis."

Colonel Sisera kicked Phobos in the ribs. The stallion leaped forward and galloped off. Taken by surprise at the sudden movement, the command staff of Legion North snapped their reins and trotted after their Battle Commander.

***

On the far side of the Medjerda River, Optio Conti and his pathfinders crossed farmland. They couldn't miss the main feature of the homesteads as they had to scale the walls of stacked stone. For decades, the Punic farmers had dug up and split boulders to clear the land. But their agriculture and efforts ended at a tree line.

Legion maps only hinted at the stones in the forest. They were reported to be numerous, but the trees blocked an accurate count and prevented the drawing of trustworthy charts. Other than the main trail through the forest, the rest of the route consisted of animal paths weaving around tree trunks and boulders.

On the far side of the cultivated fields, the scouts formed a line and entered the forest. Behind them, Centurion Keoki crossed the river and rode through the farmland with the rest of the Velites. They entered the forest on the main trail as did the second maniple a little later. Slowly, the rest of the Legion traversed the Medjerda, formed columns, and hiked along the road. It was the only straight and level surface available and one of the reasons only a single Legion could pass through the forest at one time.

***

Three miles into the march, Sergeant Conti and his scouts emerged from the forest. Several plots of land lay under cultivation, but indications of a different industry dominated a small settlement. At the village, fishing boats in various forms of repair rested on stands, fish drying on racks baked in the sun, and blankets of half completed nets hung on weaving forms.

A mile to the north of the town of Mégrine, the waters of Lake Tunis shone in the morning sun. After a brief conversation with a local, Conti learned the other lake was three miles to the northwest. With no signs of the Qart Hadasht army, the Optio waved the Fiftieth Century onward.

Slightly over a mile later, the scouts entered another forest and the start of the narrow land between the lakes. The NCO slowed the march of the pathfinders. He knew the Punic defenders were up ahead because the map showed a hill fort. But he didn't know if the fortified encampment was manned by a garrison or the entire Qart Hadasht army.

***

Jellaz Hill rose above the treetops giving the garrison a view of the main trail. While they could see far down the road, leaves and bushes hid Conti and a squad of pathfinders. The scouts crawled from tree, to boulder, to bush until they halted on the left side of the fort.

"What do you think, Optio?" a scout asked.

"I don't understand the Empire," Conti admitted. "If I wanted to defend this area, I would blockade it with every Legionary I could put in a shield wall."

"How do you know they haven't?" another scout inquired.

Conti moved a branch. From ground level, he could see a portion of the slope behind the hill fort. And the only soldiers in view were four horsemen. All four sat at a campsite with their bedding unrolled from the previous night. While they relaxed, their horses were tied to nearby posts.

"Not enough smoke from cookfires," the NCO explained. "A large force would have turned the sky to hazy."

"If it's just a garrison, the infantry can easily take the fort," a squad leader boasted. "Then we can move on Tunis."

"Tell me, Decanus, why are four men lounging as if they have no duties," Conti questioned, "but their horses are loosely tied with their saddles tightened down?"

The squad leader thought for a couple of beats before venturing, "They're messengers waiting for instructions."

"And what message will they carry?"

"Optio Conti, they will alert the Qart Hadasht army that we are attacking the hill fort," the squad leader told him.

"I need to speak with Centurion Scoedia," Conti told the squad. "Stay low and keep watch."

The Optio crawled from bush to boulder to tree until he was deeper in the forest. Then he jumped to his feet and sprinted for the main trail and his officer.

***

A shiver ran up Alerio's spine. On the road in front and behind him, the Legion marched under a clear blue sky.

"If you spend enough years at war," Senior Centurion Agoston whined, "eventually, you develop a feeling of mistrust when things go as planned."

"Got a shiver in your spine?" Alerio questioned.

"It's a cramp in my right shoulder from an old injury, Colonel," Agoston told him. "Your spine?"

"Like a cold bolt of lightning," Alerio admitted.

The shared experience between the two veteran infantry officers was confirmed when Centurion Keoki came into view. They exchanged troubled looks at the meaning of the Light Infantry Centurion's return. Keoki's horse wasn't galloping but the mount moved at the top of his canter.

"I called a halt to the march," Grear Keoki stated as he reined in. "I thought to give you a moment to think, sir."

"Not unexpected, I'll admit," Alerio told him while stretching his back. "But just what am I thinking about?"

"We expected trouble at the fort on Jellaz Hill," the Velites Centurion reminded Alerio. "Well Colonel, the Qart Hadasht army isn't there."

"That's good news. We'll send the second up and remove the garrison," Alerio repeated the plan. Then he studied the puzzled expression on Grear Keoki's face. "But that's not a reason to stop the march. Is it?"

To the front, the first maniple shuffled to a stop. When the command staff drew up, the third maniple coming from behind was forced to halt as well.

"No sir, it isn't a reason," Keoki acknowledged. "But the four messengers waiting at the hill fort are. Let me explain, Battle Commander. The Qart Hadasht General has riders waiting. When we attack, they'll ride off and alert the army."

"If we move fast enough," Tribune Invisum noted, "we can catch them unprepared."

"Only four riders?" Alerio asked.

"Yes, sir, Optio Conti, one of my best saw them with his own eyes," Keoki assured him.

"Rapti. Can you get riders around the fort and stop the messengers?" Alerio asked the Tribune of Horse.

"If they don't have any warning that we're coming," Tribune Galba replied. "I've got enough racehorses that we'll be on them before they recognize the Noric steel of my gladius."

A question floated through Alerio's mind. 'I wonder how many coins I made from the sale of the iron ore used in that blade.' He and his adopted father imported the raw material used to create Noric steel.

"What are you thinking, sir?" the head of planning and strategies asked. He assumed Alerio's delay in replying meant the Battle Commander was thinking about the information.

"If we take down their couriers," Invisum continued, "we can take our time with the fort."

"Without the messengers, their army won't know we're coming," Alerio guessed. "Isn't that the best time to approach your enemy?"

"But sir, you're proposing we leave an enemy stronghold in our rear," Griffinus Agoston warned. "Is that wise?"

"We'll run right by the fort," Alerio instructed. When the Senior Centurion scowled, he added. "They'll only be on the hill until the third maniple catches up."

"And we'll be in Tunis before the defenders can get into their armor," Invisum declared.

***

From the top of Jellaz Hill, a Qart Hadasht Lieutenant watched a pair of warriors. His orders were to keep two sentries on vigil from dawn to sunset. These two seemed especially lax, plus they were playing with long ribbons of leather.

"It's important that we alert Tunis when we first see the Legion approaching," the officer blustered. "Pay attention to the road."

"Yes sir," the tribesmen responded.

Being Crete mercenaries, they were expert slingers, specialists with valuable skills. Sitting on a dirt wall watching an empty trail was not the challenge they expected when they signed on to the Qart Hadasht army.

"How about we chuck a few lead pellets down the road, sir," one advised. He stretched his leather sling before letting it hang from his fingers. "That way we'll be sure the road is empty."

"Or if it isn't, the first Legionaries to arrive won't have a pleasant experience," the other slinger stated.

"Put those toys away," the Lieutenant barked. "Put them away now. I don't want to see them again while you're on watch."

Although they kept their eyes on the road, the slingers carefully rolled their leathers and placed them in pouches. Then they collected lead pellets from neatly stacked piles and dropped them into ammo holders.

"That's better," the Empire officer complimented the warriors. "Now…"

The trail was empty. Then in a heartbeat, ten Legion cavalrymen broke from the trees beside the road. Mounting on the run, they galloped towards the fort, raced around the hill, and vanished behind the rear walls.

"Alert, alert," the Lieutenant yelled. "Send the couriers."

He managed to rouse his garrison. But the four couriers never made it to their horses. Three died while drawing their swords. One never made it that far. The blade of Rapti's Noric steel sank into his chest and pierced his heart before ripping its way out through his shoulder.

No messages traveled from Jellaz Hill. The two miles from the fort to the town might as well have been two hundred. And so, no word reached Generals Hamilcar, Bostar, or Hasdrubal that the Legion was advancing on Tunis.

Chapter 5 – A Naked Iberian

The forest ended abruptly. In response, the scouts and Velites dropped to their knees inside the tree line. Behind them, the arriving second maniple stacked up and the Legionaries caught their breath. Although superbly conditioned, sprinting a mile around Jellaz Hill while dodging lead pellets from slingers and arrows from archers took a toll. Then running another mile to the edge of the forest, left the heavy infantrymen in need of a breather.

Battle Commander Sisera shoved between the ranks. With his First Century left behind by the speed of Phobos, Alerio traveled without bodyguards. To remain hidden from the Empire forces, he left the stallion and his white plumed helmet behind the maniple. Then he began hiking to the edge of the forest.

"Excuse me," he apologized while pushing between two Legionaries.

"Watch yourself," a Corporal said assuming Alerio was a lost infantryman. He didn't look back at the intruder when he added. "Get back to your Century, Legionary. Although, I can't imagine they're missing the likes of you."

"Excellent. A man with opinions," Alerio exclaimed. He grabbed the NCO around the neck, gripped the top of his chest armor, and began dragging the Tesserarius towards the end of the tree line.

Two men from the Corporal's Century witnessed the assault and took a step to intercede.

"Are you touched by Coalemus?" another Legionary demanded. He hooked them with his arms and held them back. "That's Battle Commander Sisera. If he wanted to do harm, he'd have cursed the Corporal and left him for dead."

"What does the God of Stupid have to do with this?" one inquired.

"Colonel Sisera is a sorcerer," the Legionary enlightened his fellow infantrymen. "I had the duty at the front gate when he swept a runaway team off the ramp and into the defensive ditch. And the scariest part. The horses lived but the driver died. Just like that with a wave of his hand. You can thank me later for saving your lives."

Alerio didn't hear any of the exchange. He was busy ordering Legionaries, light infantrymen, and scouts out of his way while towing a struggling NCO in his wake. When he could see the open farmland beyond the trees, he stopped, kicked the Corporal's legs out from under him, and sat the NCO down on the forest floor.

"Get me an Optio or a Centurion," Alerio instructed the scouts around him. Then looking at the Tesserarius, he inquired. "What are you doing sitting down on the job. Get up here, Corporal, and tell me what you see."

The NCO shoved off the ground, reached for his gladius, and stopped. His eyes grew large, and his lips quivered.

"Colonel Sisera, sir, I didn't recognize you," he pleaded.

The Battle Commander normally arrived after a head's up from First Century. But, the lack of bodyguards was no excuse for mouthing off to the commander of a Legion. The Corporal could already feel the lashes on his back from a session on the punishment post.

"Are we going to have a long conversation about feelings?" Alerio challenged. "Maybe later, over a bowl of camp stew. Right now, I brought you up here to get your opinion. Look out there."

The experienced NCO from the second maniple peered into the distance. Big tents were positioned behind rows of troops' tents. But unlike the Legion that preferred goatskin, the Qart Hadasht units had tents made of various material. Most were unrecognizable to the NCO as they came from the homelands of the mercenaries.

"Sir, what am I looking for?" the Corporal inquired.

Sergeant Conti elbowed his way through the crowd that had formed behind the Battle Commander.

"Sir, what are you doing up here?" the scout NCO inquired. Then he caught his mistake, and hurriedly added. "Colonel. Optio Conti reporting."

"You're the scout that saw the messengers, good," Alerio complimented him while directing the Sergeant's attention to the open field. "What do you see?"

Conti recognized three distinct command compounds behind the squad tents.

"What kind of cluster are you holding?" a voice demanded. "This better be a mutiny, and not a game of dice. That at least, will give me a reason to crucify the lot of you."

A gap opened in the semicircle and a big combat officer strutted through.

"People, I asked..." he stopped and saluted. "Sir, I didn't expect..."

"Out there, tell me what you see?" Alerio ordered.

The combat officer examined the command pavilions, the rows of tents, and the corrals. Then he focused on an area occupied by giants.

"That's the combined Qart Hadasht armies," he declared. "But you can see that sir. What am I looking for?"

Alerio dropped to a knee and signaled the two NCOs and the officer to follow him.

"We have one chance to take them by surprise," Alerio stated. "But I don't have all of my maniples in formation. My cavalry is spread along the line of march, my first maniple is back in the woods, and my third maniple is playing with a hill fort. But I do have a Tesserarius, an Optio, and a Centurion. You three are my council. So, advise me. Where are the Qart Hadasht heavy infantry units billeted? And how do we kill them?"

***

Left flank commander, Senior Tribune Emerens, trotted his mount from the road to the open farmland. In the distance, he noted the town of Tunis, the Empire command compounds, and the tents for the Qart Hadasht army. As if a separate city, the thousands of campsites gave testament to the size of the force defending the Empire.

Based on the number of mercenaries opposing the Legion, the flank commander assumed Legion North would be in combat lines and waiting. Hesitating in their maniples so their Battle Commander and his two Senior Tribunes could hold a strategy session. That proved to be a faulty assumption.

Stationed away from the edge of the forest, Colonel Sisera shouted and indicated directions with his arms. On either side of the commander, NCOs, and a couple of Centurions mimicked his words and actions.

"Velites to the left, second maniple down the center, cavalry right center, first maniple far right," they instructed the Legionaries emerging from the trees. "Velites to the left, second maniple down the center, cavalry right center, first maniple far right."

A quick glance at the enemy positions showed Emerens the target for each unit. He nudged his horse forward.

"What's the plan, Colonel?" he asked.

"Planning is a luxury we don't have," Alerio stated. "Velites to the left, second maniple down the center, cavalry right center, first maniple far right. Senior Tribune Emerens take command of second maniple. And flank commander, capture us a Qart Hadasht General. Go. Velites to the left, second maniple down the center…"

Emerens kicked his mount and charged after the running Legionaries. It all seemed to be madness. In the face of a force of mercenaries out numbering the Republic Legion by three to one, Colonel Sisera had split Legion North and aimed elements at narrow targets. But the flank commander didn't have time to question or protest as he approached the fighting at the pavilions for the Empire Generals.

"Second maniple, form ranks," he bellowed. "Centurions, get control of your Centuries. Second maniple, stand by to advance."

In the melee between the large tents, the Legionaries began slamming the edges of their shields together. While the personal guards for Hamilcar, Bostar, and Hasdrubal fought in clusters, the experienced infantrymen of the Legion began to form assault lines.

***

Senior Tribune Cancellus burst from the forest with Griffinus Agoston close behind.

"Senior Tribune, you're in command of first maniple on the right," Alerio ordered before Cancellus could say a word.

"Secure the Empire supplies, chase off the giants, and support Emerens and the second."

"Yes, sir," the flank commander acknowledged.

As he rode to the right, Agoston nudged his horse in behind Alerio and listened.

"Velites to the left, second maniple down the center, cavalry right center, first maniple far right."

"Not to question your judgement, sir," Agoston commented. He flung his arm out to encompass the isolated fights in the Qart Hadasht camps. "But what kind of formation do you call this mess?"

"If Fortuna is with us, a winning formation," Alerio replied. He glanced over his shoulder at the Legion's top combat officer. "What do you call a mercenary heavy infantryman without his shield and armor?"

"Sir, I don't know," Agoston admitted. "What do you call a mercenary without his shield and armor?"

"A naked Iberian," Alerio responded. "Take over here. I need to go see how our Velites are managing against the soldiers."

"Colonel, you sent our light infantry against Iberian heavy infantry?" Agoston gasped. "That's a disaster in anybody's scroll."

"Not if we caught them unprepared," Alerio explained, "and drove thousands of naked Iberians from their tents."

"Did we?" Agoston asked.

Hektor Nicanor rode up on Phobos.

"Colonel, I found your mount back in the woods," the youth reported to Alerio. He slid out of the saddle and lifted a medic's bag from the one of the four saddle horns. "I thought you might need him."

Alerio vaulted into the saddle. Before galloping off, he addressed Agoston's question, "Senior Centurion, I'm about to go seal the fate of Tunis or die. I'm sure you'll be alerted to the outcome, shortly."

The Battle Commander raced to the left where his skirmishers battled for their lives.

***

In response to an urgent message, third maniple after securing the fort, jogged from Jellaz Hill. As soon as the veterans reached the farmland, Senior Centurion Agoston split the Centuries. Reluctantly, he sent six to help the cavalry. The horsemen were having a difficult time handling the Empire warriors, and the senior combat officer feared the mercenaries would break out and get behind his Legionaries.

Conversely, he wholeheartedly directed the other six veteran Centuries to the left. His light infantry needed bolstering against a select group of Iberians who hadn't run off but had found their armor and shields.

"Where do you want the triage center?" he called to Hektor and three other medics.

The four scanned the fighting, and consulted for several beats before one replied, "Left of center, Senior Centurion."

"That's what I was afraid you'd say," he admitted. The choice meant the medics assumed the light infantry would suffer the most casualties. To a group of reserve Legionaries, Agoston instructed. "Take your shields to the combat lines and pull out the wounded. We're locating the Legion treatment center behind the Velites."

***

Senior Tribune Cancellus rode up behind the first maniple. He assumed his least experienced Centuries would require the most direction. But they didn't.

"Spare the teamsters," Centurion Aeneas ordered. Wounded in the thigh, the combat officer used a branch as a crutch to stand on a wagon full of grain. Despite the injury, he continued to issue orders. "We'll need them to drive the wagons. Use four squads to push out the right perimeter. Everyone else, shift to Optio Kalem's location."

Bodies of Empire mercenaries littered the ground. Plus, several bloody gladii showed where the Legionaries had indiscriminately killed wagon drivers. The perimeter mentioned by the combat officer was marred by footprints made by giant animals. Even after they left the fighting, the backs of the enormous creatures were visible in the distance.

On the left, an Optio had assumed command of the maniple.

"Block the front," Sergeant Kalem instructed. "Centurions, hook them around, we can't depend on the cavalry to contain the warriors."

Cancellus rode to the NCO and asked, "What's the situation, Sergeant?"

"Sir, we've set our maniple to corral their tribesmen. But half our line officers and our Tribunes are wounded and we're having trouble relaying information," Kalem communicated. "I'm glad you're here sir."

"You've done a fine job," the flank commander told him. "Get back to your Century. I'm assuming command of first maniple."

"Thank you, Senior Tribune," the NCO acknowledged while saluting with his gladius.

As a nobleman, Cancellus held a low opinion of the Plebeian class. Patricians founded Rome and only through generosity did they allow the common man to thrive in the Republic. The Sergeant's salute shouldn't have been seen as anything except a sign of respect for an officer and a better. But it was more than those.

The stiff spine of an Optio of the Legion in response to the senior staff officer, the heartfelt respect of the salute in the middle of a battle, and the voice relaying the willingness of the NCO to follow him into Hades if he so directed touched Cancellus. His heart swelled with pride, and the nobleman suddenly understood the connection between Legionaries and their combat officers.

"First maniple, standby," Cancellus called out. He listened for the warning order to be passed through the ranks. At three spots, the voices that should be relaying the message were silent. He kicked his mount and rode to the first dead spot. "Centurion, Optio, shift left, shift right, and assume command of the adjacent Centuries."

Two more times he redistributed NCOs and combat officers. Once done, he raised an arm and the evenly distributed Optios and Centurions acknowledged his signal. In that instant, he felt the power of direct command.

"First maniple, brace," he instructed. Along the line, his infantrymen locked their shields together and held their bodies rigid. The Senior Tribune smiled at the personal attachment he felt to the Legionaries. Then he announced. "Play time is over. Second rank, throw two javelins. First rank, stand by to advance."

***

General Marcus Regulus, one hundred and twenty members of his First Century, Legion East's Battle Commander Ferenc, and six Centuries of East's veterans burst from the road.

Colonel Ferenc erupted, "What level of Hades has Sisera unleased?"

On the crushed crops of the fields, discarded scutum covers were strewn in lines heading across the landscape as if markers pointing to the Qart Hadasht camp. Along with the protective covers, bags of grain, and other items Legionaries hauled but didn't want to take into combat lay on the ground.

In the distance, tents burned throwing off thick smoke that shrouded the battlefield in fog. Yet through the haze, shields, swords, spears, and helmets were visible as men dueled to the death.

"What level of Hades, indeed?" Regulus asked.

The Proconsul spotted Legion North's First Centurion. Agoston was bent over an injured Legionary, holding him steady so a young medic could sew a wound closed.

"It hurts, sir," the infantryman stated.

"Hush, Legionary," Agoston encouraged. "Be proud, you've joined the club. Not many can brag in years to come, they were sutured by the grandson of Captain Nicanor, and valet to Battle Commander Sisera. Look how pretty those stitches are sewn."

"No thanks, sir," the Legionary begged off. "I'd rather admire Hektor's work later. After, I'm healed up."

"Probably a good idea," Agoston admitted. When the legs of horses came into the Senior Centurion's peripheral vision, he glanced up then back down. "Excuse me Legionary, duty calls."

After gently lowering the infantryman to the ground, Agoston pushed to his feet and saluted.

"General Regulus, welcome to Tunis," he greeted Marcus.

"Shouldn't you be with the Battle Commander at the center of the maniples?" Colonel Ferenc challenged.

"Roughly, sir, this is the center of Legion North," Agoston reported. "And Colonel Sisera ordered me here to coordinate the shifting of Centuries."

"How does that work with you back here?" Regulus questioned.

A rider galloped from the directions of three pavilions. He reined in beside the Senior Centurion.

"Flank Commander Emerens has the Twenty-Fifth and the Twenty-Sixth Centuries available," the cavalryman informed Agoston.

"Send them to the right side," the top combat officer instructed. "The first maniple is still struggling to hold the warriors in check."

The rider kicked the mount's ribs and the cavalryman raced back into the smoke.

"I take it that is an example?" Regulus quizzed.

"It is sir. Been like that all day," Agoston confirmed. "But things are slowing down. Most of the Empire defenders have fled. Unfortunately, we don't have the assets to pursue."

"You didn't have the manpower to begin this battle," Ferenc blustered. "Which begs the question, why did a single Legion engage an army three times its size?"

"Well sir, I wasn't there. I was still deep in the forest as were all of the command staff," Agoston clarified. "But as the story was told to me, there was a Centurion of Velites, an

Optio of Scouts, a Tesserarius from the second maniple, and a discussion about naked Iberians."

Ferenc faced puffed up and his eyes bulged. The East's Battle Commander was a serious man and being answered by a joke would not be tolerated.

"If you were my Senior Centurion," Ferenc threatened, "I'd have you on the punishment post for insubordination."

"Yes, sir," Agoston allowed with a tilt of his head. "If, I was your Senior Centurion."

From the smoke where the rider had vanished, a line of five horses emerged. Walking in a row they could have been on parade. Except for the blood on their armor, the saddles, the flanks of their horses, and the ash smeared on their faces. Behind the five, Senior Tribune Emerens and Tribune Rapti Galba rode to either side of an older Punic gentleman. His extravagant robe displayed a high office, meaning they escorted an important prisoner.

"What's this?" Marcus Regulus inquired.

"General Regulus," Emerens announced with a salute. "May I present General Bostar, Senior Commander of the combined Qart Hadasht armies."

Chapter 6 – Just Too Much

Alerio swung his gladius over the infantryman's shoulder and retracted the blade after chopping into an Iberian soldier. Stepping back, he scanned the combat line for other threats. Seeing none, he allowed his blade to drop to the side of his leg. The Legionaries in this section were holding the line without difficulty.

"One doesn't expect to see a Battle Commander backing up an assault line," Centurion Grear Keoki remarked.

Between the haze and the distance, he could barely make out Alerio. But the ceremonial armor and the white comb of his helmet identified the Battle Commander. Equally, Alerio identified the top officer for his Velites by the red horsehair crest.

"Most Colonels are smart enough not to send light infantry into a fight with Iberian heavy infantry," Alerio shouted back. "So, I thought it only fitting that I join them in the fiasco."

Behind the Battle Commander, four members of his First Century stood guard while the rest fought on the shield wall. Additionally, several Junior Tribunes acting as runners kept the Colonel informed about the situation in other areas of the battle.

"We had them on the run," Keoki said. "Then their ready Companies arrived and threw up this shield wall. The second maniple saved us from the turning tide."

An instant later, the conversation broke up. Both officers rushed to the combat line. Where Alerio pulled an injured Legionary out of the fray, Keoki jumped into the fight adding his gladius to a developing breach.

The smoke saved the men of Legion North. It prevented the Iberians from seeing how few Legionaries opposed them. For all they knew, the Republic had them trapped in a three-sided box. Thankfully for Alerio and his Velites, haze hid their thin line, medium shields, and light armor.

"Sir, General Regulus would like a word."

Alerio twisted his head and squinted. An immaculately dressed Centurion stood beside him.

"I'm a little busy," Alerio informed the First Centurion of the East's First Century.

"Not for long, Colonel," the Centurion stated.

From behind him, squads of veterans jogged into view. Once they located the assault line, the Legionaries began inserting themselves into the shield wall.

Then two veteran combat officers stepped up to flank Alerio.

"We've got this, sir," one assured him.

"Take me to the General," Alerio instructed the mounted officer.

***

Out of the smoke and away from the fighting, the sky was blue and the air sweet on the tongue. Alerio marched to the mounted Marcus Regulus and his command staff.

"General Regulus, Tunis is yours," Alerio announced. He saluted, coughed to clear his lungs, and continued, "compliments of Legion North."

Marcus leaned down and studied his Battle Commander. Streaks of ash coated his face, arms, and legs. Adding to the untidiness, blood splatters dotting Alerio's armor turned the grey ash to ruby mud.

"You've created a problem for me," Marcus confessed. "My other Colonels are jealous and critical of you and Legion North. It seems you are just too much. It's not personal. But for a period, I need you out of the way."

"Sir, we took Jellaz Hill and Tunis for you," Alerio reminded the General. "And it was our third maniple who broke the blockade on the coast road. Which was possible because Legion North punched through the Qart Hadasht army at the pass. Something your other commanders failed to do on the coastal road."

"I'm aware of your accomplishments," Marcus Regulus admitted. "But I need to keep peace with my other Battle Commanders. To do that, Legion North will guard our supply route."

"Sir, that will take me out of the fighting," Alerio whined. "Why would you keep your best commander off the front line?"

"As I said," Marcus Regulus replied, "to keep peace in the expedition."

"By coddling the ineffective and punishing your most successful Legion," Alerio shot back. Then he remembered to whom he was speaking and quickly reined in his temper. "General, I protest."

"So noted," Marcus Regulus stated. "By the way. Your Senior Tribune Emerens captured an Empire General. Thank you for that."

"Again, sir, compliments of Legion North."

"I'm going to go and give him the terms of surrender," Marcus Regulus informed Alerio. "You see, Colonel Sisera, you've won the war. Something the other Battle Commanders will not have the opportunity to do."

***

On a training ground near the defensive wall of Qart Hadasht, forty Spartans drilled two thousand Celtics. Each of the Noricum soldiers possessed a sword of Noric steel from their homeland and carried a heavy wooden shield. Racing around the ranks, Spartan instructors adjusted a few feet or shields until the soldiers resembled a drawing.

"You'll note, the formations are interlocked," Spartan Tail-Leader Xanthippus illuminated the positions. "Once they take a location, leave them there to fight. It's what heavy infantrymen are for. They will hold your center."

"Very instructive, General," two of the five Punic officers acknowledged.

Without the tradition of fighting in phalanxes, the Qart Hadasht Lieutenants and their Captain had no idea or appreciation for the position of Tail-Leader. To them, a foreigner must be a General to have their respect and to get their attention.

"Wouldn't it be better to move them around to show aggression?" one Lieutenant questioned.

"We depend on the cavalry, the war elephants, and our light infantrymen to move around the battlefield," Xanthippus replied. "The only proven use for heavy infantrymen, like the Iberian and Noricum soldiers, is forward or backward. Both always in a controlled manner."

"It's been a fine demonstration," the Empire Captain assured the Spartan. "I'm positive my junior officers appreciate the knowledge you imparted."

Xanthippus saluted, spun, jumped down from the reviewing stand, and marched away. Ten steps from the platform, he spit to get the taste of wasted advice out of his mouth. It was the only sign of frustration the stoic Spartan leader allowed himself to show.

"Let me guess, sir. They want their mercenaries to scream war cries and frighten the enemy with dance moves," one of the Spartan instructors sneered. "Have they learned nothing about commanding infantry in battle?"

"Don't ever say that again," Xanthippus cautioned. "The Punics may not be great Generals. But they are most creative in finding ways of executing outspoken Spartans."

"Yes, Tail-Leader," the instructor acknowledged.

"But they do pay well for instructions they don't follow and information they don't use," Xanthippus remarked. "Let's get back to the barracks and review the lessons we learned from today's drill."

The instructor had gone four steps when a cry of alarm came from the reviewing platform. Xanthippus made a left face and took in the sight of the five officers frantically waving their arms and stomping their feet. But the Punics weren't facing the ranks of Noricum infantrymen. Rather they looked to the southwest in the direction of Tunis.

"What's the problem?" Xanthippus demanded after vaulting onto the raised stand.

The Punic Captain steadied an arm and pointed. A herd of cavalrymen and elephants thundered their way towards the Qart Hadasht Capital. Behind the fleeing animals, warriors, and men in short undergarments completed the scene of a stampeding army.

"It's not the Republic's Legion," the Spartan observed. "Those appear to be units from the blocking force at Tunis."

"That's only ten miles away," a Lieutenant stammered. "What are we going to do?"

The junior nobleman might have been talking about the Legions. But the Spartan leader was more practical. From a pouch, he pulled a small flute, placed it between his lips, and issued a shrill whistle. In response to the signal, the forty Spartan instructors focused on their Tail-Leader.

"Three lines in front of the gates to the city," he shouted. Xanthippus added hand motions to accompany his voice so the instructors at the rear of the practice field understood.

The Noricum formation dissolved as row upon row of soldiers marched away. Under the directions of the Spartan instructors, they took positions defending four gates to the city.

"That was quick thinking, General," the Punic Captain complimented Xanthippus.

"Thank you," the Spartan responded with a slight bow. "Now if you'll excuse me, I'll take my men and retire."

"What? Where are you going?" the officer demanded.

"To our barracks, Captain," the Tail-Leader answered. "As I've been warned numerous times by the Special Branch, I'm here to train your home guard. Not to assume any responsibilities beyond that. I do believe crowd control of your beaten army qualifies as additional responsibilities."

"It's the poor quality of the troops sent by our subject states," one Lieutenant moaned.

Xanthippus circled his arm to direct his Spartans to where they would form up. On the steps down from the platform, he assumed he was out of hearing range.

"It's not the poor quality of the soldiers," the Spartan commander whispered. "It's the poor quality of your Generals and your officer corps."

Unfortunately for the Tail-Leader, one young nobleman was blessed by the Greek mountain nymph, Echo. Thusly, he had sensitive ears and heard every disrespectful word.

Rank Leader Xanthippus didn't witness the glare of the Punic Lieutenant, the nobleman's hate filled eyes, or even suspected the coming troubles. For the time being, he was happy to get his Spartans away from the rushing mass of an out-of-control army. Xanthippus' joy would last for a day before he was sentenced to crucifixion for his insolence.

***

The panicked troops made it difficult for the bodyguards to keep a protective envelope around General Hamilcar and General Hasdrubal. But with continual snaps of whips and jabs with spears, they kept the warriors and soldiers away from the Qart Hadasht noblemen.

Hamilcar seethed with anger as he rode. His cousin had been in command at Jellaz Hill. A man who he believed could be trusted to send an early warning. But like so many others, his cousin disappointed the General.

He thought back on the happenings that brought him to this point.

While taking his midday meal, the sounds of battle reached Hamilcar's pavilion. At first, he assumed the clashes were shield and sword practice by the mercenary infantrymen. He almost went outside and ordered them to stop disturbing his repast. It wasn't until the Major arrived to alert him; they were being overrun by four Legions. Only then did he understand the disturbance.

"How, Major?" Hamilcar demanded. He stepped close to the officer. "How did they sneak fifteen thousand Republic Legionaries by your sentries?"

"Sir, I don't know," the mercenary officer replied.

Rage took control of Hamilcar. Between the failure of his cousin and this idiot, the General lost the war and his reputation. Drawing his knife, he sank the blade into the Major's lower belly.

"That's the last time you will disappoint me," he remarked while ripping a gash in the mercenary commander's gut. Then to the servants at the entrance of his tent, Hamilcar instructed. "Bring my horse around and have my bodyguards mount up."

General Hamilcar raced for Qart Hadasht without an army. And to make matters worse, the Legions were chasing him. Pursuing him, no doubt, to the very walls he had sworn to defend.

***

Dawn found the amphitheater of the Special Branch in full session with three visitors. One came in the person of the Suffete for domestic affairs. The second and third guests being General Hamilcar and General Hasdrubal. Noticeably absent and unaccounted for since the battle of Tunis was the old campaigner, Bostar.

"We recognize the bravery of our field commanders who escaped," the speaker exclaimed. He bowed to Hamilcar and Hasdrubal before continuing. "And we offer prayers for our missing brethren who sacrificed himself on the blades of the Republic. Let us take a moment of silence in honor of General Bostar."

No speech could be heard in the arena, only the breathing of distraught men. They had reason to worry. Scouts reported that three Legions of the Republic were camped at Tunis, just ten miles from the walls of Qart Hadasht.

"We do have some good news of a sort," the speaker announced. "A count of our army shows minimal loss. It has been suggested that we bring them in the gates and use them to defend the walls."

"Speaker, if I might have the floor," the Suffete for domestic affairs requested.

"The Special Branch yields the floor."

"After consulting with the Congress, it has been decided that bringing thousands of mercenaries inside the city walls is dangerous," the Suffete stated. "Let me remind you, the Sons of Mars were allowed into Messina. Not to protect the town but to save the struggling band of mercenaries. They turned on the city guard and commandeered Messina for themselves. It's with that threat in mind that the people's Congress voted. We will keep the mercenaries outside the city walls."

"If we can't bring them in for protection," a member inquired. "And we can't fight the Legions with them. What are we going to do with the mercenaries?"

"Isn't the real question," another member asked, "what are we going to do with the Legions?"

The speaker tapped the floor with his staff.

"Those are precisely the questions we have on the agenda for today," he informed the amphitheater. "Let us begin with a report from General Hamilcar."

Hamilcar stood and acknowledged several members of the Special Branch. However, before he could open his mouth to speak, Bostar marched through the doorway.

"I beg your attention for urgent matters," the old General proclaimed. He crossed to the center of the arena and insisted. "Matters that cannot be set aside."

"General Hamilcar, our apologies," the speaker stated. "General Bostar has the floor."

Bostar pulled a scroll from a pouch and gripped the two dowels. Then with shaking hands, he unrolled two sheets of papyrus. His chest rising and falling with emotion, the old General read.

"Citizens of Qart Hadasht, I greet you as a conqueror. Let this missive stand as both a notice of capitulation and the nonnegotiable terms for the surrender of your city," Bostar peered over the top of the scroll to be sure the attendees understood the first part of the letter. He needn't have bothered. Everyone in the amphitheater was fixated on him and the condescending words. "You will disband your forces and remove your bases of operations from Sicilia, Sardinia, and Corsica. Henceforth, the Qart Hadasht Empire is prohibited from declaring war or making peace without permission from the Senate of Rome."

Cries of anger rose from the aggressive members of the Special Branch. Others, more pragmatic, kept their opinions to themselves. Although harsh, the trade that made the Empire great could continue under the terms. For them, the conditions were acceptable. But Bostar hadn't finished reading the declaration.

"Further, Qart Hadasht will provide fifty quinquereme ships-of-war and crews to the Roman Navy. For home port defense against pirates, the Empire is allotted one ship-of-war."

Declawing the Empire put trade in jeopardy. The stipulation moved a few more members to express outrage. And still, Bostar hadn't finished with the letter.

"Qart Hadasht will compensate the Republic for war expenses and pay an annual levy to Rome. The exact amount of tribute will be determined at a future date by the Senate."

Abandoning territory and stripping them of their powerful Navy was hard to take. But the final issues were the demands for coins. In its entirety, the Special Branch screamed for the letter to be burned.

"I await your surrender. Signed Marcus Atilius Regulus, Proconsul of the Senate, Senator of the Republic, and citizen of Rome."

The speaker rapped his staff on the floor trying to get control of the rowdy assembly. When they finally settled, the Suffete for military affairs stood.

"I don't need a vote to know our answer to this outrage," he avowed. "To a man, we know the Republic Commander just wants too much. The question we face is what our response to this monster will be. We'll break into committees to formulate a series of suggestions."

"If I might," a member of the Special Branch said while standing. "Going back to the comments made by the Suffete of domestic affairs. I want to report a subversive residing in our city."

"Who poses such a danger?" the speaker inquired.

"The Spartan, General Xanthippus."

Act 3

Chapter 7 – Questionable Motives

Marcus Regulus and three of his Battle Commanders lifted glasses and saluted each other. At the other end of the banquet table, staff officers raised their mugs as well.

"It was a brilliant letter of demand, General," Colonel Balint cooed. "You've won. There is a triumphant parade through the streets of Rome in your future."

"Now that does present an interesting quandary," Marcus proposed. "I'm the first General to command marching Legions beyond his term of office. Can a non-Consul have a parade?"

"After what you've accomplished, sir," Colonel Ferenc stated. The Battle Commander stood and declared, "if the Senate doesn't allow it, you can always rip up the peace treaty and let the war continue."

The three Colonels laughed at the idea. Mimicking their commanders, senior and junior staff officers at the end of the table chuckled along with them. But one flank officer cut his fawning short.

Senior Tribune Triticeus wondered at the absence of Colonel Sisera. It seemed odd that the man who engineered the victory should be excluded. Beyond feeling badly at the slight to his friend, Triticeus was a follower of the God Mercery. And he knew, the outcome of the treaty talks would be very different if Mercery, the messenger of the Gods, and the God of Tricksters, got involved before Sancus, the God of Oaths.

At the head of the table, the General raised his hands to quiet the attendees.

"Gentlemen, a war doesn't end unless both sides agree." Marcus Regulus reminded the group. "My letter was only a wish list. Leadership in Qart Hadasht will need several days to debate the items before coming back with a counteroffer. I expect General Bostar will head the delegation."

"Still sir, this is great news. The men have missed a fall harvest and a spring planting," the Battle Commander from Legion South stated. "They're restless to get home to their farms."

"We all miss our families and our work," Marcus commiserated. "I guess I should have included transportation home for us in the letter."

Chuckles of good humor burst from the assembled officers. It must have been the sounds of merriment that drew the God Mercery's attention.

***

As the sun climbed into the sky, Alerio stretched and hiked to the top of the earthen battlements.

"Not much to see, is there?" he questioned the Legionary on watch.

Suspicious of any question from a Colonel, the Legionary on duty gave a cautious reply.

"Sir, it's not my place to say," the infantryman begged off.

From the top of Jellaz Hill, the view included the treelined main road, a peek at the green water of Lake Tunis and, to the north, the upper reaches of the pavilions at Tunis. In fact, there were things to see from the hill fort. But none of it held interest for the homesick Legionary and his outcast Battle Commander.

"Keep sharp," Alerio said. "There might be a caravan of drama girls coming up the road."

"Really, sir?" the sentry gushed.

Alerio laughed and picked his way down from the ramparts.

"Anything new up there, Colonel?" First Centurion Palle inquired.

"Nothing but greenery," Alerio replied. "I think I'll ride to the Medjerda River and check the coastline."

"Tunis is closer, sir," Pelle advised.

"I don't think I'm welcome there," Alerio responded. Then he questioned while slipping on his armor. "Tell me Rabbit, is there such a thing as being too successful?"

"I never thought so before," Pelle answered. "But seeing the petty response to you, I'd say yes, there is such a thing as being too successful. Like Zeus and Semele."

"Was the God jealous of her accomplishments?" Alerio asked.

"No sir. It was Hera, Zeus' wife, who was jealous," Pelle answered. "The beautiful Semele had a nightmare about dying from a lightning strike. A priest advised her to sacrifice to Zeus to counter the omen. Later, she went to the river to wash away the sacrificial blood. Zeus spotted the beauty and fell in love."

"So far it sounds like a bawdy song from a minstrel," Alerio complained.

"It's not, Battle Commander," Hektor assured him. "Allow the Centurion to finish the story."

"Is the moral, a handsome man like me shouldn't bathe in the river lest a Goddess find me irresistible?" Alerio teased. Seeing the frowns of disapproval on the faces of his valet and the First Centurion, he agreed. "Fine. Finish the fable."

"Semele emerged from the tryst pregnant with a divine child. After a few months, she gave birth to Dionysus, the God of Wine Making and Fertility," Pelle continued. "But Hera, Zeus' wife learned of the affair. Disguising herself as a confident, Hera counseled Semele and suggested a test of Zeus' love."

"I'm not given to testing Gods," Alerio observed. Then he thought of his complicated relationship with the Goddess of Death. "Not most of them, anyway. And I don't believe I'm in a position to sire a God."

"No, sir. But you have birthed success after success," Hektor told him. "And there are people jealous of you."

Hektor made hand signs to urge Pelle to tell more of the tale.

"By asking him to appear in his armor at full power and with his lightning in hand, Semele would know if Zeus truly loved her. She begged and Zeus did as she asked. However, Zeus in his magnificence accidently burned Semele alive. And so, as her nightmare predicted, Semele died by lightning."

"The two of you can be assured that I don't have nightmares," Alerio informed them. "And if a storm comes up, I'll seek shelter and avoid standing in the lightning."

"It's fate, sir," Hektor pointed out. "We're all tools of the Gods. Jealousy is but one road to the preordained."

"Beyond being a medic and my valet, now you're a seer?" Alerio challenged.

"No, sir. I'm a youth who worries about how you're being treated," Hektor replied.

"Furthermore Colonel, we've apprehensions about what fate their jealousy is driving you towards," Pelle added. A Legionary walked into the command area and saluted. The First Centurion returned his salute and informed Alerio. "Sir, your escort is waiting at the corral."

Without thinking, Alerio reached to his neck and touched the Helios pendant.

"The fates have their job to perform, as do I," Alerio remarked to Hektor and Pelle. "And mine is to get as many of my Legionaries home as possible. To do that, I need to be sure the Empire doesn't row an army across the Gulf of Tunis and land them along our supply route."

He slung a red cloak over his shoulders and marched down the hill. At the bottom, a mounted troop from First Century and a handful of Junior Tribunes waited to accompany Battle Commander Sisera on his patrol.

***

Rank Leader Xanthippus inhaled the morning air of Qart Hadasht. In the crowded city, the heady aromas of spices and unwashed bodies assaulted his nostrils. It was much different than Sparta. There, the pleasant smells of freshly turned soil and growing crops drifted in the air.

'I miss that,' he thought while tossing a scarlet cloak over his shoulders.

The commander acknowledged his Spartans while marching through the exercise yard. Paired off, they drilled with spears, shields, swords, or wrestled or tried to outdo one another in calisthenics. Exercise was a daily ritual instilled in them since they were seven years old. Lean and hard, the

Spartans took pride in their martial abilities and in their appearance. Especially in a growing city with a large female population.

At the gate to the street, a Helot bowed and slung open the door. From a pleasant morning, the Spartan Commander's day transition into a struggle. From the street outside, a Punic Captain and fifty infantrymen attempted to shove their way into the compound.

Although a slave, the Helot was trained in battle tactics and instantly shouldered in beside the Tail-Leader. Together, they held the doorway. While he pushed against the intruders, Xanthippus dropped a hand behind his back.

The Hoplites had stopped their exercises and were sprinting towards the entrance. But Xanthippus' hand pivoted at the wrist. With spread fingers, he rotated the palm from side to side.

It was the same motion used to sow seeds over a prepared field. And it served as a sign for the Spartans to disperse around the city. With spies and lovers in every quarter, the highly visible Hoplites could easily vanish among the population. And they did.

By the time, the Commander and the Helot backed up and allowed the gate to swing open, the practice field and buildings were empty. Immediately, the Qart Hadasht officer and his detachment raced in.

"Where are your Spartans, General?" the Empire Captain demanded.

"I gave them a few days off," Xanthippus responded. He pointed to the buildings around the exercise area. "Go see for yourself. You'll find the barracks are empty. As all infantrymen do, my Hoplites enjoy a variety of things in their leisure time."

"You're under arrest for insolence among other more serious crimes," the officer charged.

A slight quiver in his voice ruined the effect at projecting authority.

Xanthippus jerked his sword from the scabbard and his knife from its sheath. The nearest soldiers and their Captain jumped back. With a smile, the Spartan spun the blades on his palms and offered them hilt first.

"I trust you'll take care of these. I'll want them back in the same condition when this is over," Xanthippus directed. Then to the infantrymen, who had been trained by the men from Sparta, he ordered. "Detail, forward march."

With the Spartan Commander out front, the infantrymen filed from the compound and proceeded up the street towards Byrsa Hill and the Special Branch. Meanwhile, the Captain remained in place. Mesmerized by holding the Spartan's weapons, he was oblivious to the movement of his detail.

Long moments later, the Helot cleared his throat and noted.

"Sir, your detachment has left."

***

The walls of the amphitheater rang with the voices of men attempting to talk over each other. A cacophony of words and phrases bounced back on the bleachers, drowning out new comments and the same arguments.

"We have the army, isn't that enough?" the military Suffete shouted.

"Apparently not against the Legions," a Special Branch member yelled.

"Nonsense, we have to fight," Bostar exclaimed.

Around the arena, the same type of discussion was repeated over and over. Yet, neither the unsure, the fearful, nor the hawks could take control. Then a voice bellowed out the question no one wanted to broach.

"You lost, General," a member accused Hamilcar. "Who will lead us? I ask you, who will lead our forces and defeat the Republic?"

It might have been exhaustion from the morning of debate or the booming voice of a powerful speaker cutting through the racket. In either case, the questioning hushed the Special Branch. When they fell silent, a rustle of cloth and hard boots on the tile floor drew the members' attention.

Tail-Leader Xanthippus marched through the doorway. Tucked under his left arm was a Greek helmet with a long red and yellow crest that cascaded from the top. Swept out behind him, his cloak billowed before he stopped, and the scarlet material folded around him as if the wings of a giant bird-of-prey.

Seeing an opportunity to change the topic and bring the members together, the speaker rapped the floor with his staff.

"The Special Branch has voted, General Xanthippus," he informed the Spartan. "You have been convicted of subversion. From this moment onward, you are designated an enemy of the people of Qart Hadasht. Before your arrival, you were tried, convicted, and sentenced to death by crucifixion."

Still heated from the debates, the Special Branch erupted in cries for an immediate execution.

"Do I get a say?" Xanthippus asked. "Or is justice as gone as reason from the Empire's Capital?"

Several members called for openness and a chance for the Spartan to make a comment. After getting a sign from the Suffete, the speaker rapped for order.

"The Special Branch will hear from General Xanthippus," he announced.

Xanthippus turned and walked to the bench where guests sat. He placed his helmet on top of the backrest with the eyeholes and slit down the front facing the assembly. Blackness under the helmet filled the holes giving the orbs the appearance of dark eyes peering out and observing the bleachers of the amphitheater.

While adjusting the headgear, he inquired, "Can you see?"

"General, we can't hear you," the speaker directed. "If you want to address the Special Branch, please give us the courtesy of looking in our direction."

He didn't respond to the speaker. Instead, the Spartan unclipped his cloak, fluttered it through the air before guiding it down and around the helmet. Now the cape resembled a distorted body wearing a phalanx Tail-Leader's helmet.

Once the display met his approval, Xanthippus turned to face the Special Branch. But he didn't talk. Instead, he pulled a leather tie free and unbound his mane. After lifting a brush from a pouch, he began combing his long hair.

"Let me tell you a secret," he imparted in a conspiratorial tone. He combed in long even strokes while talking. "Yes, the Spartans are great warriors. In battle we fight as if possessed and we win. But is that from years of training? Or something else?"

He stood in one spot, brushing with one hand, and making eye contact with different members. It wasn't lost on them that for a condemned man, Xanthippus was relaxed and holding a one-way conversation.

"On the day of a battle, we cut our toenails, trim our fingernails and, as you can see, we comb our hair," he enlightened the members. Waving the comb in the air brought chuckles from several of them. "Why you ask? Because a Spartan has already sharpened his blade, polished his shields, and repaired his armor and helmet. There is nothing else to do on the day of battle except to groom and be bored while waiting."

The Tail-Leader stopped brushing and raised the comb in the air. Holding it aloft for several counts, caused the assembly to stare at the bristles as if the comb were going to change form. Once he had everyone's attention, Xanthippus moved the comb in an arc, and pointed it at the helmet and cloak.

"We are relaxed because we know our enemy did not sleep well the night before," he stated. "Maybe they got a little sleep, but it was troubled. Maybe they woke and drank wine or beer all night. Or, maybe they stayed awake, quivering, and praying to their Gods. In every case, they didn't get a good night's sleep. Unlike Spartans."

Xanthippus bowed to the helmet and resumed combing his hair.

"How can we know our enemies are weak from lack of sleep?" he asked. "Because Epiales, the God of Demons and Nightmares follows Spartans wherever we go."

The Tail-Leader dropped to a knee and bowed to the helmet.

"He enjoys the terror Spartan Hoplites cause during the daylight," the Tail-Leader described. "And in return, he delivers terror to our enemies during the night."

Still bent in the helmet's direction, Xanthippus cried out.

"Oh God Epiales, why have the Gods deserted Qart Hadasht?" he demanded of the helmet and cloak.

There had been no talk of the Gods abandoning the city. But now that the Spartan mentioned it, a few members decided it was true. Every member of the Special Branch locked their eyes on the Spartan and his cloak and helmet.

"Why, God of Nightmares do you deliver terror to the Empire?" the Spartan thundered. "Give us a sign so we can right the wrong."

The only sounds in the amphitheater were those of quick breathing in anticipation and the thumping of racing hearts as the members waited for a sign.

"I am Xanthippus, a Spartan Commander," he roared. "In the names of the Kings of Sparta, tell me."

Undulating as if a spirit moved beneath the scarlet cloak, the material lifted and fell in waves. Then, as if the God Epiales bowed his head, the helmet slid from the top of the backrest, skated down the cloak, hit the seat, and bounced into the air. It crashed to the floor and spun a half revolution before coming to rest on its side.

The Spartan remained stooped over his knee as if overcome with emotion.

"What does it mean?" members cried. "Please, tell us the meaning. Why have the Gods deserted our city?"

Xanthippus remained as still as a statue except for the movement of breathing. Finally, he finished stealthily wrapping the thread around his left hand and he regained his breath. Blowing hard enough into a gap in the material to make it move had left him lightheaded.

He picked up the cloak and clipped it around his neck. Then with the helmet under his left arm, the Tail-Leader broke the thread off from the helmet. He stood and faced the Special Branch.

"What did the sign mean?" the Suffete demanded.

"It seems obvious to me, sir," the Spartan replied. "You have thrown the savior of your city to the floor. Discarded him as if he were nothing but a fallen piece of gear."

"Who, who have we overlooked?" the speaker shouted.

"Me," Xanthippus informed the Special Branch. "Make me the commander of your army and I will crush the Legions for you. However, there is one stipulation."

"What stipulation?" the Suffete asked.

"It'll cost you gold," Xanthippus told the assembly. "Lots of gold."

Chapter 8 – Winds of Regret

The forty Hoplites took the entire afternoon to regroup at the barracks. Most came with smiles, but a few arrived wearing frowns. The difference told on the faces of the ones who indulged in pleasure while hiding and the Spartans who worked.

"I don't know what you did Tail-Leader," one said, "but Congress has created a committee to investigate stripping you of all your property."

"Stay on that source," Xanthippus urged. "I'll need to know when the talk shifts to taking a contract out on me."

In addition to the Spartan's fighting abilities, they were experts at information gathering. Through their network of paid informers and supporters, the men from Sparta kept tabs on persons of interest and events around the city. Of special interest were political moves that affected the phalanx.

Another Spartan examined the Tail-Leader from head to toes.

"How did you convince the Suffetes to make you a General," he inquired, "and us Captains of the army?"

"It wasn't me," Xanthippus protested. "They were persuaded by the God Epiales."

"Sir, those are tricks we all learned as boys," the Hoplite remarked. "But the Punics fell for it?"

"The Punics have never been boys training in the agoge," the Tail-Leader laughed. Then he got serious. "We have a lot to do before we take their army to war. First, find us a ship and reserve it."

"It'll cost bags of coins to convince a merchant Captain to wait around for us," the Sergeant in charge of transportation informed him.

"With the gold the Special Branch is paying us, we can afford to be generous," Xanthippus remarked. "Also, we need to secure horses for the phalanx. I can't have my Captains hiking all over the battlefield."

"With the number of horsemen and extra mounts brought in to fight the Republic," the procurement Rank-Leader reported, "buying horses will be easy."

"How many cavalrymen have they hired?" Xanthippus asked.

"Four thousand horsemen, plus one hundred war elephants," the NCO charged with keeping track of the Qart

Hadasht army listed. "Heavy infantry consists of three thousand Noricum and twenty-five hundred Iberian soldiers. The rest are a mixture of light infantry, warriors, archers, and slingers numbering around sixty-five hundred."

"And the Legions?" The Tail-Leader solicited the Hoplite detailed with evaluating the Legions. The man looked perplexed, so the Commander inquired. "Is there a problem, Rank-Leader?"

"More of an enigma, Tail-Leader," the Spartan NCO responded. "Their best Battle Commander, Sisera, and his Legion North have been assigned to guarding the supply route."

"He doesn't have the honor of having a seat at the negotiation table?" another of the Spartans inquired.

"Legion North and Battle Commander Sisera have been exiled to Jellaz Hill," the Legion expert stated. "I don't believe he'll be at the negotiations."

"That is a problem," Xanthippus contemplated. "Rank-Leaders, work up a plan to stop Legion North. I don't want to isolate the Republic's leadership only to have their best Commander show up and stab me in the back."

***

In anticipation of the arrival of the Qart Hadasht representatives, the treaty tent went up a safe distance from the Legion lines.

"Do you think they'll feel secure enough?" Marcus Regulus inquired.

"That's not the question, General," Colonel Ferenc said. "My worry is, will our committee be safe that far away?"

"I can't imagine General Bostar will allow any trickery," Regulus stated. "Before he left with the demand list, I felt we bonded over the need for peace. Didn't you?"

"I did, sir," Ferenc confirmed. He indicated his left flank commander. "I'm sure Senior Tribune Triticeus is honored to be selected to represent the Republic. I know, I am. We'll do our best to get a good treaty."

"You've been my primary Battle Commander since my election. I can't think of anyone else I'd trust to negotiate for us," Marcus told him. "As for your senior staff officer, he's shown himself to be a stellar officer. I only wish I could be present in the tent."

"General, you're the authority figure," Ferenc reminded him. "If you're in the tent, who are we supposed to blame when we don't agree on an article."

"I envy you," Marcus admitted. "Sitting across from an adversary, looking him in the eyes, while haggling over points of contention. The act of parleying is exhilarating."

"I just need to remind myself not to give away too much of our advantage," Ferenc confessed. "I'm as homesick as a raw recruit on the third day of Legion training."

"Why the third day?" Marcus asked.

"By day three, the recruits are exhausted from running, exercising, and lack of sleep. And they are missing home." the Colonel said. "It's then the Legion issues shields. The regret for joining the Legion gets very real when the recruits start getting bashed around by the heavy scuta."

"Just be sure you, Triticeus, and the other staff officers don't get pushed around by the Qart Hadasht emissaries."

"That won't happen, General. You can count on us."

"I am," Marcus said before walking to his horse.

Mounted, he had a better view of the isolated tent and the Punic delegation as they approached.

"Colonel Ferenc, duty calls."

Battle Commander Ferenc, Triticeus, his right flank commander, and the Legion's Tribune for planning and strategies, plus five Junior Tribunes mounted and rode to meet the Punic officers. The youths were included so they could witness the great negotiation that ended the war with Qart Hadasht.

***

The First Centurion of Legion East positioned his twenty veterans on one side of the treaty tent. Once his Colonel and the staff officers dismounted and entered the open sided pavilion, the commander of Ferenc's security detail searched for his opposite number. While twenty Qart Hadasht soldiers mirrored the formation of his Legionaries, none wore an officer's headgear.

"I don't expect trouble. They didn't even bring a line officer," the Centurion commented before asking a squad leader. "Isn't that Noricum armor they're wearing?"

"It is, Centurion," the Decanus confirmed. "But aren't the Celts big men?"

"Everyone I've faced required me to reach up when we fought," the veteran officer remarked.

"Not them," the squad leader pointed out. "They're muscular, but don't have the mass and height of the typical Noricum. Maybe they select their bodyguards by running marathons."

"Now there's a terrible selection process," the Centurion joked, "picking your security detail by who can run the farthest and the fastest."

***

On the far side of the tent, the Rank-Leader examined the Legionaries.

"They shouldn't be a problem," he observed.

"I agree," another Spartan confirmed. "I like this armor. Noric steel is solid."

"You can buy some with the gold from this assignment," the NCO stated.

***

When all the negotiators arrived, the Legionaries of the security detail relaxed. Behind the Legion line, their General, Marcus Regulus didn't.

"Our Legions need this treaty," Marcus remarked to an aide.

"I'm sure they'll work it out, General," the staff officer replied.

The negotiation teams had entered the tent, exchanged salutes, and poured beverages. As they sat, a wind rose from the north.

Riding on the winds, the Goddess Victoria came to collect on Marcus' pledge.

"This day, Victoria, grant my warships the strength to be triumphant," Regulus had prayed during the sea battle at Cape Ecnomus. "For that blessing, if you choose, I offer myself as a sacrifice."

In response to Regulus' oath given during a time of crisis, the Goddess of Victory joined the discussions. Along for his own caustic reasons, Mercery, the Trickster God, also inserted himself into the negotiations.

Blowing directly into the faces of the Legion team, the flying dust forced them to squint or to look away from their

Empire counterparts. Fatally, servants lowered the sides of the pavilion to block the windstorm. In doing so, they hide the Republic negotiators and observers from the Legion security detail.

***

Moments before, the participants had strolled into the airy tent to face the opposition.

"General Bostar, nice to see you again," Ferenc greeted the Qart Hadasht officer with a salute. Holding out an arm, he indicated Triticeus. "This is my Senior Tribune and left flank commander. He'll be helping me during the talks."

"And this is General Xanthippus, an adviser to my city," Bostar introduced the Rank-Leader.

Scowling at the Spartan, Ferenc commented, "I didn't realize there were Spartan units in the Qart Hadasht army."

For several heartbeats, Xanthippus' bland face considered the Legion Battle Commander.

"There weren't," he stated after the long pause.

Feeling tension in the pavilion, Senior Tribune Triticeus asked, "Can we offer you a libation?"

"Wine for me," Bostar ordered.

"Water," the Spartan Commander snapped.

The four principals placed their helmets on the cloth covered table. Then with beverages in hand, they sat across from each other. No one spoke until the wind sent the tablecloth flapping over their mugs and helmets.

"Drop the sides," Ferenc instructed the servants. Remembering Regulus' concern that the Qart Hadasht delegation wouldn't feel comfortable close to the Legion line, he inquired. "If that's alright with you, General Bostar?"

Rather than Bostar, the Spartan replied, "It's fine to drop the sides."

"Seal the tent against the weather," Ferenc directed.

The snapping of blowing tent material and the howling wind prevented coherent speech. All four negotiators sipped and waited for the sides to be lashed down.

"That's better," Ferenc stated when the wind was sealed outside. "Now we can get started with…"

The sica sliced the air in an even straight line. From the edge of the table, the blade cut Triticeus' windpipe before severing Ferenc's left carotid artery. While the Senior Tribune and the Battle Commander fell to the floor, their life and blood pumping from the wounds, the Spartan leaned back. He cleaned the blade on the tablecloth and stood. After examining the hilt to be sure it was spotless, he slid the long knife into a sheath beside his kopis. The Spartan sword had never left its scabbard.

Even though the Junior Tribunes yelled out in horror and the Tribune from planning and strategy bellowed with rage, Xanthippus ignored them. Strolling to the back of the tent, the Tail-Leader addressed his NCO.

"Rank-Leader. Signal the cavalry," he directed, "and dispatch the Legion security detail. I don't care about the junior staff officers."

"Yes sir," the Spartan NCO replied. He raised an arm overhead and rotated the large bronze shield while ordering his Spartans. "Shields up. Draw. Charge."

The sun reflected off the bronze surface, flashed across the distance, and into the eyes of several mounted Spartans.

"That's the signal," they reported to their sections.

"Cavalry. Forward," the Rank-Leader instructed.

Two thousand horsemen jumped onto their saddles and nudged their mounts into motion. Soon, they were galloping towards the bloody negotiations tent and the Legion lines.

***

The First Centurion of Legion East had survived plenty of battles. During season after season in marching Legions, his experience and responsibilities had expanded under different Consuls. Always a professional, he initially thought fire when the young staff officers ran from the tent.

"Sir, what's the matter?" he attempted to asked one of the fleeing noblemen.

But panic blinded them to the duty of informing the combat officer. Rather, they sprinted for their horses. Still thinking it was a natural disaster caused by wind and fire, he stepped to the entrance of the pavilion.

The Centurion's Legion knowledge and battle reflexes failed him. From around the side of the tent, a kopis stabbed under his chest armor. Gutted by the blade, the veteran combat officer dropped to the ground holding his sliced abdomen.

After stabbing the Legion officer, the Spartan finished racing around the tent. The sneak and stab cost him. Out of place, the Hoplite had to leap to get his shield in place at the Spartan wall.

If he were alive, the First Centurion would have taken back his barb about a marathon. The security detail for the Qart Hadasht delegation was fast. Before the Legionaries knew they were under attack six infantrymen died on kopis blades. The rest of the veterans from First Century stumbled backwards using their scuta to ward off the other blades.

Pursued every step by the soldiers of Sparta, it seemed hopeless.

But then, the Spartans gained some combat knowledge about Legion veterans. It started with a single word issued by a Legion Decanus.

"Brace," the squad leader bellowed.

From retreating targets, the Legion shields snapped into a solid wall of hardwood. And the kopides stopped doing damage to the infantrymen and began beating harmlessly on the scuta.

"Advance."

Only training from a young age saved the twenty Spartans. They flexed rather than resisted. And yet, they had to jump back when the gladii stabbed from between the shields.

"Advance."

The duty of the Rank-Leader and his Spartans was to take the Legion security detail out of the fight. When he realized his files were getting into a slug fest with veteran infantrymen, he ended it.

"Fall back," the Rank-Leader directed.

The Legion Lance Corporal snorted and peered over his shield at the retreating Spartans. He wanted to go after them. He wanted payback for his dead Legionaries, the murder of his Centurion, and for the treachery inside the treaty tent. But the horizon boiled with dust from a wall of racing horseflesh and their riders.

"Fall out," the Decanus shouted, breaking the formation. "Now run. Run hard."

Chapter 9 – Rules of Fate

Marcus Regulus screamed in frustration when the junior staff officers sprinted from the treaty pavilion. He understood immediately their panic had nothing to do with a fire or a failing tent. Teenagers would have fallen against each other laughing at a freak accident once safely outside. It was something more sinister that sent the young noblemen running from the pavilion.

Before the Junior Tribunes mounted up, the First Centurion from Legion East died on a Qart Hadasht blade. As the officer fell, the rest of the Empire's security detail attacked and killed six of his Legionaries. The broken negotiations and the unexpected attacks caused Marcus mental stress. It heightened as the surviving infantrymen scrambled away from the Noricum soldiers.

To Marcus Regulus, the sight of his veterans taking flight crushed his soul. Sensation fled his limbs with each staggered step as they retreated. His throat went dry, and he couldn't even moan in his agony.

But then, the fourteen remaining Legionaries locked their shields together. A rush of adrenaline surged through Regulus when the shields hammered forward. The numbness faded and he began issuing orders.

"Get me the Senior Centurion from Legion East," Marcus ordered.

In a matter of heartbeats, the Legion's top combat officer rode up.

"Sir, we have Empire cavalry heading our way," he informed the General. "I've taken the liberty of deploying the first maniple to our combat line. I hope that meets your approval."

"On most days, I need you to help staff officers with administration work. Today, I don't. You're the new Battle Commander for Legion East," Regulus informed him. "Appoint a left flank commander from your Tribunes and move your oldest Junior Tribute to the left maniple. Qart Hadasht didn't break the treaty to further negotiations. They'll be coming for us."

"I agree, sir," the new Battle Commander acknowledged. "And they'll come hard. You do remember, sir, you have a fourth Legion in reserve?"

Marcus Regulus paused and wondered if Alerio Sisera had been in the tent, would the outcome be any different. Deciding it didn't matter as the tent had little to do with the Punic army, he directed, "Send your youngest junior staff officers to Jellaz Hill."

"Is it that bad, General?"

"That's up to the Gods," Marcus replied. "I just want the children out of here until it's over."

As the new commander rode away, Marcus sent messengers to Legions West and South and a longer missive to Colonel Sisera at Legion North.

***

The Qart Hadasht horseman reached the Legion defensive ranks. Rather than attempting to breach the lines, they pulled their mounts to the side and raced along the rows of shields. Besides the yelling which was unnerving, and the danger of a sudden attack from the proximity, the Empire cavalry hadn't attempted to breach the Legion shields.

Behind the combat rows, Centurions called for two javelins. A cry of 'Rah' echoed from the ranks of Legionaries at the command. Following the confirmation, first one than a second flight of javelins soared into the sky. When the barbed iron heads dropped, horsemen and their mounts fell. The volleys drove the cavalry back. The cheering of Legionaries followed the javelin attacks.

"What's the purpose of the hoard of riders?" General Regulus asked his staff.

No one had an answer. Unfortunately, as the horsemen pulled back, Marcus Regulus received the answer. Two Legion officers appeared. They rode from among the horsemen and began parading back and forth in front of the Legion. However, the way Colonel Ferenc's helmet and arms flopped it was obvious a dead man sat on a horse. The same was true for Senior Tribune Triticeus. Plus, each of their horses was led by another rider.

The riders stopped pulling and let the horses for the Colonel and the Senior Tribune stand still.

"Why an exhibition of the dead?" Marcus questioned.

The 'why' shouldered aside horsemen as he rode to the front. Stopping just out of javelin range, he straightened his scarlet cloak. It flowed from his shoulders, down his back, and over the hindquarters of his horse. When he pivoted his head, a red and yellow crest flipped like the hair of a maiden flirting with a hero. The long crest cascaded from the top of the Greek helmet.

"A Spartan," several of the General's staff uttered.

"Be quiet," his chief aide ordered.

The Spartan Commander lifted his arms and indicated the propped-up corpses of Ferenc and Triticeus.

"I walked into the Legion camp and took their lives," the Spartan bellowed. He paused as men in the crowd of riders repeated his words. When they grew quiet, he continued. "I, personally, took the lives of two senior Republic officers."

Again, his speech got repeated by men placed there to be sure every horseman heard the Spartan's brag.

"And, I took their souls," he announced.

As if the words were a signal, the riders leading the dead men, resumed walking the bodies back and forth in front of the cavalrymen.

The horsemen shouted war cries and the Legionaries yelled challenges. As quickly as he appeared, the Spartan turned his horse and trotted away. The bodies of Ferenc and Triticeus traveled in his wake. No doubt for display and bragging rights at other units of the Qart Hadasht army. As the Spartan rode away, the crest was visible bouncing and swaying from side to side as were the bodies of the Legion officers.

"Because you need to convince your troops that you are invincible," Regulus answered the question of why the Empire Commander displayed the dead officers. Then in an undignified outburst, he shouted. "We beat them before you, Spartan. And we'll beat them with you."

Cheering from the defensive lines rose in response to the General's assertion. Heartened by the infantry's reaction, Marcus Regulus kicked his mount and raced to consult with his Battle Commanders for Legions South and West.

***

Alerio unrolled a scroll and read a report. On the backside of the papyrus, the ink from an earlier scouting report had faded.

"Tell me, Senior Centurion, if a Legion runs out of writing material and can't keep records for the Senate," he asked Griffinus Agoston, "is that a good enough reason to sail for home?"

"Colonel, in years past, my commanders always said if there was no record, the event didn't happen," The top combat officer replied. "That went for accomplishments and punishments. But they never said anything about ending a mission for lack of paper."

"How about for lack of activity?" Alerio grumbled. He tossed the scroll onto the camp desk. "The supply route is safe. We haven't had so much as a robbery by a band of thieves."

"Colonel, you need a good soak," Agoston recommended. "We don't have a proper bath. But there are two bodies of water an easy ride from here."

"Seeing as all Legionaries can swim," Alerio stated while standing, "I believe we need to requalify Legion North in the swim or drown test. I volunteer to be the first in line for the examination."

"A truly brave gesture, Battle Commander," the Senior Centurion acknowledged with a smile.

"It's a sacrifice I'm willing to make for the good of the men," Alerio announced. Then he yelled to another room of the hill fort. "Hektor. Get my combat armor, three javelins, a spear, a scutum, and a mule. While you're gathering, collect soap, some rags, and clean tunics for you and me. Then meet me at the corral."

"Is something wrong with the one you're wearing, sir?" the boy inquired. "I can bring you a fresh tunic."

"Do as you're told," Alerio barked. To the duty infantryman at the door, he instructed. "Alert Centurion Pelle and the entire First Century. We're riding to the west lake for a Legion swim test."

The Legionary left the doorway and ran to alert his officer and his Optio. He didn't smile until he was out of sight of the Colonel and the Senior Centurion.

***

Although soap was used in abundance later, the test was dangerous, grueling, and hated. Not just by weak swimmers but hated by everyone as they got their leather wet, their iron and steel damp, and their shields soaked. All of that required drying, waxing, and maintenance after the test.

"They're good swimmers," Alerio remarked.

"That they are, sir," Pelle confirmed.

The two officers floated in waist deep water while watching the latest group of swimmers.

Out on the lake, six Legionaries in armor swam to where a pair of squad leaders were treading water. The infantrymen would swim around the unarmored Decani before heading back to shore. Forced to use powerful strokes to counter the weight of their armor, they also towed their scuta. But tied to each shield was a helmet, gladius, armored skirt, a spear, and three javelins. The pulling required them to swim fast to keep the shield from sinking below the surface. For slow Legionaries, the drag of the submerged scutum increased the difficulty.

But after the test, there was fire for drying, grease and wax for polishing, and wine for drinking. Plus, soap to scrub the skin clean and an allotment of leisure time for a long soak.

Alerio kicked and water exploded into the air.

"I've never seen you swim with equipment, sir," Hektor remarked. "Very impressive."

"Every Legionary can swim with his war gear," Alerio told him. "How else could a Century cross a river or a lake to reach the enemy?"

"But not every Colonel could have passed the test," Pelle added.

The one hundred and twenty men of the beefed up First Century tested, cleaned, then floated while drinking. As hard as the swim was, test day always ended in a celebration.

Feeling relaxed and comforted by the companionship of infantrymen, Alerio dunked under the surface and swam underwater. On the fourth stroke, his right arm stiffened, and he felt pressure on his right shoulder blade. The sensation announced the presence of the Goddess Nenia. Alerio came up quickly and peered at the bank. Men reclined or worked on their equipment while chatting in a casual manner.

"Centurion Pelle, get half your Century dressed," Alerio instructed. "And post guards."

"What is it, Colonel?" the Rabbit inquired.

"Something is wrong," Alerio told him. He didn't admit it was a premonition delivered by the Goddess of Death. Instead, he said. "It's just a feeling."

"Yes, sir," the Rabbit stated. He waded to shore. On the bank, the First Centurion ordered six squads to gear up and spread out in a semi-circle.

While the Legionaries hustled into defensive positions, Alerio pulled on his armor, tied the armor skirt around his waist, and dropped the straps to his gladius over his shoulder.

"Get out your medical kit," he instructed the boy.

Hektor jogged to the mule and began undoing the knot securing the medic's bag. Before he finished, Legionaries screamed.

***

Galloping along the curve of the lake, horsemen lanced and slashed a pair of Legionaries at a position to the south. But even wounded, they did their job. Issuing cries of pain, the pair warned of the approaching danger. In response, undressed Legionaries snatched up shields, grabbed spears or gladii, and fell in on either side of Alerio. Further down the lakeside, Pelle set the center of another line away from the water. And the squads sent to stand sentry, consolidated inland.

Two abreast, fifty Empire cavalrymen raced along the bank. But their route ended at a wall of thirty-five shields. Although the riders urged their mounts forward, the stack of scuta appeared to be the side of a building to the beasts. The horses veered away putting the cavalrymen sideways to the Legionaries.

Veterans jumped from the end of the hasty formation and pulled five riders off their horses. With the way along the bank blocked, the Empire cavalrymen veered away only to face Centurion Pelle's wall of hardwood. When the three groups of Legionaries ran inward, screaming, and jabbing with spears, the horsemen began to run in a circle. That's when the second rank in each formation broke from the attack line and ran to stacks of drying javelins.

Maybe it was the rage at disturbing a pleasant day, or the horsemen injuring a pair of Legion sentries. Or, maybe the frustration at being relegated to guarding the supply route is what drove the Century. A little of each, perhaps, went into the nightmare unleashed by the Legionaries on the Qart Hadasht cavalrymen.

"Rabbit. To circumvent the lake, those horsemen started before dawn," Alerio pondered while watching the last of the Empire horsemen die. "Where do you suppose they were going?"

"Coming up from the south," Pelle guessed, "they could have been heading for Jellaz Hill. Which made you, their objective. Or they were trying to sneak up and attack the Legions at Tunis from the rear."

"Both tell me Qart Hadasht isn't going to sign a peace treaty," Alerio decided. "Send messengers. Any Centuries north of the Medjerda are to rally at Jellaz. Those south of the river, I want to form a blocking force on the far side."

"You're thinking the Legions may need to retreat?" Pelle inquired.

"The Empire is fighting for their Capital," Alerio explained. "What would you do if you were fighting for Rome?"

"I'd put you in command," Pelle responded. "And we'd fight to the death."

"Exactly."

***

Three Legions stretched across the fields of Tunis. With two hundred feet between commands, the Republic forces controlled twenty-eight hundred linear feet of ground. Within each Legion, the first maniple stood at the front in a three-rank formation. At the rear, the veterans of third maniple held the same three-rank shape. Not that the veterans expected to rush into the battle anytime soon. The first and second maniples would take the brunt of the attacks. However, before the sides joined in conflict, all three maniples displayed even rows of shields, signifying their readiness to fight. As the instructors in recruit training taught, "Intimidation of your foe starts when they see you are ordered and prepared for battle."

Legion South held the left side of the Republic's formation. That position put them in front of their marching camp, and more than a quarter of a mile away from their supplies.

At almost the exact center of Legion South, Tapeti Elateris scratched his neck while staring to the right. The two hundred feet between South and Legion East was occupied by Republic cavalrymen and skirmishers. Beyond Legion East was another two hundred feet of cavalry before the start of Legion West. But he wasn't focused on the infantrymen, the horsemen, or the Veles. Tapeti Elateris had his eyes on the waters of Lake Tunis.

"What are you thinking about?" the Centurion for the Nineteenth Century inquired.

Tapeti reluctantly pulled his view back from the water and the neighboring Legions.

"My family is in the shipping business," Tapeti Elateris replied to the combat officer. "When I was younger, we lost two ships to Illyrian pirates. Although my father wanted me to become a Captain in his fleet, after suffering the loss, he needed one of his sons to learn how to handle a shield and a sword."

"And he signed you up to a Regional Legion, so you'd be close to home?" the officer guessed.

"Not even close," Tapeti corrected. "I joined four years ago and was promptly shipped off to Sicilia. At Thermae, we witnessed the Empire sweep in and murder four thousand of our allied troops. Before we could chase them down and get revenge, the campaign season ended. Harvest time came and the Senate ordered us home."

"At least you learned to handle a scutum and a gladius," the line officer said.

"More than that," Tapeti Elateris informed him. "After a few months sailing and rowing on my father's ships, I joined another marching Legion. As much as my heritage was the sea, my heart fell in love with the infantry."

"It's a sickness, I fear," the Centurion joked.

"Like all Legionaries who return to their trade between campaigns," Tapeti continued. "I went to sea. But as soon as a Consul formed a new Legion, I signed up. Having missed last year's trading season, I keep looking at the water like a farmer views a freshly turned field."

"It's understandable," the officer agreed. Then he stated. "I better get back to my squads."

"May the God Occasio bless you this day," Tapeti Elateris offered.

"For what," the officer inquired, "opportunity, luck, or favorable moments?"

"Based on the size of the army approaching us," Tapeti responded, "let's pray to him for all three."

The officer of the Nineteenth walked back to his Century and Tapeti looked behind him at the Legion's stockade. Wagons had been wheeled onto the ramp at the gate. Teamsters, supply men, and tradesmen stood on the platforms drinking wine and observing.

"I hope you enjoy the drama," Tapeti spit out before turning back to examine the Empire army.

The hoard had warriors, light infantrymen, and soldiers in good armor. They would be a problem. And although he couldn't get a count, their ranks appeared to be deep. At least based on how far back their cavalry rode.

"If nothing else, they don't have elephants," he whispered.

"Sir, did you need something?" his Optio asked.

Centurion Tapeti Elateris scanned the three ranks of his Twentieth Century. Seeing the infantrymen neatly arranged, he replied to his NCO in a light manner.

"A fat bellied trading vessel," Elateris replied while slipping on his officer's helmet. "And a contract for a port-of-call somewhere over the horizon."

"Sorry, sir," the Sergeant answered. "There's nothing here except good farmland, and bad Empire steel."

"Anybody here ever see an elephant?" Centurion Elateris questioned. He walked along the line of his infantrymen examining their gear. They had already been checked by their squad leaders and his NCOs. But, Tapeti became an officer because he didn't neglect details. "They are huge beasts. I saw a couple in Sicilia."

"Did you ever face one in combat, sir?" a Legionary asked.

"It's been twenty years since the Legions battled war elephants," Tapeti informed his infantrymen. "Legions of Consul Manius Dentatus had taken the field to stop Greek King Pyrrhus. But at Beneventum, General Dentatus was driven back by war elephants, Pyrrhus' cavalry, and Greek soldiers. During the retreat of his Legions, Manius Dentatus called on his rear guard to throw javelins. They lobbed several flights but didn't hit any of the giant beasts and just a few of the soldiers. Then a lucky throw sliced a calf. Wounded and afraid, the baby elephant bellowed and ran through Pyrrhus' army searching for its mother. The other war elephants heard the calf, became agitated, and they began running through the ranks searching for the baby. In the mania, Consul Dentatus advanced his Legions and drove Pyrrhus back to Greece."

"Sir, in that story, is there a lesson on how to fight the beasts?" his Corporal inquired.

"If you locate a calf during the battle, injury it, don't kill it," Centurion Elateris answered. "Other than that, get out of the way because war elephants are huge animals."

"Are they more dangerous than those, sir?" a squad leader questioned.

Tapeti gazed beyond the first maniple to the Empire army. Where the soldiers had been in line with the warriors and light infantrymen, they had begun to crowd together. Forming up in loose ranks, the armored men were a few steps from establishing phalanxes. The combat officer did a quick count of the front rank and the numbers of groupings.

"Sir, we have five Greek phalanxes coming out of the hoard," he shouted to the staff officers for the first maniple.

Using his hand, he indicated the five areas.

"I don't see any," one staff officer snapped. "If we want the opinion of the second, we'll ask for it. Stay with your maniple."

Another reason Tapeti Elateris reached the rank of combat officer, he was persistent and confident. Spinning, Tapeti signaled his right flank Tribune.

"Sir, there are five phalanxes forming," he described. "Looks to be five across but I can't tell how many ranks deep."

"I don't see any spears, Centurion," the staff officer commented. "Are you sure?"

"If I'm wrong, what's the harm Tribune?" Tapeti asked. "But if they suddenly acquire long spears, we need to be prepared."

"Good call," the Tribune acknowledged.

He waved over a Junior Tribune and instructed him to carry the news to his flank commander. Centurion Elateris faced his Century.

"What do we do about the phalanx, sir," another of his squad leaders asked.

"Remember when I said to stay out of the way of war elephants?" Tapeti Elateris reminded his infantrymen. They all shook their heads confirming the elephant lesson. "Well, to keep a phalanx from busting our lines, we do the opposite. We stand in their way."

Act 4

Chapter 10 - The Battle for Tunis

"Second maniple, move up," the staff officers ordered.

The Tribunes' instructions came after long spears appeared in the ranks of the grouped soldiers. When the spears tips were shoved to the fore of the formations, and the shields overlapped sealing the front, top, and sides, the phalanxes became identifiable.

"Javelins," the Tribunes from first maniple called out.

The phalanxes were close, allowing the second row of Legionaries to chuck their javelins over the line and directly into the enemy shields. Iron barbs punched through, slid along iron shafts, until the heavy wooden frames slammed into the shields. As designed, the javelin shafts bent making the shields unwieldy. The weight dragged the barriers downward.

Instead of stopping the progress of the formations, the soldiers with the dangling javelins rolled away and the files continued forward.

"Javelins."

Barbed iron heads drilled through, long shafts bent, and the javelins pulled down shields. Again, the affected soldiers stepped aside, allowing the phalanxes to continue.

"First maniple, second maniple, brace," the Tribunes and Centurions yelled.

Five files wide and twelve men deep, the Spartan trained phalanxes pushed into the Legion line. Countering them were Legionaries stacked six deep and pushing just as hard. For a few heartbeats, the struggle became a stalemate. The sides ground their shields together, both immobilized, with neither the Empire nor the Republic winning.

But, just as small cracks were the biggest threat to a dam and not the flow of the river, it wasn't the mighty phalanxes that broke the Legion line. On either side of the armored encased formations, mercenary light infantrymen shoved against the scuta. As if they were prying open a stuck door, they placed their backs against the shields of the soldiers and pushed the Legionaries with their legs. Warriors leaped into the gaps, forcing the Legionaries back. Then as if waterproof seals gave way on a ship's hull, Empire forces flooded through the breaches and crashed into the Legion.

"Rally, rally," the second maniple officers screamed.

They backed away from the chaos, trying to establish a new defensive position. Tapeti Elateris glanced back to judge the distance to the third maniple. To his dismay, the veterans stood right behind him. The entire Legion line, as if a falling fence, had collapsed. The veterans were creating the next and last hardpoint for Legion South's defense.

Then Tapeti noted the dead men far to the rear lying beside the wagons on the ramp. Qart Hadasht horsemen rode in and out of the Legion's fortified bivouac.

"Where's our cavalry?" he asked.

"They ran, Centurion," a Legionary answered. "Hard to blame the noblemen. The Empire brought eight times their number to the party."

Tapeti scanned towards the two-hundred-foot gap between his Legion and Legion East. Before the battle, the area held Legion horses and Veles. Now, horsemen and warriors of the Empire crowded in and battled both Legions.

A flash caught his eyes and Tapeti looked back at the stockade again. Flames engulfed the wooden posts and upright boards of the sides. And from within the marching camp, smoke boiled into the sky as their tents and supplies burned.

"I miss the sea," Tapeti whispered, "but still it's…"

"Excuse me, sir," a veteran asked. "Did you say something?"

Centurion Elateris drew his gladius, shoved aside several Legionaries until he reached the spot for his final stand. Then he braced his legs and waited for the Empire formation to come to him.

Seeing an officer, desperate infantrymen flanked him creating a short combat line.

"I said," Tapeti Elateris announced as the spear tips of the phalanx reached him, "it's a good day to die."

***

Marcus Regulus watched as Legion South vanished under the Qart Hadasht army.

"Thirty-eight hundred sons of Rome," he said grinding his teeth. "May the judges in Hades see their valor and rush the heroes to the Elysian Fields."

"General, maybe we can shift right and link up with Colonel Balint," an aide recommended.

Frozen in place by the forces opposing them, Legion East feared to move left in support of Legion South. Besides the threat of soldiers in front, the move would have abandoned

Legion West. But after the destruction of the Legion on his left, Marcus Regulus had no choice.

"Order the maniples to join with Legion West," Marcus instructed. "Put the veterans in the lead."

They had two hundred feet of Empire horsemen and warriors to clear before linking with Legion West. And to be sure the way was open, their battle-hardened veterans jogged to the right side. Where five ranks of Veles had held the side, three rows of heavy infantrymen were charged with moving the line.

***

Until the Legion on the left was dead and buried, the Spartan Commander held some attackers in reserve. Now he could add the victorious Companies to the assault against the other two Republic Legions. When South fell and East began shifting, he ordered the rest of the Qart Hadasht army and the phalanxes to engage. His army's moral peaked and he used it for the final push. But to assure the momentum, he needed to dishearten the Republic.

"Let's take away their safe havens," Xanthippus instructed. "Send the cavalry around and burn the other two Legion forts."

***

Alerio Sisera trotted up Jellaz Hill on a captured horse. Pulling on the reins, he stopped in front of Griffinus Agoston, and dismounted.

"Did you get my message?" he asked.

"We have twelve centuries of infantry, two Veles, and once hundred cavalrymen south of the Medjerda," the Senior Centurion reported. "The rest of the Legion is on this side and awaiting your orders, sir."

"That should be enough for the blocking force," Alerio announced. "I'm going to Tunis and speak with General Regulus. To keep you and Centurion Palle from throwing fits, I plan to take three Centuries and elements of the First with me."

"An excellent idea, Colonel," Agoston agreed.

A courier galloped from the direction of Tunis. Spotting the Legion's staff, he drove his mount up the hill before reining in.

"Where is Colonel Sisera?" he asked.

Alerio laughed and raised his arm. For all the saluting and sirs, when dressed in his battle armor, but without the white combed helmet, he could be any of a half dozen staff officers. He had left it in his room as the Battle Commander's helmet was too valuable to be sacrificed to a swim test.

"That's me, what do you have?"

"Sir, compliments of General Regulus," the courier stated while passing over a rolled scrap of parchment paper.

Taking the piece of parchment, Alerio thought again of the dwindling supplies. Not food, they could forage for that, but for harder to replace consumables such as paper, aged hardwood, and quality steel.

"Senior Tribune Emerens, you and I are moving up to engage the Qart Hadasht army," Alerio directed after reading the message.

"What about me, Colonel?" Cancellus inquired.

"You're staying here," Alerio informed the right flank Senior Tribune. "There are going to be wounded and staff coming this way. Don't let them block the road or stop at Jellaz Hill. I want all of them pushed back to the river."

"Sir, the Medjerda is six miles from here," Cancellus protested. "Wouldn't we be better staging them on Jellaz Hill."

"The hill is only a mile and a half from Tunis," Alerio reminded the Senior Tribune. "It's too easy a target. Move supernumerary personnel to the river. Understand?"

"Yes, sir."

When fifteen Junior Tribunes rode into view, Alerio swept his hand in Cancellus' direction as if shuffling an object to the senior staff officer.

"We have a force at the river," Cancellus shouted at the young noblemen. "Keep moving."

They followed directions and passed by the hill. Then, cavalrymen came from the forest. Half were wounded and slouched over the necks of their mounts.

"Rapti, if they can ride, hold them here," Alerio directed his Tribune of Horse. "If they might bleed out, treat them here, but find a wagon and move them as soon as you can. And get me a report."

Rapti Galba jumped on his horse and along with four of his horsemen rode down to meet the newly arrived cavalrymen.

"Grear, send a Century up the road to the end of the trees," Alerio instructed the light infantry officer. "I've a feeling we're behind on a developing situation."

Grear Keoki saluted and jogged to several Centurions of Veles. While he talked with one of the officers, Alerio focused on his senior combat officer.

"Griffinus, disregard the order to wait here," he stated. "We're moving all available Centuries up to Tunis."

"Yes, sir, probably a good idea," Agoston commented.

He pointed to the trees. Walking wounded, struggling to carry stretchers, limped along the road.

Alerio noted Hektor racing down the hill with his medical bag flopping against his hip. While he watched, an aide brought Phobos from the corral.

"Sir, will you be changing armor?" the Junior Tribune inquired.

Alerio took the reins, looked down at his scratched and dented battle gear, and replied, "I don't think so. But I'll need the Battle Commander's helmet. And thank you for bringing my horse. Very thoughtful of you."

"Sir, I would like to take credit, but it was Master Nicanor's idea."

Another aide ran from the hill fort with the Battle Commander's helmet.

"Let me guess," Alerio remarked as the identifiable headgear was handed to him. "Hektor's idea?"

"Yes, sir."

***

Legion North rushed towards Tunis but stopped at the edge of the forest. There appeared to be no clear path to victory or even an identifiable destination beyond that point. The forest ended while the road continued to a dark and forbidding place.

The landscape and the town of Tunis were obscured by thick smoke. The bulk of it coming from two burning Legion camps while a little drifted in from the charred remains of a third. Alerio studied the scene and a knot formed at the pit of his stomach.

"The shadows in the smog are Empire warriors attacking the Legions," Centurion Miklos of the Forty-Sixth Century reported. "Or else, they're being hounded by the three-headed dog, Cerberus. If only the gates of Hades would open and swallow them."

The shapes he referred to were shadowy figures in the distance.

"If anyone is at the gates to Hades, it's our Legions," Alerio submitted. To his left flank commander, he instructed. "Emerens, we aren't going to rush out and join the Legions."

"If we aren't fighting, sir, why are we here?"

"I didn't say we weren't going to fight," Alerio clarified. "I want double files of shields running from the trees to the Legion line. They're surrounded and we're going to provide a corridor for their retreat."

"I've collected another two hundred cavalrymen, sir," Rapti Galba told Battle Commander Sisera. "We'll keep their horsemen off our infantry as much as possible."

"Hektor, Centurion Lophos, Tribune Invisum, Centurion Gratian," Alerio called to his support staff. "You four escort our Junior Tribunes to the river."

"Sir, I can't leave you," Hektor insisted. His breathing came hard either from the forced march or from emotion. "I swore an oath."

Alerio leaped off Phobos, handed the Battle Commander's helmet to Agoston, and walked to the defiant boy.

"I appreciate you wanting to keep your word to the Goddess Hera," Alerio consoled Hektor. "But my parents, and Gabriella need to know what happened here."

"But your unborn child," Hektor pleaded. "I promised he wouldn't grow up without a father. Respectfully, sir, I'm staying with you."

Alerio lifted the necklace with the pendant of Heilos over his head and let it dangle between his fingers. The image of the Sun God swung back and forth.

"Take this and Phobos home to Rome," Alerio instructed. He wrapped an arm around Hektor and squeezed affectionately. Dropping the pendant over the boy's head, he told him. "Know this, Hektor Nicanor, I will come back for all the things I love, including you."

With tears in his eyes, Hektor climbed onto the big stallion and nudged it into motion. He rode away with the rest of Legion North's admin staff.

"Senior Centurion, where do we stand?" Alerio inquired.

"The Forty-sixth is taking the lead," Agoston answered. He held the gaudy helmet up to Alerio. "We'll follow with the Sixth Century and create the corridor with the remainder of Legion North."

"Why the Merchants of Mayhem?" Alerio questioned.

"Sir, they want revenge for Corporal Philetus," Agoston replied.

"Retaliation or an oath. Both are good enough reasons to die," Alerio stated. He pushed the Commander's helmet back to Agoston. "You wear it Senior Centurion. It'll draw too much attention to me."

"Colonel, I don't understand," Palle dared even though he had an idea. "What does draw too much attention mean?"

"Rabbit, I'm going forward with the Sixth," Alerio responded. He grabbed an infantryman's helmet from a Legionary and placed it on his own head. "You're now a stretcher-bearer and don't need a helmet."

"Yes, sir," the stunned infantryman acknowledged.

"Forty-Sixth Light and Merchants of Mayhem," Alerio boomed at the two lead units. "I am late for an appointment with General Regulus. Can you get me there?"

"Rah," the Veles and the heavy infantrymen responded.

"But the way is full of peril," Alerio challenged. "Empire blades, clawed monsters from the netherworld, and only the Gods know what else stands in my way."

The men howled their willingness to take the Battle Commander through the hazards.

Centurion Miklos called to the Forty-Sixth, and Centurion Aeneas addressed his Sixth Century.

"Century, attention," they instructed.

The Legionaries braced. Barely breathing, they waited for their Colonel.

"Glory and the Qart Hadasht army await us," Alerio announced. To Senior Tribune Emerens he remarked. "I'm going in. It would be pleasant to have an exit corridor in place to get out."

"Yes, sir, you'll have a walkway," the Senior Tribune assured him, "as nice as any pathway in a temple garden."

"I don't seem to be any closer to the General," Alerio informed the Centuries. "Forward."

The light infantry stepped from the woods and jogged into the smoke. Close behind Alerio with the Sixth Century followed in their wake. While they began running, Legion North shuffled out in two lines, forming a channel of shields. Agoston and Emerens trotted down the center. Rapti Galba's cavalry split and began patrolling along the line of march.

It was a good strategy for the extraction of the surviving Legions. A fine plan with an excellent chance of success.

Except, the Spartan General was prepared for Legion North and their successful commander, Colonel Alerio Sisera.

Chapter 11 – Too Much Territory

Alerio ran with the Sixth Century. Glancing back, he noted the double line of infantrymen extending from the woods. Alongside the Legionaries creating the escape route, Rapti Galba's cavalrymen kept Empire horsemen away. Unopposed, the walls of the passageway formed quickly.

A sudden stop brought Alerio's attention back to the front. The Centuries were approaching the backs of the warriors assaulting Legion East. A couple of mercenary NCOs saw the fresh Republic forces. Although they waved and yelled, their warnings were lost in the din of battle.

Off to the side, a Spartan Captain observed the danger. But, seeing as the reserve Legion was forming a corridor and not attempting to reinforce the besieged Legions, he ignored the threat. It was worth a few hundred dead mercenaries to lure Legion North out of the forest.

"Throw one javelin," Centurion Miklos ordered his skirmishers, "and disburse."

From leading the way across the field, the Veles released javelins, divided, and created endcaps for the heavy infantry.

"Form three ranks," Centurion Aeneas instructed. "Cut them away from our boys."

Now bracketed by the skirmishers, the Sixth Century was able to deliver the concentrated power of their shields and gladii to the attackers.

Bodies dropped by the javelins of the skirmishers defined a section. The Sixth Century stomped over the dying warriors as they hammered into the rest. As if a hand dropped and scraped away grains of wheat, the Legionaries scraped away soldiers exposing fifty-five feet of Legion defenders.

"Where's General Regulus?" Alerio demanded while pushing to the front of the Sixth Century.

From blocking, stabbing, and fending off wave after wave of Qart Hadasht mercenaries, the men of Legion East found themselves facing the shields of Legion North. They paused but kept their scuta interlocked.

"Stand down," Alerio shouted. "Make way."

But the tense and embattled infantrymen held their positions.

"Allow me, sir," Centurion Aeneas interjected. His helmet, unlike Alerio's, had the distinctive horsehair comb. Recognizing him as an officer, the defenders responded to his instructions. "Make a hole for the Battle Commander."

Shields parted and Alerio walked through.

"I should have kept my Colonel's helmet and dressed the part," he scolded himself. A projectile slammed into the side of his heavy armor. Alerio stretched to the side to give relief to the bruised spot. His heavy battle armor had stopped the lead pellet. In his flashy Battle Commander's armor, on the other hand, he would have had a broken rib. Looking down, he located the squashed lead missile from the Empire slinger and stated. "Or not."

Spying a Tribune standing with a rear rank, Alerio jogged up and inquired, "Where's General Regulus."

Before the staff officer answered, a horse charged through the Legion ranks. The rider, his face a mask of fear and terror, rode towards the corridor. Infantrymen had to jump out of the way as Tribune Ostentus Colonna galloped between exhausted infantrymen. Alerio spit in the direction of the horse and rider. They reached the opening, galloped through, and escaped.

"Limp mentula," Alerio cursed at the retreating noblemen.

"You know Tribune Colonna?" the staff officer questioned.

"Enough to know him as a coward," Alerio remarked. "Where's the General?"

The Tribune indicated an area to the left of the command tents.

***

From the edge of the forest, a Qart Hadasht soldier stepped into the clear. He waited to be sure the Republic troops leaving the woods were more than a patrol. Once sure the reserve Legion was committing, he pulled flags from his back and began snapping them through the air.

Hidden by the flames and smoke from a burning stockade, a Captain, one of Xanthippus' hoplites, waved a flag in reply.

"Get them up," the Spartan officer shouted to his Lieutenants. "Sisera's Legion is on the march. They embarrassed you once. Now it's time to return the favor."

Sprawled on the ground, his two thousand Iberian infantrymen stirred then jumped to their feet. Held out of the earlier attacks, they were assigned to take on Legion North.

"Form ranks," the Spartan Captain instructed. "Wedge formation. Forward."

In a broad sweeping movement, the soldiers circled from behind the burning structure. Once on a collision course into the side of the corridor formed by the Legionaries, the center elements stepped out front and the ones on their sides drifted back. Before the Iberian heavy infantry were ten steps towards the flank of Legion North, they formed an arrowhead designed to slice through the corridor.

***

In a defensive square, one would expect to spot specific units. But the combined Legions of East and West created a massive perimeter. Ranks of Legionaries and officers waited for another trip to the front, medics worked on wounded, and water carriers raced to quench the thirst of men just rotating from fighting at the front. Between the smoke, dust, tents, and wagons, Alerio might have wasted precious time without directions.

"Get back to your Century," an NCO from First Century ordered.

He and five veterans blocked access to Marcus Regulus and his staff with spear heads. Alerio unstrapped the infantry helmet, tossed it to the ground, and pointed to the crescent shaped scar on the crown of his head.

"If you don't recognize me as Battle Commander Sisera, I suggest you examining the mark. Most people gossip about it," Alerio challenged. "But If you don't know it's me by the scar, I will have to murder you all, then go speak to the General."

"Stand down and let the Colonel through," First Centurion Nugari instructed. "Battle Commander Sisera how are you here?"

"We punched through your southern wall," Alerio replied. "Pass the word. Get the wounded loaded and moving in that direction."

"Yes, sir," Nugari told him. "The General is with Colonel Balint beside his tent."

Alerio pushed aside the spears and jogged to Marcus Regulus and Balint, the Battle Commander for Legion West.

The General and the senior officer were bent over a map.

"There is a gully here," Balint pointed out. "If we form in blocks, we can get some Centuries out."

"You'll have to leave your wounded, and you'll lose more men than you'll save," Alerio stated while marching up and saluting. "General Regulus, good afternoon."

"Sisera? Come to gloat?" Balint growled. Then he challenged. "Think you could have done any better?"

People under stress will sometimes revert to a time when they felt safe by acting out. Colonel Balint had reverted to when he had the luxury of being jealous.

"I'll gladly cross blades with you later, Colonel," Alerio acknowledged. "But right now, we need to plan a withdrawal."

"And how do you propose to do that?" Balint demanded.

Marcus Regulus hadn't said a word. He just gawked at Alerio as if looking at a specter.

"Legion North is holding open a corridor to the woods," Alerio reported. He ignored the other Battle Commander and continued. "Centurion Nugari is moving your casualties. Which Centuries do you want to move next, General?"

Marcus Regulus glanced down at the map, ran a finger to the signature of the cartographer, read the name, and smiled.

"For an instant, I thought you really were a sorcerer," Regulus informed Alerio. "Just being here is magic, but at least this isn't one of your maps. That would have been too much of a coincidence."

"Who drew the map, sir?" Alerio asked.

"Centurion Lophos made this one," Marcus answered before addressing the other Battle Commander. "Colonel Balint, move our admin staff members out after the wounded. Then start with Legion West. I'll leave the order of march up to you."

"Yes, sir," Balint stated. He saluted and jogged away.

"He and Colonel Ferenc have a problem with me," Alerio remarked, "and I can't figure out why."

"Ferenc and Triticeus are dead," Marcus informed Alerio. "I know you and the Senior Tribune were close."

Alerio's hand reached for the hilt of his gladius, and he felt a pressure on his back.

'No Nenia. I'm a commander now, not an infantryman. My revenge will need another approach.'

He wasn't sure how long he stood in thought, but it must have been long enough for Marcus to worry.

"Colonel Sisera, are you okay?" Regulus asked.

"Yes, sir," Alerio answered although he wasn't steady on his feet. "Did Senior Tribune Triticeus go down in a charge? Did he at least have a glorious end?"

"I don't have details," Marcus confessed. "But Triticeus was part of the negotiation's team. He and Ferenc were murdered in the treaty tent."

A shiver ran through Alerio's core, and he wanted to lash out. But he had a Legion to manage and Legionaries depending on him.

"If you don't need me, General," Alerio said excusing himself, "I'll go and oversee the retreat."

"Go. And Colonel Sisera," Marcus Regulus offered, "thank you."

***

Alerio jogged around the defensive square alerting medics to pack up their wounded. Eventually, he arrived at a line of wagons, clerks, and exhausted infantrymen. They shuffled forward heading into the corridor.

"How many have we gotten out so far?" he asked Centurion Miklos.

The skirmisher officer rested a stick on his shoulder while consulting the ground. Lines, drawn by the stick, covered a good portion of the dirt around his feet.

"About eleven hundred, Colonel," Miklos replied. He used the stick to point at the sides of the passageway. "Aeneas and the Sixth are taking a beating. You might want to get some veterans over here."

"I know just where to get them," Alerio stated.

He ran back to the command area intending to send General Regulus through. Once the Proconsul made it to safety, Alerio could use Balint's First Century to hold the opening against the encroaching soldiers.

This time, the veterans recognized Alerio. They waved him through.

"We have a steady flow going into the forest, sir," Alerio reported to the Marcus Regulus. "I believe it's your turn."

"Not while I have Legionaries in combat," Marcus responded. "I can't leave them behind."

"I'll stay in command until the end," Alerio volunteered. "But I need Balint's First Century at the opening."

"Send Balint through and put his bodyguards on the passageway," Marcus instructed an aide. Then to Alerio, he said. "I'll stay with you until the last of us retreats."

"Not ideal, sir," Alerio admitted. "But you are the General."

If the battle for Tunis had been fluid and the Legions able to maneuver, the General and Battle Commanders would be ordering adjustments. But as a static fight, the details fell to Senior Tribunes, maniple staff officers, and Centurions. That didn't mean messages with reports from sectors didn't come into the command area.

"General, the west side is pulling back to reestablish their combat line," a courier reported.

"Good. Shrinking the formation will make it easier to consolidate our forces," Marcus Regulus responded.

"General, the northeast corner is pulling back," another courier informed him.

"Advise the rest of the east line to fall back with the corner," Marcus instructed.

Alerio listened, agreeing with the few orders the General issued. Mostly, Marcus Regulus took in the news and weighed it against other reports. His job required an overview of the battle with an eye to where trouble was developing. Alerio laughed.

"Is something funny, Battle Commander Sisera?" Marcus inquired.

"It's the turn of a phrase I was thinking of, sir," Alerio replied. "With an eye to where trouble is developing. Seeing as we have trouble on all sides, developing trouble is an overstatement."

Before the General could comment, Centurion Miklos sprinted into the command area.

"The corridor is gone, sirs," he stated. "We managed to get over two thousand men out before a horde of Iberians crashed the walls of the passageway."

"Where did they come from?" Alerio asked.

"I've had no reports of the Empire holding a large unit in reserve," Marcus told him.

"Before we knew they were there, they came out of the smoke," Miklos answered, "probably from behind Legion West's bivouac."

Alerio went to the General's map of the area. He studied the location of the road through the forest and that of the marching camp. After a few beats, he stepped back.

"They were waiting for us," Alerio stated. "Staged and waiting for Legion North to come out of the forest. Who thought of that?"

"The Spartan," Marcus answered.

"What Spartan, General?" Alerio asked.

"Qart Hadasht put a Spartan in command of their army," Regulus said. "He's orchestrated everything from the slaughter in the treaty tent to the destruction of Legion South and everything since. His intelligence is solid enough, it seems, he targeted you, Battle Commander."

"Me, sir," Alerio questioned. "Why me?"

"For the reasons Balint and Ferenc envy you," Marcus informed Alerio. "You are successful and a threat."

Centurion Nugari marched up and saluted.

"Tell me something good, First Centurion," Marcus requested.

"General, we're pressed on all sides and trying to cover too much territory," the veteran combat officer informed him. "We should collapse into a proper defensive square and pray, sir."

"Or beg for peace," Marcus added. "Pass the word. Pull all units back and don't engage unless defending yourself. Let's see if the Spartan will consider a surrender."

Chapter 12 – Not the Spartan

At first, warriors and soldiers chased after the withdrawing Legionaries. But after a few steps and unanswered strikes, they allowed the Legion formation to shrivel into a mound of shields. But left in the open were thousands of dead or wounded Republic infantrymen.

"I've murdered four Legions," Marcus Regulus uttered in a weak voice. His back bent as if his spine was failing. "Had we stayed in the valley, Mount Boukornine would have provided a barrier. But I didn't and now I've executed fifteen thousand men."

"Sir, you have almost a Legion left alive," Alerio whispered. "Those men need your strength."

Marcus Regulus stood a little straighter.

"You're right. I'll negotiate for their release. And I'll work at sending as many home to Rome as possible. Even to my own detriment," Marcus promised. "Let's see what the Spartan has to say."

But it wasn't the Spartan who rode to the forefront. The Spartan was there. Sitting on his horse among the ranks of Noricum infantry with the scarlet cape and the crest on his helmet motionless.

Taking command for the Empire were General Bostar and General Hamilcar. They walked their horses through the army to stand before Marcus Regulus.

"Have your men lay down their arms," Bostar demanded from horseback.

"What do I get in return?" Marcus inquired from the ground.

It was symbolic that the victor should be on a higher elevation than the vanquished.

"You will submit, or you will die," Hamilcar responded.

"What are my terms for surrender?" Marcus questioned.

"Drop your weapons. Or this will continue to its inevitable end," Bostar threatened.

The three men considered each other with blank faces and stiff necks. Finally, Hamilcar shifted in the saddle and allowed a lighter expression to cross his face.

"Maybe, there is a term," Hamilcar proposed.

Grasping for any sign of conciliation, Marcus asked, "What term?"

"Qart Hadasht is growing. Unfortunately, the building trend is due to the war industry," Hamilcar apprised him. "But growing as it is, we need craftsmen. Perhaps some of your infantrymen have skills we can use."

Alerio stood several paces behind Marcus. When an object pushed between his hip and wrist, he glanced back to see Nugari shoving the rolled-up command map into his hand.

"If they take craftsmen," the First Centurion whispered. "Our men will need a staff officer among them. And you're the only one here not in officer's armor."

After the map, Nugari handed Alerio a felt petasos.

"Do what you want, sir," he challenged. "But the men need you."

Alerio had no interest in becoming a slave. To be an officer without authority over slaves with no freedom was useless. Despite his misgivings, he held onto the map and the hat.

"I offer myself as a hostage," Marcus stated. "Take me. I'm more valuable than a hundred craftsmen."

"How about five hundred?" Bostar questioned.

"We'll take you and five hundred men to work on buildings in the Capital," Hamilcar stated. "But first, order your infantry to lay down their arms."

After a few beats, Marcus Regulus turned to the three thousand remaining Legionaries. He bowed his head before lifting it and peering around at the sweat lined and blood-stained faces.

"It has been an honor to lead you, sons of Rome," Marcus announced. "Men with building skills, report to your Centurions or NCOs. Those in command, pick the ablest and bring them to the front."

Alerio put the hat on his head and nodded to First Centurion Nugari.

"Every construction site needs the building drawn on the plot of land, and the structure pictured," Alerio informed Nugari. "I'm Alerio 'Lophos' Carvilius and I am a cartographer. You can see my name on this map, it's Lophos."

Understanding the ploy, the First Centurion took Alerio by the elbow and guided him to a Centurion.

"Where is Colonel Sisera?" Bostar called to the Legionaries. "I want to meet the heroic commander of Legion North."

Because none of the other Battle Commanders had been singled out, Marcus and Nugari froze. If anyone pointed to Colonel Sisera, he might be put on trial and executed. Marcus Regulus glanced around. He saw a man with a felt hat on, which he thought odd, but didn't see Alerio. When no one answered Bostar, Hamilcar added his own solicitation.

"Come, step forward, Battle Commander Sisera," the Empire General encouraged. He waved an arm as if inviting Alerio forward. "Come, claim your just reward."

A silence fell over the army and the Legion. No one responded until an officer of skirmishers spoke out.

"Colonel Sisera died at the escape corridor," Centurion Miklos lied. "If you search the dead, you'll find the Colonel's helmet with the white horse-hair crest among the bodies of his command staff."

"That is a shame," Bostar grumbled. "I so looked forward to crucifying the cowardly dog."

***

The afternoon was taken up by Legionaries filing by a growing stack of discarded shields and piles of gladii, javelins, and spears. Further away, helmets and armor were taken off and dumped.

Another area had a line of combat officers and NCOs standing with men who had building experience. The craftsmen were interviewed and judged by Qart Hadasht managers. Some marched through the ranks of the Empire army to a holding area. Others were turned away and sent back to their Centuries.

"Name and specialty?" one manager asked.

"My name is Alerio 'Lophos' Carvilius," Alerio reported. He unrolled the parchment and displayed the map. "I'm a map maker. You'll notice the exactness of the elements and my signature in the corner."

The manager inspected the work, nodded his approval, and turned Alerio over to an escort. They walked through the army to a shaded area where other Legion builders sat.

"They're taking five hundred of us to Qart Hadasht," a man protested. "I got picked because my officer doesn't like me."

"I can't blame your Centurion," another Legionary with building skills responded. "I don't know you, and already, I don't like you."

Both men began to rise.

Fearing a fight and repercussions, Alerio asked, "Has anyone ever been to the city? I hear it very cosmopolitan."

"What does that mean?" the complainer demanded.

"Spices and women," a third build submitted.

"From all around the known world," Alerio added. "All in one place."

"But we'll be slaves?"

"Working building sites," Alerio said. "It's not like we're digging in mines. They need our skills. Just stay calm, and everything will work out."

Later in the afternoon, Marcus Regulus and an Empire cavalry escort appeared. The horses reached the five hundred and stopped.

"You people, get on your feet," a horseman ordered.

Alerio and the builders stood and faced towards Qart Hadasht. It was an easy ten-mile hike for the Legionaries.

Generals Bostar and General Hamilcar rode from between the ranks. Following the Empire commanders were a company of Iberian soldiers. The Generals reined in beside

Regulus, but the soldiers continued until they crowded around the Legionary builders.

"What about my Legions?" Marcus asked.

"That's right," Bostar admitted. He looked around as if he had lost something. Then he spotted the Spartan, sitting quietly. "Xanthippus. Kill them all."

The Spartan shook the scarlet cloak from his arms and signaled left and right. In response, the Empire army leveled spears, roared, and rushed forward.

Marcus shouted in horror, but a horseman rapped him in the head with a sword. Regulus collapsed onto the horse's neck.

The cries of the dying filled the air. And yet, the pleading from individuals drifted above the shrieks. Alerio felt every voice begging for mercy and suffered with each until a thrust silenced the infantrymen. Iberians poked and prodded the Legion builders into motion. They shuffled away from the massacre. All of them angry, and grateful to have escaped with their lives.

Half conscious, Marcus Regulus seemed unaware of the slaughter of twenty-five hundred unarmed Legionaries. Almost the opposite of the Republic Proconsul, the Spartan Commander watched intently as if he was memorizing and learning from each death.

Act 5

Chapter 13 – Spartan Control

The building had holes in the walls. And at one end, the wall was tilted and fractured. An irregular crack in the floor divided the flat segment from the part dipping below level. Above, the roof threatened to collapse. The broken support rafters were obvious through the openings in the ceiling of the first and second floors.

"Do you think the second floor will handle a load?" one of the Legion builders asked.

"I wouldn't trust it to store hay," Alerio replied.

"Well, it's home for now," another Latian stated. "We should figure something out."

Most of the five hundred Legionaries waited in the courtyard. A few had ventured into the dilapidated structure to survey the damages.

"If I had a choice," another offered, "I'd demolish it and start over with a better foundation."

The Iberian overseer, who greeted them when the prisoners arrived, came in and overheard the comment. Two massive bodyguards carrying clubs followed him. They flanked the manager and made a show of holding their herding clubs with two hands when he stopped.

"The building's owner wants this floor for storage with apartments on the second story," he instructed. "There will be no demolition. You Latians need to get creative."

"Any chance of food while we work up a plan? How about bedding?" Alerio asked. "And we'd like to inspect the tools."

"No food. No blankets. No tools," the manager asserted. He turned to leave but stopped and forewarned. "You will show progress, or you will be beaten before your mob is broken up."

"Broken up?" Alerio questioned.

"Yes. I'll send each of you to work at a different project," he replied. "Keeping you Latians together is a mistake."

After the Iberian overseer and his guards left, one Legionary kicked the dusty floor.

"He reminds me of my Master when I was an apprentice," the Latian builder said. "Never enough time or supplies. And every project is a rush job. I hated that guy, too."

"What's your trade?" Alerio asked.

"I'm Tullius, a Master Carpenter," the Legionary replied.

"We need to show progress, or the Iberian will separate the Legionaries," Alerio remarked. "Where would you start?"

"We have a few daggers hidden away, but no real tools," Tullius responded. He reached out and took the large piece of parchment from Alerio. "We can start by designing something the Punic owner wants. No. Make that something he desires."

"If you plan to go higher," another Legionary stated. "You'll need to rework the foundation."

No one had ventured the idea of adding to the tilted building. No one did as the building was half sunken, uneven, and obviously unstable.

"Who are you?" Alerio inquired.

"Naevus, a foundation mole," the man bragged. "From deep beneath the earth to the top of the sky, if it needs to be structurally sound, you want me in the hole."

"I hadn't considered adding a level," Alerio admitted. "The second floor is barely there as it is."

"I've put a third floor on worse," another man stated. "But it took a lot of shoring up. Where do I get the lumber?"

"Name and occupation?" Tullius the carpenter asked.

"The name is Didacus," the Latian stated. "I've been a foreman on projects since I was a teen. Learned structure and bracing, scheduling, and material handling from my father."

"Find me a piece of cinder or a soft stone," Alerio requested. "Let's clear a spot on the floor and draw up something."

With a branch, Naevus, the mole, swept an area clean. Then in the fading light, the men sketched a three-story structure on the rough stone of the floor.

"That's not a pretty building," Tullius observed. "It looks more unsteady than this one."

"I'll work on it," Alerio commented.

Then from outside a voice ordered, "Stay back."

Alerio and the Legion builders rushed to the doorway. Armed men with torches pushed back the Legionaries to make room for a trio of wagons. The overseer stood off to the side with a scowl on his face.

"They haven't done anything to earn food, bedding, or tools," he protested.

A man dressed in a scarlet cloak stepped from between the soldiers. For a beat, Alerio thought it was the Spartan Commander. But once the man was bathed in the flickering light, he could see it was a different Spartan.

"Master Bagarok, answer this. How can a man accomplish anything if he falls ill from starvation?" the Hoplite questioned. Then he added. "As long as General Xanthippus is in command, these men will be guarded closely, worked hard, but treated well."

"Spartans," Bagarok said it as if it was a curse.

The overseer and his thugs walked away. Then a figure stepped forward with a tablet.

"Who is in charge?" he asked. "I need someone to sign for the equipment."

Alerio took Didacus by the arm and marched the foreman to the scribe.

"Master Didacus is in charge, sir," Alerio stated. He emphasized the words master and sir, hoping the NCO would catch on to the meaning.

Corporal Philetus, formerly of the Sixth Century, blinked in the weak light. The speaker was familiar but couldn't place him. Then his mouth fell open when he recognized Colonel Sisera.

"Here, sir, use me as a writing surface," Alerio said quickly. He spun around and bent, offering his back as a flat surface so Didacus could sign for the wagon loads of supplies.

"You are who?" Philetus inquired.

"Alerio Lophos Carvilius, a simple draftsman," Alerio replied.

"I see," Philetus remarked. "You and Foreman Didacus are lucky."

"We know," Didacus agreed, thinking the NCO was talking about Tunis. "It's terrible."

"What's terrible?" Philetus asked. "I was referring to having the Spartans in command. Before they took over, workers were starving because the guards didn't care. Most didn't bother showing up for duty. Yet when they got in trouble for the lack of progress, the soldiers took it out on the captures. Since Xanthippus got control, we're treated better."

"The butcher of Tunis is our benefactor?" Alerio inquired. "How can that be?"

"All the guards and managers are foreigners," Philetus informed him. "This is Qart Hadasht and it's complicated. My next delivery here is in two days. What do you need?"

"A layout of the city, a schedule for the gate guards," Alerio whispered, "and some drawing materials."

"That won't get the structure rebuilt," Didacus scolded. "We need buckets for water and material hauling, axes, hammers, shovels for digging, and hand trowels."

***

The morning found Alerio sitting on the rickety roof with a flat piece of board and the nub of a burnt stick. To his front, he could see the eastern defensive walls of the city. Somewhere in the distance lay Tunis and the bodies of Legionaries.

To the north, orchards started at the bottom of the hill, outside the ring of fruit trees, vegetable gardens spread to the defensive walls, and beyond the tall structures, fields of grain stretched to the horizon. Behind him, Byrsa Hill rose to a collection of government buildings and a market. Just below the crest of the hill, tall buildings encroached on the heights. Wrapping around the hill were the flat roofs of buildings. Almost as if giant stair steps, the residential and commercial structures marked the falling elevation of Byrsa Hill. And finally, along the southern edge of Qart Hadasht were beaches, docks, and warehouses. Plus, there was an odd watercourse in the form of a round harbor cut into the shoreline.

Obviously manmade, the circular harbor housed several ships-of-war on an arched beach. Immediately, Alerio grasped the significance. The shape offered a safe harbor from severe weather and protection from enemy warships. And, as he could tell by the activity, ship repair personnel had access to the clustered vessels. Unlike pulling them onto a straight beach, where the boats were in a long line, in the circular harbor they were close together and accessible.

A section of roof a few feet from him fell in, leaving a hole. Alerio remained still, thinking if he moved, he too would fall through the weakened structure. But shortly after the collapse, Tullius appeared in the opening.

"Carvilius, I didn't know you were up here," the carpenter greeted Alerio.

With his torso half out of the hole, Tullius seemed to be floating in the air.

"I wanted to get an idea of what people would see from the third floor," Alerio informed him.

"And what will they see?"

"Most of the city and the harbor," Alerio answered. "How did you get up here?"

"We salvaged boards from the second floor and built ladders," Tullius clarified. He looked down and shouted. "Put another ladder up here. Carvilius needs a way down. Him? He is our draftsman."

"I could scale down on the side," Alerio indicated the edge of the roof several feet away. "That's the way I came up."

"We've already taken out a lot of roof supports," Tullius warned. "It's better if you use a ladder."

Although he had seen enough to know the setting, Alerio took another look at the landscape. Then, after tucking the board with the sketches into a pouch, he carefully crawled to the hole in the roof. Looking over the edge, he realized it was a long way down to the cracked floor.

***

On the third day of captivity, Bagarok, his two guards, and a tall swarthy man in flowing robes walked onto the plaza. Unlike the thugs with the overseer, the Punic nobleman was accompanied by men with steel blades and dressed in uniformed armor.

"Noricum soldiers," Didacus announced. "I heard their steel is the best."

"I heard the same thing," Alerio agreed.

The Iberian manager whined as the group approached the ruined building.

"Sir, they don't know what they're doing," Bagarok grumbled. "Let me send them to projects around the city where we have more oversight."

"I'm considering it," the Qart Hadasht citizen responded. "I don't see any progress. As a matter of fact, they've destroyed my roof."

Alerio picked up several sheets of the parchment Corporal Philetus provided. With the drawings of the redesigned building in hand, Alerio started for the owner.

"Sir, if I might have a moment," he called out while crossing the courtyard. Two guards blocked Alerio's way, forcing him to plead. "Master, I only want to show you the drawings for your new building."

"New?" the Punic owner turned on Bagarok and exploded. "I told you I didn't want the expense of rebuilding the structure."

The overseer stammered trying to organize his thoughts.

"Our plans use everything here, sir," Alerio blurted out before Bagarok could respond. "And we've added a third floor. That will give your tenants a view of the harbor."

The nobleman ceased his tirade, stroked the hair on his chin, and contemplated Alerio.

"Harbor views fetch a higher lease rate," the Punic admitted. He reached out and grabbed the drawings. While shuffling through the stack and admiring the solid look of the building, he asked. "How much more will this cost me?"

"We'll need clay, rocks, straw, sand, and lumber," Alerio listed. "All of those are available in the Tunis area. So, your cost will be for guards, wagons, and donkeys, sir."

"And you'll build this structure?" the owner asked. He pointed at a symbol located on the face of the building just below roof level. "Will this be visible from the harbor?"

"It will be sir. Although, we'll have to create it from clay which doesn't catch the rays of the sun," Alerio expounded on the limitations of clay. "Unless you want the Helios image made of bronze. In that case, we'll need copper and tin to cast the image of the Sun God."

"I want it in bronze," the Punic noblemen instructed. "The other business owners in this district will be eaten up by jealousy at the sight of it."

"Then we have your approval to construct the building, sir?" Alerio asked.

"Yes. You have my permission to make me the envy of my competitors," the Punic owner gushed. "Come along Bagarok.

I want to inspect my other properties. I can only pray the other sites are as inventive as this one."

Alerio relaxed. He had created a building the owner had to have and in doing so he kept his Legionaries together. Once work began, he needed to locate General Regulus and report on the progress.

"Tell me, Alerio," Naevus, the foundation mole, inquired. "Why did you add an image of the Sun God to the facade?"

"To mark the building," Alerio replied. "Someday, the Legion will land in Qart Hadasht. When they do, I want them to tear down this structure and throw the rubble into the bay."

"Because we built it as slave labor?"

"No. Because it was paid for by the deaths of four Legions."

***

With the weight of the roof and the second floor gone, Naevus selected fifty men. He placed them on a line fifteen feet from the lopsided wall.

"We'll dig a slope down to this section of the foundation," he said while scooping air with his hands to demonstrate the operation. "Dirt gets stacked behind you and rocks go on the far side of the mound."

They began the task with enthusiasm. It was better than sitting around doing nothing. While the Legionaries dug, Alerio sketched from the top of the wall to ground level, then stopped.

"The soil looks good," he noted. "Why is the wall tilting and cracking?"

Naevus hopped over the growing mound of dirt, selected a large rock, a small stone, and a handful of dirty sand. He brushed off the surfaces while carrying them to Alerio.

"This site has been filled in to make it level," Naevus explained. He displayed the large rock, held the handful of sand over it, and dribbled the sand over the curved surface. As expected, the fine grains hit the rock and slid off. "Imagine this rock to be the bedrock under Byrsa Hill and the sand the landfill where we're standing."

"You're telling me, the land under our feet is sliding down the rock face?" Alerio questioned. "How is that possible? I can't feel movement."

"It's not the earth moving," Naevus corrected. "It's the weight of the building pushing the foundation through the soil. Think of it as if you were plowing your foot through loose dirt."

Alerio nudged his boot forward. The dust separated but after the heel passed, the material fell back, filling in behind his foot.

"How do we prevent it from happening again?" Alerio questioned.

"The Mole will fix it," Naevus boasted. He used the stone to chip steps in the large rock. Then he poured sand onto the flat risers. Unlike before when the sand slid down the curved surface, the notches caught grains until each flat place held a pile. "We'll cut steps and build columns to support the end walls of the building."

"For three stories?" Didacus questioned.

The foreman and a group had walked over to check on the digging.

"After my work," Naevus pledged, "you could build it five stories tall. And it will stand until the Goddess Hestia tears it down."

Without thinking, Alerio injected, "Three stories will serve our needs."

"Just what needs are you talking about?" another builder demanded. "You don't look like a Priest so it can't have anything to do with Hestia, the Goddess of Architecture. Who are you to tell us what we need?"

The foremen stepped between the two men.

"This is Remus our Master of Clay," Didacus introduced the man asking the questions. Then he pointed to Alerio. "And this is Alerio Lophos."

"I heard about you, Lophos," Remus sneered. "They described you as being fat. I guess Battle Commander Sisera worked the weight off you. But they also said you were lazy and a coward. And lazy is a trait that's hard to lose."

Alerio wanted to tell the Master of Clay that he was Colonel Sisera. But prisoners have needs. And if the captivity lasted long enough, a weak man might trade the knowledge that the infamous commander of Legion North was one of the Legionaries. He'd hate to be exposed for an extra portion of stew meat.

"I'm just a simple cartographer, Master of Clay," Alerio humbled himself by bowing. "If I can help, please let me know."

"Then give me that hat," Remus ordered.

Of all the scars Alerio had picked up over his life, the one that stood out among men who made their living with blades was the one on his head. It might not be recognized and connected with Colonel Sisera at first. But eventually, someone would connect the scar with the senior officer.

"Do you like my petasos?" Alerio remarked. "If you want it, I'll box you for the hat. Apollo's sport is how I lost the weight."

Remus noted the muscles and scars on Alerio's arms and his willingness to fight.

"Maybe later," Remus said. "Right now, I need the rocks they dug up and all the soil with sand."

Didacus organized a work party, and they began selecting from the overburden excavated by the diggers. Alerio went to the backside of the building and began drawing in the lower section of the wall. Not surprising, the foundation as it was exposed, lay on the slope of the rock. As he watched the deeper foundation get uncovered, Alerio noted stitches on one of the diggers.

"Come over here," he called. "Help me with something."

Having reached the correct depth for the upper section, the Legionary had finished digging. He climbed the slope and strolled over to Alerio.

"What do you need, draftsman?"

"The stitches in your thigh," Alerio pointed out. "Those are tight and professional. I bet it healed up quickly."

"Thanks to Hektor Nicanor," the man stated. "If I hadn't been in so much pain when he washed the open wound with vinegar, I would have stabbed him. I'm glad I didn't. The Greek boy's sutures were so tight, I never got even a trace of the rot. With some of our other medics, the wounds leaked for days."

"Leaked and healed up looking like a blind man did the stitching," Alerio sympathized. He lifted his tunic to display the uneven stitch marks rippling along a scar on his hip. "I wish I had Hektor when this happened."

"A Legion special," the infantryman stated, referring to the rustic suture work. "What do you need?"

"I want to organize our escape," Alerio told him. "But not for just a few. I want all of us to get home. To accomplish that, we need to organize an escape committee of trusted men."

"And you want me on the committee?" the Legionary guessed. "Why me?"

"Thanks to Hektor, I know the type of man you are," Alerio replied. "You see, Hektor only treats men with the will to survive. Find other patients of Hektor and have them come see me."

"They have Spartans and Noricum soldiers," the infantryman reminded Alerio. "Yet, you believe we can get out of Qart Hadasht?"

"And back to Rome," Alerio assured him. "They do have Spartans. However, I have Republic Legionaries, and a secret society."

"The Friends of Hektor," the infantryman confirmed.

Chapter 14 – The Generals' Aides

Marcus Regulus had one wish and a mission. He wanted to see and hold Marcia Regulus once more. His wife had been by his side for all the important events of his life. With her, he had become a father, a respected Senator, a successful General, and had twice been elected a Consul of the Republic. Without her, he had lost four Legions and been taken captive. If not for the wish, Marcus Regulus would throw himself from the building.

"General Regulus, you must get dressed," the servant encouraged. "We have attempted to clean the helmet and the armor. If they are not to your satisfaction, kindly let us know. But for now, please, sir, do get dressed. The Suffete and his guests are expecting you."

"Another showing of their prize peacock," Marcus growled. He looked out on the ships in the harbor. He peered at the roofs of the buildings coming up Byrsa Hill. One caught his eye. Off to the side, he couldn't help noticing a large structure with a collapsed roof. Lastly, he stared straight down to the courtyard at the base of his prison. Before turning to the servant, he addressed Alerio Sisera's personal Goddess. "It must be a fall of at least sixty feet. Is that far enough for you, Goddess Nenia, to free me from my humiliation?"

"Sir, your armor, please," the servant begged.

He held up the armored skirt, but it was inside-out. Despite his predicament, Marcus laughed, making a short, hard sound that lacked humor.

"A proper aide-de-camp would know the correct way to hold it," Marcus complained. "Give me that."

Snatching the armor piece, he spun it around, and secured it to his waist. Then he slipped on the ceremonial armor and dropped the leather truss with his medals and the Proconsul tab over his head. After adjusting the leather bands, he tucked the General's helmet under his left arm.

At first glance, he might have been a commander going to review his Legions. Except no Consul would go before his Legionaries without a gladius. As a prisoner he was going unarmed to entertain Punic noblemen. If not for his wish, Marcus Regulus would end it. If not for his mission to return to Rome and tell the story of his brave Legions, he would have jumped from the window.

Stowing away the thoughts of suicide, General Regulus swallowed his pride, and marched for the doorway.

***

"Marcus Atilius Regulus, Senator, Consul, and General," the greeter announced when Marcus arrived at the banquet hall. "A Citizen of the Republic, direct from Rome by way of defeat at Tunis, Suffete Paltibaal bids you to make his guest welcome."

Applause and sounds of amazement rose for the crowd of Punic dignitaries. Here was a living example of the upstarts from Rome. Terrifying in his armor with the stern look of a defiant man, Marcus Regulus both attracted and repulsed the noblemen and women of the Qart Hadasht Empire.

"My other guests can't stop ogling you or refrain from making comments behind their hands," the Suffete for Military affairs informed Marcus. "General Regulus, you are the hit of the social season."

"I would be of better use to you in Rome," Marcus told him. "Who better to secure the release of your noble brats, than the man who made them slaves of the Republic."

"Ah General, you seek to rise my ire," Suffete Paltibaal remarked. "Unfortunately for you General, you lost. So much waste, I could barely finish reading the reports from the final battle."

"If it's so final," Marcus insisted, "send me home with your demands."

From behind, a voice broke into the exchange.

"But you are so entertaining," Bostar commented. He walked up to Marcus and asked. "How can we ever let you go?"

"General Bostar, I trust you're having a pleasant evening," Marcus professed while saluting the old campaigner.

"You never cease to amaze me, Regulus," Bostar asserted. "I killed fourteen thousand of your soldiers and personally ordered the murder of another three thousand or so. Yet, you treat me like a long lost, and even revered, uncle."

"Nemo dat quod non habet," Marcus quoted a phrase in Latin. "No one gives what he doesn't have."

"I do love word games," Paltibaal gushed. "By that, you mean what?"

"I have no blade nor harsh words for General Bostar, as he has taken everything from me."

Hamilcar and the Suffete for Domestic affairs strolled up.

"Very well stated," General Hamilcar complimented Marcus. "And very true, I might add."

"I hate to break up this private party," the Domestic Suffete apologized. "But I need Bostar for a matter of some importance."

"Please, don't let me or this fascinating Latian keep you," Paltibaal said. "We'll go elsewhere. There are guests who simply must meet General Regulus."

They were three steps from the trio when Marcus stopped a servant carrying a tray crowded with glasses of wine. He paused to liberate one just as an Empire Captain marched up to Paltibaal. The officer whispered angrily to the Military Suffete.

"General Regulus, stay right here," Paltibaal instructed. "I'll be right back."

Left alone and happy for the reprieve from being both complimented and insulted, Marcus took a step towards the Domestic Suffete and the Generals Bostar and Hamilcar. Not seeing the Republic General, they continued their conversation.

"It's too much," the Suffete grumbled. "Our bank is depleted because of a rash decision by the Special Branch."

"What can we do?" Bostar questioned. "He asked, they agreed, and the Spartan got his gold."

"And remember, he's not only protected by his gang of Spartan Hoplites," Hamilcar added. "But Xanthippus trained the Iberian and Noricum soldiers. They practically worship him."

Marcus Regulus wanted to feel hot anger at the mention of the Spartan. But inside, he was dead. Only the wish and the mission held him together. For vengeance to grow, it needed to cling to a matrix of feelings. But inside Marcus Regulus, there was nothing to support the hate.

"Suppose the finance committee withdrew funding for the mercenaries," the Domestic Suffete pondered. Then he gave the results. "In a matter of days, the Iberians and Noricums would sail away. What then?"

"The Spartan did murder the Legionaries after they surrendered," Hamilcar stated. "Did he have written orders, General?"

"Nothing in writing," Bostar assured them. "And we have boat loads of witnesses to the horror. Once he's convicted, all the Spartan's possessions will be confiscated."

"And go directly into the city's coffers."

A hand landed on Regulus' shoulder and guided him away from the conspirators.

"My apologies, Marcus," Paltibaal stated as they crossed the room. "We have a report on one of my Generals. In Gades, that's far to the west of Iberia, he has declared himself King of the Region."

"A General cut off from his administrators is bound to make bad decisions," Marcus stated.

The truth of it cut deeply into the Republic General's heart.

"It is ever so. Or so it seems," Paltibaal projected. Then he asked. "The servants assigned to your quarters. Are they satisfactory?"

"I would prefer Legionaries who understand how armor and leather are supposed to be cleaned," Marcus responded. "And who know the correct order for the display of medals."

They approached a group and the Military Suffete boomed, "Come here and touch the Republic General. He's relatively tame. Just don't hand him a sword."

The group shouted in mock horror before bursting out in good natured humor. Marcus stood stone faced, accepting the ridicule. He was after all, dead inside.

***

Late midmorning, two days after the dinner party, Bagarok and his henchmen strutted onto the plaza. Spying several men wrapped in blankets and asleep under an awning, he went directly to the sleeping area.

"Get up," he screamed at the Latians. "Get up and be busy. You are not to sleep away the day."

Kicking one of the sleeping men, the overseer backed away quickly and directed his bodyguards to beat the men awake.

The kick woke one of the sleepers. But still half-awake, the Legionary rolled over, threw off the blanket, and pushed to his feet. He might have been angry enough to fistfight. But it wasn't a fist coming at his head. It was the knot of a hardwood club.

Too late to duck, Remus realized the danger but could only throw up his arms to ward off the strike. A flying body came racing around the building and dove between the Master of Clay and the club. Absorbing the blow with his shoulder, Alerio fell as Remus jumped back. Rolling twice, he came up on his knees holding a shoulder that already showed signs of bruising.

"Him. Use him to set an example," Bagarok yelled while pointing at Alerio. "Show these Latians that crossing me has consequences."

With his right arm tucked into his ribs to ease tension on the shoulder, Alerio circled with the bodyguard keeping his left arm out.

"I enjoy a good fight as well as the next man," the Spartan Hoplite stated. He stopped a few feet from the combatants, drew his kopis, and tossed it to Alerio. "Here, let's see how the guard feels about facing a blade."

Already hurt and angry at the attack, Alerio forgot he was only a draftsman. After a smooth catch, he brought the sword down to the back of his thigh. For an instant, the thug lost sight of it. Then Alerio's wrist snapped the blade up ninety degrees, putting the tip on a direct path to the thug's gut. All it would take was a simple stab to…

"Enough," the Spartan roared.

Alerio froze and the guard stared at the short distance between the steel blade and his lower belly.

"I guess that answers one of the questions," the Spartan said. He marched to Alerio and took his sword. "Walk with me Latian."

"Wait. Why were these men sleeping?" Bagarok demanded.

Remus walked to a rough mud and stone mound, lifted a door off the front, and exposed racks of tiles.

"My team and I were up all-night firing flooring tiles," the Clay Master stated. "The fire needed to be at a constant temperature and that required feeding in wood and manning the bellows. We just laid down when you showed up, overseer."

No one expected an apology and Bagarok didn't offer one. He and his two guards stormed off.

"Come," the Spartan directed Alerio. They had gone several feet and were away from the men gathering around Remus when the Hoplite remarked. "We have a bet in the barracks. Are you a Lieutenant or a Sergeant?"

"Why do you ask?" Alerio inquired.

"We Spartans observe everyone," he said. "It's hard to miss your influence no matter how hard you attempt to disguise it. I thought an NCO. But after your foolish interference, I'm changing my wager to a Tail-Leader."

"How does getting clubbed make me an officer?" Alerio asked.

He massaged the shoulder. Nothing felt broken, but based on the pain deep in the muscle, he knew it would be a week before he could use his right arm.

"Your willingness to sacrifice for your men," the Hoplite replied. "And only a swordsman trained since birth could have caught a spinning sword left-handed, transited to a feint, and brought the blade to a killing plain that quickly."

"It's a natural talent," Alerio told him. "What now? Now that I've been discovered."

"Nothing. We don't care," the Hoplite answered. "But there is a message. If any of your people escape, we will march to this courtyard and gut the ones remaining."

"I understand," Alerio assured him. "Until I can take them all out, you won't have trouble with us."

"We thought not, Lieutenant," the Spartan commented.

He walked out of a side entrance and Corporal Philetus came into the courtyard from the opposite side.

"Did you guys plan that?" Alerio asked when Philetus crossed to him.

The Corporal blinked as if the comment caught him off guard. Recovering after a pause, he asked, "Plan what?"

"Never mind," Alerio told him.

He still gripped his shoulder, favoring the right arm.

"Do you need to lay down?" Philetus inquired. "If so, I can talk to Didacus about the General's need."

"I'm fine, tell me what the Proconsul requires."

"The Qart Hadasht Suffete wants to assign a Legion aide to him," the NCO reported. "Any idea who to use?"

"Absolutely," Alerio assured him. "I have just the man for General Regulus."

***

In the early evening, two Legionaries climbed the stairs towards the top floor of the apartment building.

"The General is living good," Vitus observed.

"He's a General," Tutus reminded the other potential aide. "Aren't they supposed to live good?"

At the top floor, the pair approached an Empire guard. One lowered his hood and addressed the soldier.

"Which apartment is General Regulus' quarters?" Vitus asked.

There were three doors off the landing. None were marked to identify the occupants.

"All of them," the soldiers stated. He leaned a spear in the direction of one door. "Most servants use that entrance. VIP guests use the other."

"What about the center door?" Vitus inquired.

"No one ever uses it," the sentry replied.

Titus and Vitus walked to the center door and pushed it open. To their surprise, Marcus Regulus stood at a window with his back to them.

"Sir, we are assigned as your aides," Tutus announced.

"Assigned by whom?" Marcus asked. "General Bostar?"

"No sir, Centurion Lophos sent us," Vitus replied.

"Lophos? Isn't he the fat cartographer from Legion North?" Marcus Regulus questioned. He turned to face the door. Looking from Tutus to Vitus and back again, he inquired. "Are you brothers, half-brothers, or cousins?"

"No, sir," Vitus answered.

"As far as we know, our family villages are over a hundred miles apart," Tutus stated.

"With no shared relations," Vitus said.

"We've talked it over, sir," Tutus added.

"And can't find a connection," Vitus assured the General.

Marcus Regulus blinked. Vitus and Tutus were lean and of average height. Besides their similar forms, they had small noses, wide set brown eyes, high foreheads, and full lips.

There was nothing extraordinary about their looks except they were identical in appearance.

"How did you come to be assigned to me?" Regulus asked.

"We are both Friends of Hektor," Vitus responded by holding out an arm and displaying a line of neat stitches along his bicep.

"And Centurion Lophos advised that a Latian couldn't blend in around Qart Hadasht," Tutus clarified. He raised the hem of his tunic and showed Marcus a thigh wound with the same professional sutures.

"So, he decided, the next best thing was for us to be in two places at once," Vitus informed Marcus.

"If that meets your approval, sir?" Tutus inquired.

"Where did you come from?" Marcus asked. "I thought they broke up the five hundred Legionaries."

"No sir. Thanks to the Centurion and the Spartans, we are all on the same worksite," Vitus related.

"The Spartans?" Marcus asked. "You can be aides later. Pour us some vino and give me a full report."

"Yes, sir," Vitus and Tutus replied.

Chapter 15 – Raw Materials to Coins

Ten wagons rolled through the main entrance along with twenty mounted warriors. A shudder ran through the unarmed Legionaries at the presence of the riders, until Corporal Philetus jogged into view. He waved to Didacus but walked to Alerio.

"I have the ink you wanted," he stated while handing over a clay container.

"What's with the wagons?"

"Lumber, rocks, stones," Philetus listed while indicating pairs of wagons. "And the last four are for your clay and sand."

"It seems the Punic nobleman wants this building done quickly," Alerio guessed. "I'll assign Captains for each work site."

"I thought you might," Philetus remarked. "Are you going to let Didacus pick the teams?"

"Yes," Alerio told him before walking towards the building. On the way, he waved two men into his wake.

The three vanished into the structure. Moments later, they reemerged. The two Legionaries went through the courtyard pulling Friends of Hektor to the back of the assembly for conferences. Alerio went to stand with the crowd, but Didacus stormed up to him.

"See here, Lophos," he scolded. "I'm the foremen for this building. I make the decisions. I may have given you the impression that you're special. But you aren't. How dare you force managers on my work sites?"

"Didacus, you run the teams working on the building," Alerio cautioned while taking the foreman's arm and pulling him in close. "Otherwise, stay out of my business."

Didacus swung wide. The fist traveled across Alerio's chest and punched his right shoulder. Doubling over with shooting pains crippling his arm, Alerio stumbled a step before a pair of hands caught him.

"Steady there," Remus comforted him. "Let me handle this."

The Clay Master didn't challenge or threaten. He released Alerio and drove his knuckles into Didacus' belly. As the foreman bent, Remus punched him in the side of the head.

"If you want to fight, pick on someone with two good shoulders," the Clay Master threatened. "I have both and I'm right here. Come for me."

"My argument isn't with you," Didacus responded. He held the side of his head trying to clear his thoughts.

"You are the foremen because the craftsmen back you," Tullius remarked. "Don't fool yourself. You can be replaced."

The carpenter stepped up and stood shoulder to shoulder with Remus.

"Being prisoners of the Empire is hard enough," Alerio said. Although bent over and nursing the shoulder, he coached. "The last thing we need is to start fighting amongst ourselves. Until we're all free, let's focus on the tasks in front of us."

Tullius and Remus contemplated the comment and stared at Alerio without saying anything.

But Didacus questioned, "Do you think we'll ever get out of Qart Hadasht?"

"Yes," Alerio responded. He uncurled and grimaced from the pain. "When it's time."

"And when is that?" Didacus demanded.

"When I tell you," Alerio barked at the foreman. He started to walk away but stopped and directed. "Pick work crews to go with my captains."

***

Seven miles south from the defensive walls of Qart Hadasht, the two wagons and twenty-seven Legionaries stopped. Next to the trail, a hill of stone waited to be quarried.

After unpacking tents, wedges, and hammers, twenty men began clearing off the soil to give them access to more stone. While they worked, seven of them pulled poles and nets from the wagons and marched towards Lake Tunis.

"Where are they going?" a mounted guard asked.

"Going fishing," one of the two captains of the stonework party replied. "We'll have fresh fish for dinner."

"I like fish," the second guard stated.

"They are my best fishermen," the captain told him. "I would guess there will be plenty for everyone."

***

A second set of wagons moved east along the coast. At an area between the Gulf of Tunis and the northern end of Lake Tunis, the sand team unloaded shovels and baskets. The guards got excited when seven men pulled bows and arrows from the wagons and walked towards the lake.

"They're armed," one warrior remarked.

"How else are they supposed to hunt birds?" a work captain inquired.

***

Eight miles southeast of Qart Hadasht, a third team stopped at the southern end of Lake Tunis. They pulled curved pieces of iron from the wagons and baskets for the reeds. Seven men took spears from the wagons.

"Stop right there," a guard ordered. His horse danced backwards. "Spears are not allowed."

"How are my hunters to take down the hartebeest, if we're lucky enough to locate a herd?" one of the captains challenged. "Do you want to chew mushy grain. Or feast on roasted meat?"

A few heartbeats later, the guards waved the armed Legionaries away.

"If they escape, you all will die," the other guard threatened.

"We are aware," the captain assured him.

***

Twelve miles from the Capital of the Empire and three miles from the hill fort at Jellaz Hill, a fourth expedition set up camp at the other lake. Their wagons held straight iron slats that resembled unformed sword blades and blunt tipped shovels. In with the tools were boards for carrying cut blocks of white clay.

"The fort is close," the guard stated when he saw the big bows and iron tipped arrows.

"So it is," a captain acknowledged. "Between there and here are red deer. But don't tell the men in the fort. They'll want our venison. Unless you want to share your portion with them?"

"Go hunt," the second guard instructed.

***

The last work team rolled beyond the hill fort before angling off into the woods. On a trail that was almost too tight for the wagons, they camped at a grove of cork oak.

"They aren't good for building," a guard pointed out. "The wood is too soft."

"That's true," one of the captains agreed. "But we have Eucalyptus trees nearby. That's hardwood we can use for construction. Plus, the leaves make good herbal tea for the throat."

"Then why stop here?" the guard asked.

"We'll cut the bark off the cork oak," he said, "and punch out stoppers for clay jugs from the cork."

"What good is that?" the warrior inquired.

"A cork plug is reusable after opening a jar or a bottle," the other Friend of Hektor's described.

"I don't see the value in that," the guard admitted. "But as long as nobody escapes, I'll allow you to cut bark as long as you harvest hardwood."

***

Over the next week, no one ran away. Logs of hardwood and rolls of cork bark arrived at the compound. Wagons with clay blocks, others filled with reeds, and still more came in with slabs of stone or piles of sand came from the work sites.

In addition to the raw materials, dried fish, smoked venison, beef, and fowl arrived. They provided better food than the overseer allotted. Enough meat and fish came in that the Noricum guards were invited to the daily feast. As a result of proper feeding, unlike most slaves or prisoners, the Legionaries maintained their stamina and their muscle mass. Another benefit, the happy guards allowed Alerio to go outside the courtyard so he could sketch the surrounding buildings.

"We want this structure to be special," he explained while the guards chewed on pieces of duck or maybe goose. "I need to see how it fits in the neighborhood."

"Just don't try to escape," they cautioned between greasy bites.

Every day, he had the same exchange with the guards. And each time, Alerio assured them he had no intention of running away.

***

A week after he sent Vitus and Tutus to General Regulus, Alerio sat on a wall behind the building site. On his lap was a board with a sheet of parchment on top. But he wasn't drawing. He hadn't been for most of the afternoon. Now as the sun sank low in the sky, he prepared to pack up and return to the courtyard.

"Centurion Lophos, I'm glad I caught you," Vitus greeted Alerio as he strolled from an alleyway. "General Regulus sends his congratulations for organizing the Legionaries. He did ask if you had any word on the whereabouts of Colonel Sisera."

"He didn't make it to the five hundred," Alerio lied. As far as he knew, the Empire and the Spartans wanted to see Battle Commander Sisera dying slowly on a high cross. "What else does the General need?"

"The General was surprised the Spartans were taking care of our men," Vitus reported. "He said if it will help you, the Qart Hadasht finance committee is getting ready to dismiss the Iberians and the Noricum soldiers."

"How does that help us?" Alerio questioned.

"Because once the infantry leaves, the Special Branch will charge the Spartan with murder," Vitus answered. "They want their gold back from General Xanthippus. Can you use that information?"

"That will be useful. But I could use some funds," Alerio told him.

"The Empire is keeping the General poor and dependent on them," Vitus informed Alerio.

"Take this to the harbor," Alerio instructed. He lifted a strap from around his neck and handed a large pouch to the aide. "There are pieces of cork in there and clay pots of herbal tea made from eucalyptus leaves."

"Raw materials to coins," Vitus confirmed.

"Yes. Now you better get back before you're missed."

"That's not a problem, sir," Vitus said. "Tutus is getting the General and himself ready for a banquet. I need to stay out of sight until they get back to the apartments."

"I need to get back to the courtyard," Alerio stated. "I'll be here every other afternoon if you need to contact me."

"One of us will leave the coins at the base of the wall," Vitus commented as he walked away. He turned and asked. "Will you take us with you when you go?"

"That is the plan, unless something else comes up," Alerio promised.

The two went in separate directions. One heading for the harbor to sell the items in the pouch and the other to spend the night speculating when, or if he should use the information.

***

General Marcus Regulus had adopted a slightly different attitude. Not enough to be forceful with the Empire noblemen or to resist them. But the knowledge that five hundred of his Legionaries lived, gave him a tingling of pride in his chest.

"You look splendid," Marcus said while admiring his aide.

Titus wore a bright pink tunic with gold trim and a shoulder scarf with an Optio's rank on it. From the way the Legionary admired the garment, it was obvious he had nothing like it in his wardrobe at home.

"It's a bit much, sir," Tutus murmured. He touched the NCO medal, the expensive trim, and ran a hand down the vibrant colored linen. "We don't wear expensive cloth on the farm."

"I would hope not," Marcus said. He held back explaining the too flashy color, the ornate trim, and the rank were intended as insults. It represented a washed-out version of the red Legion cape, the gold trim the captured wealth from the Legions, and one misconception. His Punic handlers didn't understand it was an honor for a Sergeant to be a servant to his General. Hoping the insults were over the head of his aide, Marcus reminded the young man. "They will offend you and me with slurs and affronts. But fighting and getting beaten down for the entertainment of the Qart Hadasht guests is not our assignment for tonight."

"Yes, sir," Tutus assured him. "Our job, General, is to be stoic enough that we frustrate them, and they send us home."

"I couldn't have said it better myself," Marcus agreed. "Grab my helmet and let's go parade around for the nobility."

***

Marcus Regulus and Optio Tutus were out of the apartment building, and down the street at the banquet hall when someone noticed the Republic General's aide at the harbor. Thinking he discovered subterfuge on the part of the captured Latian, the Punic nobleman rushed to the party.

"See here, General Bostar, I saw the aide for your pet General at the harbor," the man asserted. "I think you might want to question Regulus."

"It seems he has abused the freedom we allow him and his aide," Bostar responded. "Come with me. We'll confront him this very instant."

"An excellent idea," the nobleman agreed.

As they crossed the ballroom, the Punic noble signaled others to come along and join in the fun. By the time Bostar located Marcus, they had ten couples following to watch the public scolding.

"General Bostar, good evening to you," Marcus greeted the Qart Hadasht Commander with a slight bow. "I trust you are in good health."

"I was having a pleasant evening until I learned your aide was at the harbor," Bostar charged. "What was he doing there? Trying to hire a boat to spirit you away?"

"My aide, sir?" Marcus questioned. He stepped aside and extended a hand towards Tutus. "Have you been to the harbor?"

"Me sir?" Tutus asked. He held the General's ceremonial helmet in two hands as if prepared to lift it as a display or to hand the headgear to Marcus. "General, I've been with you all afternoon, sir."

Marcus got a serious expression on his face and stared down into Bostar's eyes. The Punic General shifted uncomfortably. Having this conversation in front of so many witnesses, was not a good idea after all.

"Is that the youth you observed at the harbor?" Bostar questioned the nobleman.

Bending forward, the Punic stared at Tutus and admitted, "I thought it was. But now that I look closely, and seeing him here, it couldn't have been him at the harbor."

Bostar started to back away, but Marcus Regulus held up a hand to stop him and to hold the crowd of witnesses in place.

"I am confused, sir," Regulus commented. "I beat your fleet and sank your best ships. Then I made prisoners of the sons from your noblest houses and shipped them off to Rome as slaves. But when I offered to present your demands to the Senate for their release, you ignored me and their plight. And when I recommended that I deliver your terms to end this war, you turned a deaf ear. And now, instead of taking advantage of my position, you accuse my aide of nefarious activities? Sir, I am confused. Just where are your priorities?"

The novelty of having a captured Republic General and his dressed-up aide ended with the speech. In the morning, the Special Branch met to draw up their formal demands for the Senate of the Republic.

***

Just after sunrise, Alerio decided to use the information about dismissing the mercenary soldiers and charging the Spartan with murder. Or rather, Bagarok decided for him. With six bully boys in tow, the overseer charged onto the courtyard. He went directly for the stockpile of meats.

"What's this?" he bellowed. "It's food too good for the likes of Latians. Impound it all."

The six thugs punched and beat Legionaries as they crossed the courtyard. Then they filled their arms with the stored meats and followed Bagarok to the wall.

Before he vanished through the exit, the Iberian manager announced, "Every day, I will hold an inspection for contraband food. And every time I find any, I will confiscate the meat."

He and his six bodyguards left. Once they were gone, the Noricum guard at the exit, who had enjoyed feasting with the Legionaries, shrugged and made a rude gesture in the overseer's direction. He wasn't the only one frustrated by the event.

Alerio brushed off a piece of flat rock and sat. He waited there for the building site's Spartan to arrive. Not sure how timely his information was, Alerio hoped it would get his Legionaries some relief from the beatings and stop the theft of their provisions by the overseer.

Act 6

Chapter 16 – Freed from an Oath

"Spartan, a word if you please," Alerio called to the Hoplite.

As the Spartan marched towards him, Alerio stood, brushed off his rear, and straightened his tunic. It wouldn't be right begging for help with his butt covered in rock dust.

"That's a relief," the Hoplite stated when he was an arm's length from the Latian. His hand fell away from the hilt of the kopis. "I didn't want to kill you."

"Why would you do that?" Alerio questioned.

"That dagger you have hidden in the small of your back," the Spartan pointed out. "When you reached back, you might have pulled it."

"I don't usually go around killing people that I need help from," Alerio told him.

"And why would I help you?" the Hoplite inquired.

Alerio was relieved when the Spartan didn't question him about the Golden Valley dagger. It would be awkward asking for assistance by starting with a lie.

"I've come across some information," Alerio told him. "A finance committee is going to remove funding for the Iberian and Noricum mercenaries."

"We've been expecting it now that the threat is neutralized," the Hoplite remarked. Seeing the pained expression on Alerio's face, he added. "In Sparta, we say it's the business of war. And business is good. You lost."

"It still hurts," Alerio admitted. "But here is the information I hope to trade. After the mercenaries leave, a special branch will issue an arrest warrant for your Commander."

"That as well was expected," the Hoplite commented. "Come with me."

"Where are we going?"

The Spartan didn't reply. He marched away and Alerio had to run to catch up. Outside the courtyard, they mounted horses and trotted away from the building site.

***

When the Legionaries arrived in Qart Hadasht, the streets were dark, the men exhausted from fighting, angry at the murder of their comrades, and confused about surviving. Almost drowning in the flood of feelings, they failed to note streets, turns, and landmarks. Putting one foot in front of the other, they passed through the defensive walls, and tramped up and across several streets before entering the courtyard.

Alerio had seen the defensive walls from the top of the dilapidated building. Distance in roof tops was different from the experience of riding on streets. Narrower in person and encroached upon by the limbs of trees and canopies from both sides, the roads had shade but little width.

"In Rome, we have directional boulevards," Alerio observed. "The thoroughfares allow our Legionaries to move quickly to any location at our defensive wall."

"In Sparta, we have no walls to protect our city," the Hoplite bragged. "Our soldiers are the walls."

"It appears Qart Hadasht is the worst of both," Alerio ventured when he noted the absence of Empire soldiers.

"They have walls surrounding a labyrinth of impassable and unguarded streets."

"It would be difficult to move a force through this," the Hoplite stated. "Either for an invasion, or for a pursuit of escaping prisoners."

To Alerio's delight, they turned on several streets taking a circuitous route. In fact, on two occasions, he saw the entrance to the construction site's courtyard between houses. By the time they left the area, he had a good idea of the streets surrounding the work site.

"We have a plan to contain your breakout," the Spartan informed Alerio.

They took a road heading east. Between gaps, Alerio saw the blue water of Punic Bay. Then they angled south and headed downhill towards the defensive wall.

"There's a company of Noricum soldiers housed around here," the Hoplite informed Alerio. He drew back on the reins, stopped his horse, and pointed farther ahead. "You can make out their headquarters from here. It's the building backed up to the city's final defensive wall."

Alerio didn't talk. He was too busy mapping the location in his mind. It was obvious why the Spartans had soldiers stationed there. A long ladder could easily span from the roof of the structure to the top of the defensive wall. Then a chill ran down Alerio's spine. There were only two reasons to show him this escape route. The Spartans were going to let him get away. Or, they planned to execute him, rendering the knowledge useless.

The door to a long, low building opened, and a Noricum NCO walked out. Seeing the Spartan, he saluted.

"Captain," he questioned. "Can I help you?"

"How goes the transfer?"

"We need more wagons," the Sergeant complained. He pointed at the building. "With only two carts, it'll take us two weeks or more to move all the Republic's battle gear."

"Two wagons are all that were assigned," the Hoplite asserted. "If the Empire isn't worried about how long, then neither should you."

"Yes, sir," the Noricum acknowledged with a salute.

The Spartan cocked his head and peered at Alerio for a few beats before kneeing his horse forward. Alerio shivered from the emotionless gaze.

***

Across the city, Alerio followed the Hoplite through the gates of a compound. In a practice yard, three squads of scarlet cloaked men drilled by smashing their shields together. Following the collision, the Spartans marched at each other. Chunks of earth flew with each step, yet their foot movements generated no forward progress. Neither side moved from the site of the impact.

"That's how men from Sparta relax," the Hoplite told Alerio. He slid from the saddle and handed the reins to a servant. "Come."

Once Alerio and the Hoplite entered the main building, a Rank-Leader on the practice field instructed, "That's enough."

The Spartans stepped back, shook dirt from their legs and boots, and broke formation.

"Is the show always necessary?" a Hoplite inquired.

"We don't have walls around Sparta," the phalanx NCO replied. "Our Hoplites are the walls. Plus, the ferocious reputation of the Spartan soldier keeps enemies away from our city."

"Besides, you needed the work. You were sloppy in the push," another Hoplite accused the first. "You fail in combat, and I'll gut you myself."

The show might maintain the mystique to outsiders. But the training and skills learned from a young age assured that the Spartans were able to back it up with their shields, spears, and kopides.

***

General Xanthippus uncrossed his arms and allowed them to drift down to his sides. Then as if a statue, he watched Alerio, and the Hoplite come into his office.

"Sir, may I present Alerio Lophos Carvilius, of the Republic Legion," the Hoplite introduced Alerio. "He has news."

"Take off your hat," the General ordered. When Alerio hesitated, the Spartan warned. "I can have a couple of my phalanx remove it. But they usually take a layer of skin. I suggest you do it yourself."

Trapped in a compound full of Spartans and about to reveal his identity, Alerio prayed.

"Goddess Nenia, make it quick," he begged while removing the petasos.

"And now, your real name?" the Spartan General inquired.

"I am Colonel Alerio Carvilius Sisera, Battle Commander of Legion North," he announced while expanding his chest.

"Hermes bless me," the Hoplite uttered.

At the mention of the Greek Messenger of the Gods and their Trickster, Xanthippus laughed.

"Lost the bet, did you?" the General inquired.

"Yes, sir, I had him as a combat officer in command of an eighty-man infantry unit," the Hoplite replied. "Of course, I never saw the scar on his scalp."

"It's just as nasty as reported," Xanthippus observed. He sat and pointed to the chair across from him. "Now that that's settled, Colonel Sisera. What news do you bear?"

Dropping into the chair, Alerio debated whether to tell the General what he knew or to bargain for his life. After looking into the cold eyes of the Spartan Commander, he decided the direct approach was best.

"A finance committee is pulling funds and dismissing the Iberians and the Noricums," he explained. "Once they're gone, something called a special branch will charge you with murder. But you might be executed for the punishment if you turn me over to them in exchange for your freedom."

"Not a finance committee, Colonel, but The Finance Committee," Xanthippus corrected. "I wondered why they were meeting behind closed doors this morning. But I have no plans to turn you over to the Empire. You see, Sisera, they don't really want me. They want the gold I extracted from them for defeating the Legions. And while they would enjoy torturing you, you aren't worth that much gold."

"Then why am I here?" Alerio asked.

"To settle the bet about your rank," the General stated. "And seeing as you're here, let me tell you something. The Special Branch is meeting to put together a list of demands. I can only surmise that General Regulus will be sent to Rome to deliver them."

Once Marcus Regulus sailed for home, Alerio would be free. Although not the exact parameters of the oath, the event would stand as a resolution to the promise sworn by Senior

Tribune Sisera to Consul Regulus. Of course, Alerio's death would also free him from the oath.

"Are you unwell?" Xanthippus questioned. "You suddenly went pale."

"It's a relief, sir," Alerio responded. "With my General safe, I can die in peace with just one regret."

"Hold that thought," Xanthippus instructed. "Hoplite. Go see if anyone wants to wager on what the Latian's regret is?"

At a hand sign, a servant brought in a pitcher of wine and a glass plus a glass half filled with water. The man poured wine into both vessels. Reputation hinted at it, but now Alerio had confirmation that Spartans avoided strong drink.

"We are a long way from home and in enemy territory," the Spartan Commander told Alerio. "One diversion is betting on the strange things we see and other mysteries."

"Like me?" Alerio asked.

"Yes, just like you."

***

The courtyard and the repaired and practically new building came into view. Alerio dismounted and handed the reins to a Noricum soldier.

"Orders, Captain?" an NCO asked the Hoplite. The Spartan waved the Sergeant over, bent, and whispered to him.

Alerio braced his legs preparing to be attacked. Xanthippus knew he was the Battle Commander for Legion North. And although it would deprive the Empire of entertainment, Alerio expected the Spartan to murder him all during the meeting and on the ride back to the courtyard.

"It was a good day, Master Lophos," the Hoplite commented. "Don't ruin it by resisting a return to your prison."

***

With long strides, Alerio marched through the entrance and into the construction site. He was greeted by a slim Legionary with burn marks on his arms.

"We have something to show you," Albin, the Master Tool Maker, invited Alerio. "Come see."

The metal worker walked behind the kilns to an area with an open forge. In the center of a cleared space rested a boulder of clay. The bands around it and a line bisecting the structure identified it as a mold.

"Bronze casting?" Alerio questioned.

"Of Helios," the Tool Maker confirmed.

Four helpers untied the mold and Albin pried around the center until the top loosened. Then two helpers shoved poles under the top section and lifted it off the mold.

In the bottom half of the clay form, a bronze disk of the Sun God glowed in the afternoon sun.

"You did an amazing job," Alerio complimented the metal worker.

"I worked from your drawing to carve the face and the four horses," Albin stated. He pulled a small medallion from a pouch. "And I cast a small pendant to test the look."

He held out a Helios medal that dangled from a leather band.

"For you, sir," Albin justified. "Without your leadership, we wouldn't be together, treated as well, or be as well fed."

Alerio took the leather thong and dropped it over his head. He ran his fingers over the bronze disk. The feel of

Helios and the God's four winged steeds told of Albin's talent as a metalworker. He dropped it down the neck of his tunic and saluted the tool maker.

"I thank you for the gift," Alerio acknowledged. "It'll remind me every day of something I do not plan to regret."

"What's that, sir?" the tool maker asked.

"Not looking into the eyes of my child," Alerio confessed. "As far as being well fed, I did my best, but probably failed."

"The bronze won't be cool enough to handle until the morning," Albin told him. "We should eat the meat that came in today."

Chapter 17 – Freedom Sailing Away

For two days, the overseer marched his thugs onto the courtyard and searched for extra meat, fish, and fowl. But after each inspection, Bagarok walked away empty handed. It wasn't that the Legionaries consumed all the food sent from the five work camps. To deny the Iberian manager, Alerio fed the Noricum soldiers and gave them extra to take back to their barracks.

"See here, Lophos," Didacus objected, "you're giving away provisions to our prison guards. I think that practice should stop."

"Would you rather the food go to the overseer?" Alerio questioned.

"No, of course not," the foreman remarked. "We could hide the meat around the job site. There are plenty of places to conceal the excess."

"Feeding the Noricum soldiers serves a purpose," Alerio assured him without explanation. "I've told you before, do not get into my business."

The foreman made fists and glared at Alerio.

"My shoulder is healed. If you want to fight, let's do it," Alerio said calling his bluff. "I need the exercise."

Didacus snorted and stomped off.

***

On the third day, Corporal Philetus arrived with packages. His appearance from the opposite side of the courtyard seemed to be a poetic balance to Bagarok and his bodyguards leaving from the other exit.

"I have trowels for finishing the exterior," the Legion NCO informed a group of men. "Where's Alerio Lophos?"

The group pointed up to the building. Six men stood on a framework of beams and boards. Interconnected, the wood created tiers that reached to the top of the facade. The six stood three stories up on the highest level.

"A little to the left," Albin instructed.

Two metalworkers shifted the bronze image of the Sun God to the left.

"Perfect. Master of Clay," he invited the next man on the scaffolding.

Remus used a chisel to cut an oval in the stucco to match the size of the bronze casting. When he had deepened the cut enough, a helper handed him a bucket of wet clay. Remus filled the shape with fine white clay and moved out of the way.

Albin and his assistants positioned the bronze medallion then pressed it into the wet mass. As it sank in, Remus cut away the excess clay.

"What do you think?" Albin asked when the casting of Helios was firmly in place.

Everyone on the platform agreed it looked magnificent. Except for one, who didn't offer an opinion.

"What no praise or corrections, Alerio?" Remus asked.

"Sorry. My mind wandered," Alerio answered. He scanned the image quickly and added. "It's very nice."

"Such high acclaim," Albin joked. "You make us blush with your untethered praise."

From the height of the scaffolding, Alerio had a view of the area outside the compound. What he witnessed in an alleyway off a side street forced him to question several notions. Specifically in doubt and the cause of his distraction, were the ideas of trust, honor, and duty. While climbing down, Alerio replayed the scene in his head.

***

Bagarok and four thugs, one toting boxes, sauntered up the road while Corporal Philetus strolled towards them from the other direction. The two were on a collision course and Alerio feared for the Legion NCO. But when they met, the overseer and the Corporal stepped into an alleyway. They talked for several moments before shaking hands. At the exit from the lane, the bodyguard handed Philetus the boxes. And while the overseer headed for the courtyard, the NCO sorted through the containers, investigating the contents. After checking, he marched across the road and entered the compound.

***

At the bottom of the scaffolding, Alerio ambled in the direction of Philetus and the boxes.

"Corporal, what have you brought us?" Alerio asked.

"Trowels. I noticed you were starting to apply stucco to finished areas," Philetus responded. "I thought they might come in handy."

"Any news from the outside world?" Alerio asked while reaching in and taking a tool from the box.

The grooved edge of the flat iron could easily rip flesh. Alerio ran a finger over the notches while waiting for the response. But the Legion NCO didn't tell Alerio about the move to relieve the Noricum and the Iberian mercenaries. Things that should have been common knowledge at this stage.

"Nothing to report, but one never knows everything," Philetus assured him. "This is Qart Hadasht, and it is complicated."

"As you've reminded me," Alerio stated. "Are you getting enough food? We have extra ham coming in from the stone quarry. They've been smoking it for two days. I expect it tomorrow."

"I'm fed grain mostly," Philetus told him. "Ham would be nice. But isn't the overseer taking all your extra?"

"Not this time," Alerio whispered. "We're going to hide it in a kiln with our weapons."

"Weapons?" Philetus questioned.

"Yes, we've made spearheads with extra iron," Alerio said bringing the NCO into the conspiracy. He bounced the trowel on the palm of his hand, "and the bronze runoff from casting the medallion. When we have enough, we'll make spears for our escape."

"Very clever," the NCO confirmed before excusing himself. "I better go, they're expecting me at another worksite."

The Legion NCO marched away. When Philetus moved by the Noricum guard, Alerio turned towards the forge and said, "I wonder how long it will take Albin to forge a few spearheads?"

***

Late in the morning of the next day, the wagons with the raw materials arrived and Alerio located a smoked rump roast.

"Where are you taking that meat?" a Legionary inquired.

"It's to replace the ham," Alerio said as he started for the clay firing area.

"What ham?" the confused infantryman asked.

Alerio didn't answer. He carried the roast to Albin who was busy hammering out spearheads.

"You could just ask him," the tool maker advocated.

"A compromised man is already living a lie," Alerio responded. "Giving false testimony isn't a challenge to a dishonest reality. Besides, I need evidence before I accuse a Legionary that I…"

Alerio stopped.

"That you what?" Albin asked between strikes with his hammer.

"A Legionary that I suspect of conspiring with the Empire," Alerio lied.

He almost said a Legionary that I promoted to Tesserarius. But it was too soon to reveal that he was Colonel Sisera. And that was the other reason he didn't confront Philetus without more proof. The Corporal knew Alerio's identity but hadn't turned him over to Qart Hadasht authorities. It was a good sign, unless the NCO was saving that piece of information for a bigger reward.

***

It might have been Bagarok changing tactics and him telling the truth.

"I've just come from another worksite," the overseer announced. He put a hand on Remus' back and propelled the Master of Clay to the kilns. "I was bragging about the quality of your tiles. How do you make them?"

Alerio and the other craftsmen followed the overseer and his guards.

"It's just a mixture of clay, water, and sand blended with reeds to hold the bricks together," Remus expounded on the simplicity of the formula for the durable finished product. "For walls we sun dry them. For tiles, we make them flatter and bake the elements in the ovens."

"Ah, yes the ovens," Bagarok repeated. He walked between the mounds, placing a hand on several. At one, he left the hand flat on the clay and rock exterior. "This one seems cooler than the others."

"The tiles have finished baking," Remus detailed. "We'll allow them to cool naturally before taking the hardened tiles out."

"I'd like to see them," the overseer stated.

"If they cool too fast, they might crack," the Clay Master counseled.

"Still, I want to see the tiles for myself," Bagarok insisted.

Remus called over a pair of helpers with rags wrapped around their hands. They grabbed the door and pulled it away from the kiln. Bagarok shoved his face close to the oven but was driven away by a wave of hot air.

"Close it," Remus instructed.

Bagarok walked behind the oven and kicked at the ash. Then he used his foot to brush away the remnants of the fire. His motions revealed a flat stone.

"Lift that," he instructed.

Two of his bodyguards used sticks to pry the rock up and expose a hole. When the other guards began lifting spearheads from the depression, the overseer hopped around in shocked amazement. A collection of roughly constructed spearheads and a wrapped package came out of the hole.

"What's this? Weapons?" the overseer accused. "And a ham?"

With the contraband in baskets, Bagarok marched his bodyguards from the kiln area and out through the courtyard. He never checked the wrapped meat.

"What are you going to do about the Corporal?" Albin asked.

"I'm not sure," Alerio replied.

Even if he had a plan on how to deal with the NCO, Alerio could do nothing about Philetus until he returned. Given time, he'd work out the details. But Janus, the God of Beginnings, Gates, Transitions, and Endings decided to intercede.

***

The morning routine had developed over the weeks they spent rebuilding the structure. Work parties gathered around their Master Craftsman and shared a meal while discussing the priorities for the day. After the meal, the crews gathered tools or prepared supplies. Then the job site became a hive of activity.

"I need a drawing of the arch for the third floor," a carpenter notified Alerio.

Grateful for a chance to be useful and to take his mind off Corporal Philetus, Alerio grabbed his parchment and ink and headed for a ladder. He climbed three rungs and froze.

The pressure against his right shoulder blade felt as if someone was crowding in behind him and attempting to peer over his shoulder. Alerio looked up for danger from above then from side-to-side checking for hazards. With no obvious threats in sight, he held the ladder and swung around. On the far side of the courtyard, the gate opened slowly.

***

The early morning sun came in the window and formed a square on the floor of the apartment. At the knock on the front door, Vitus shuffled through the square of light heading for a back room while Tutus cut across the light moving to the door.

"Good morning. General Regulus is presently indisposed," the aide said as he opened the door. "May I take a message."

In the hallway, a uniformed courier handed him a pouch, a bag of coins, and an unsealed letter. Then he spun on his heels and marched for the stairs. Tutus closed and barred the door.

"Sir, you have messages," he called to another room.

Vitus and Regulus came into the parlor from opposite sides.

"What is it now?" Marcus whined. "More invitations to galas?"

Vitus took the pouch and pulled out a stack of papyrus sheets while Regulus reached for the letter. They read then stopped.

"General Regulus, you need to read…" At the same time Vitus spoke, Regulus said, "Vitus, you need to read…"

"Sir, if I may," Tutus inquired, "what's going on?"

"We're going to Rome," Regulus explained. "There's an Egyptian trading vessel leaving at midday for Syracuse. The coins are for passage from there to home. What's in the pouch?"

"Empire demands from the surrender of Qart Hadasht hostages," Vitus answered while scanning the pages. "And it seems, their terms include the surrender of Sicilia by the Republic."

"Sir, should we tell Centurion Lophos?" Tutus asked.

"We've barely time to pack and get ourselves to the dock," Regulus directed. "Go collect what you can and anything you can't carry, leave behind. Being on that Egyptian ship when it rows out of the harbor and into Punic Bay is the most important thing."

"Yes, sir," both Vitus and Tutus confirmed with a pair of salutes.

***

Twelve miles from the harbor of Qart Hadasht, a Greek merchantman set the fore and midship sails. Once the oars were stowed, the ship's Captain directed his lead rower.

"I think we're far enough into the bay," he instructed. "Open the cargo hold."

With a crewman on each end of the heavy deck board, they hoisted it and carried it to a side rail. They went back and removed a second. As the pair shuffled sideways to the rail, a Greek helmet with a long crest of red and yellow appeared. Shortly after, scarlet cloaks and four more men dressed in the bright capes came out of the opening. Before the Greek Captain could assure the Spartans there was no danger, forty capes, forty shields, and forty spears defended his deck.

"General, there isn't an Empire ship-of-war in sight," he assured the commander.

"I hate that meaningless title. Inept men and politicians hide behind Generalships," Xanthippus stated. "I am a Spartan Commander and a proud Tail-Leader of a mighty phalanx."

His forty Spartans cheered.

Then a Rank-Leader offered, "And a wealthy one as well, sir."

"There's enough Empire gold to share with each of you," Xanthippus confirmed. "You can say it's a bonus, courtesy of the Special Branch."

With the wind's cooperation, the Greek trader hauling the Spartans sailed away from Qart Hadasht. None of the Hoplites would ever again take a contract to train or fight for the Empire. As one Spartan complained, "Verbal orders aren't worth the parchment they're written on."

***

Alerio knew nothing about General Regulus sailing for Rome or Xanthippus and his Hoplites sailing for Sparta. He was focused on the gate to the courtyard. Too early for his material haulers, there was no reason for the gate doors to open.

Responding to the alert from the Goddess Nenia, Alerio jumped from the ladder, dropped his supplies, and raced towards the gates. He wasn't sure what he planned to accomplish when he got there. But it turned out to be a moot point. He never arrived.

His run ended abruptly when a squad of Noricum soldiers marched through the opening. Whatever he had in the back of his brain, it didn't involve getting into a barehanded fight with armored soldiers.

They came in shoulder to shoulder and Alerio backed up. Inhaling deeply, he thanked the Goddess for the warning. Then he began to call out and have the Legionaries prepare to defend themselves.

Just before he got the warning vocalized, the soldiers reached the center of the courtyard and stopped.

"Men of the Republic," a Noricum NCO shouted. "Another day, another battlefield. Until we cross blades again, goodbye."

The ten soldiers turned about and marched out of the courtyard. Left behind was a cart with a goatskin tarp over the bed. Alerio sprinted to the wagon, slid to a stop, and flung the cover off the cargo.

"Remus. Albin," Alerio shouted to the Master Craftsmen, "send me ten Legionaries who aren't afraid to get their blades wet."

While he waited, Alerio pulled an armored skirt from the pile of Legion war gear and strapped it around his waist. Before the ten men arrived, Alerio had a gladius in one hand and was pulling a scutum from the bed of the wagon.

"What's this?" Didacus demanded.

"Parting gifts from the Noricum soldiers," Alerio replied.

"Parting gifts?" the foremen questioned. "Where did they go?"

"That's not the question," Alerio countered while strapping on a section of chest armor.

"What is?" Didacus asked.

Alerio answered with the question, "Who is coming to take their place?"

Chapter 18 – The Violent Trail

At midday, the answer to who was next arrived in the form of the Iberian overseer and fifteen armored irregulars. Accompanying the manager and his force was Corporal Philetus. His presence solidified the suspicion about his loyalty and revealed the level of trust his new masters had in him. He was unarmed.

"Where is Colonel Sisera?" Bagarok bellowed as he came through the open gateway. "I'm here for Battle Commander Sisera. If you turn him over, life will be good. More freedom and better food."

"But you've been stealing our meat," a solitary Latian called from the roof deck of the building.

One by one, he was joined by ranks workers. They appeared on either side of the man until the roof deck was lined with men. As if winking, rays of sunlight flashed across the face of Helios, blinding the overseer.

"A misunderstanding," Bagarok suggested while squinting. "Where is Sisera?"

Behind the overseer, the gates moved. Swinging away from the fence as they closed, the gates revealed seven armed and armored Legion infantrymen. Then, at the entrances on either side of the courtyard, pairs of Legionnaires stepped through, blocking the exits.

"Your greed has put you in a bad situation," a Legionary to the right of the gate stated. He removed his helmet. "I believe you're looking for me."

Bagarok spun to face the speaker and charged, "Battle Commander, you are under arrest."

Although some suspected Alerio, the rest of the men on the work site gasped. Alerio Lophos the draftsman was in fact Colonel Sisera, Commander of Legion North.

"Greed, overseer, was your undoing," Alerio professed as he took three steps towards the irregulars. "If you had reported me to your superiors, they would have swooped in with a company of soldiers and a troop of cavalry. But they haven't because you didn't report me."

"There are more men coming," Bagarok stammered. "Lay down your arms."

"The reward must be huge," Alerio submitted. "But wait. They think I'm dead. There isn't a standing reward. Aha, you planned to negotiate after capturing me. Bad choice, have your warriors lay down their arms."

Philetus bolted for an exit. An infantryman violently blocked his escape, knocking the former NCO to the ground. As if an order had been issued, the action triggered the irregulars. They lifted their tribal shields and leveled their spears at the Legionaries.

In response, Celso, a recently appointed Legion squad leader, barked, "Step up. Form a wall."

The infantrymen marched four steps and came abreast on Alerio's left. On the far left, Master Carpenter Tullius anchored the far side of the formation. Making clicking noises, the seven scuta overlapped, shrinking the width of the Legion formation. Across the courtyard, the fifteen warriors straightened their shoulders. With the numbers in their favor and the Legionaries cowering behind their big shields, the irregulars felt confident.

"Cover," squad leader Celso instructed.

Alerio and the six Legionaries went from peeking over the tops of their shields to ducking down behind them. An instant later, volleys of stones flew from the roof of the building.

While the irregulars were distracted dodging and attempting to block the barrage of rocks, the Legion squad leader shouted, "Forward."

***

From the right side of the formation, a rough, out of tune voice sang.

I want to dream of home and hearth
To donate at the Temple of Vesta
Witness the eternal flame
See a Vestal Virgin
Be in Rome again

Alerio's shield rocked from strikes by a pair of spear tips. Judging the location of the warriors, he angled outward. As he sang, he bent at the knees, and exploded off the combat line.

I've got seventy miles of hike
Just to reach the beach
Seventy miles of fight
Just to launch a ship

Hammered by the veteran infantry officer, the pair of warriors fell back. One spear got pushed downward while the other was moved upward by the shield. Charging behind his scutum, Alerio stomped the lower shaft, ripping it out of the warrior's hands. He slammed the unarmed tribesman inward towards the assault line and leaped at the second.

On the far side of the Legion formation, Tullius also used his shield to hem in the irregulars, preventing them from circling behind the Legion assault line.

Pivoting his hips, Alerio ducked under the second shaft. In mid step, he felt the warrior resist as he set his feet, preparing to stab over the shield. Before Alerio had to start dodging a spear's tip, he hacked the tribesman's arm. Screaming in pain, the man dropped the shaft, sunk to his knees, and held the dangling portion of his severed arm.

Alerio stepped back, rejoined the Legion combat line, and crooned.

Eight hundred miles to sail
Just to see Ostia
Eight hundred miles of sea
Just to be free

Five warriors were wounded or dead. Three had run for an exit, rather than face the moving barrier of hardwood and sharp steel. The last seven circled Bagarok, defending the manager. Heavy infantrymen hated having to chase down the enemy. Which made the positioning of the irregulars perfect for an assault.

My destiny is of travel and trouble
The Goddess Hybris has the traits
Her blessings are my guide
Outrageous behavior
To Reckless pride

Alerio pushed the warrior in front of him, crowding the man backward. The tight rounded formation of irregulars allowed for no give, letting Alerio pin the man in place.

Any stationary target in a shield wall fight was vulnerable. Alerio stabbed and his gladius found flesh.

I've got seventy miles of hike
Just to reach the beach
Seventy miles of fight
Just to launch a ship

Somehow from the press of bodies, the overseer was ejected. He fell on his face, gathered his hands under his chest, pushed off the gravel of the courtyard, and managed one step. Then the hands of five unarmored Legionaries grabbed Bagarok and shuffled him off to the side.

Eight hundred miles to sail
Just to see Ostia
Eight hundred miles of sea
Just to be free

Realizing there was no room or need for his blade in the final push, Alerio stepped back. Scanning the courtyard, he located the overseer in the hands of a group of Latians.

"I need his robe," Alerio informed them. "Don't get blood on it."

The robe came off as daggers and tools came up. Bagarok, the overseer, was stripped before being executed.

***

At one exit, three irregulars lay dead while at the other, Philetus moaned as he bled out.

"Put him down," Alerio directed.

One of the guards stepped forward and ran his blade through the former NCO's throat. There would be no punishment post for the traitor.

"Non capimus!" Alerio ordered when the fighting in the scrum slowed. "We can't leave witnesses behind. Take no prisoners!"

The warriors attempted to fend off the blades and shields of the Legionaries. But light infantrymen were at a disadvantage against heavy infantry in close quarter's fighting.

"You are blood thirsty, Colonel Sisera," Didacus observed. "After this mess, we have no alternative. The Empire will want us all on crosses."

"Did they ever want anything else?" Alerio inquired. He indicated the bodies. "We need their armor and uniforms. Oh, and Master Foreman, if you think this was extreme, remember, we're just starting on the violent trail."

Mere heartbeats later, the battle for the courtyard ended and the escape of the five hundred captives began.

***

Five irregulars marched in front of an empty wagon and five followed. Driving the mules were a pair of men in dirty tunics. Behind the teamsters, a manager in his robe of office strolled along with the wagon. At an intersection, the overseer waved his arm indicating a turn.

The detachment lost the view of Punic Bay when they left the east-west facing street. Moving south and downhill, they saw a three-story building at the bottom of the street and the city's defensive wall behind it. Rather than go to the building, the manager scurried to the lead and called a halt at a warehouse.

"Force it open and make sure we're alone," Alerio directed. As the disguised Legionaries cut the hemp binding the door, Alerio walked to the teamsters. "Master Tool Maker, you only have until dusk to sort the gear."

"Don't you worry, Colonel," Albin assured him. "I'll have helmets with helmets, gladii with gladii, and shields with shields."

Facing the other teamster, Alerio asked, "Can you find your way back to the compound?"

"As easily as if it was the foundation for Jupiter's Temple," Naevus assure him. "Aren't you coming?"

"I'll be along later. Right now, load this wagon and get the gear back to the courtyard," Alerio told him. Legionaries appeared in the doorway and cut the air with their hands. At the all-clear signal, Alerio told them. "Give me five men. The rest of you help load the wagon."

Once he had his volunteers, Colonel Sisera marched downhill to the building adjacent to the defensive wall.

***

Alerio pushed open the unbarred door and marched into the building. The bottom floor held a couple of barrels and a trough for watering livestock. He took mud bricks steps to the second level. Crossing the floor, he located an inclined ladder and climbed to the third floor. From there, he moved to a hole in the ceiling and accessed the roof by a steep ladder.

The city's defensive wall were seven feet higher than the building and ten feet away. At six feet across at the top, there was room for a double row of archers to fend off attacks. Of course, the Qart Hadasht wall was designed to keep an army out, not to prevent one from escaping.

"Can we do it, Colonel?" a Legionaries asked when he reached the top of the ladder.

"That depends on how much rope we have," Alerio replied. "You and the men secure this property. I'm going to the warehouse to see if Albin has any there. Then I'm going to the courtyard to check on the welcoming committees."

"Yes, sir," the infantryman acknowledged. "The building will be yours, Colonel Sisera, when you return."

"It best be ours, or we'll be in a bind," Alerio told him while placing a foot on the ladder. "Since this roof is the only way out of the city."

In truth, the Battle Commander's observation wasn't totally accurate.

***

Legionary Chigi snapped the reins to keep the mules moving towards the checkpoint. He squinted at the defensive wall then, glancing back, he examined his wagon. Once sure his load remained level, he looked to the wagon following behind.

For months, the two men chosen from the work crew as teamsters, hauled blocks of clay to the city. At first, the men cutting the material from the quarry were envious. Then after several occasions where the drivers returned dirty, bruised, and bandaged, the diggers changed their opinion.

Isolated and without backup, the pair of infantrymen turned teamsters ran a gauntlet on every trip. Iberian soldiers who hated the Legion, might stop the wagons, pull the drivers down, and beat on them. One thing saved them, if they could call it that, their mounted guard broke up the punching and kicking before the teamsters were unable to continue.

Another problem had to do with the stacks of clay blocks. When the blocks shifted, the teamsters were forced to unload and reload the entire shipment to balance the loads. Often, the imbalance was caused by the Iberians. It left the bleeding and injured Legionaries alone to put the clay blocks back on the wagons. Thus, it wasn't simple curiosity that caused Chigi to look both ways.

"You're in luck, Latian," the mounted guard observed. His words oozed sarcasm. "Your Iberian friends have been replaced by light infantry. Maybe the soldiers will be at the third barricade."

"Missing the show, are you?" Chigi muttered so the horsemen couldn't hear. Then louder, he questioned. "Would Qart Hadasht use warriors on the inner wall?"

The first wall in the city's defense was a ditch with an earthen embankment. It gave defenders the high ground to fend off raiders. Chigi had never seen guards at the ramp running over the ditch. When the wagon rolled up and onto the higher level, he could see what the mounted guard saw.

"Those are Empire irregulars," Chigi noted. "What happened to the Iberians?"

At the second wall, the ditch was deeper, and the wall was composed of a rock structure supporting higher ground behind it. From the heights, soldiers could hold back tribes of invaders. Irregulars stood at a raised barrier designed to drop and seal the wall after removing the ramp.

"If you miss the soldiers," the cavalryman teased, "I could ask a few of the light infantrymen to thump on you."

"No, thank you," Chigi declined.

The clay caravan rolled up the ramp and through the gate. On the next level, the Legion driver noted the third wall. Constructed of a mountain of earth and fronted by slabs of stone, the city's primary defense soared forty feet from the ditch. Chigi peered off to his right towards the waters of the Picnic Bay.

For all the sanctuary provided by the triple walls along the western side of the capital, near the bay the defenses differed. Figuring the water would limit any attack, the Empire allowed the three to meld into a single wall of stone. And Legionary Chigi wasn't looking at the harbor's defenses. He focused on where the three western walls joined. If there was a weakness in Qart Hadasht's defenses, it lay in the area where the walls merged at the edge of the bay.

On the ramp of the first wall, the mules fought to climb to the level of Qart Hadasht. Once there, they wheeled through the thirty feet of wall before stopping at the gates.

"What are you hauling?" an irregular NCO asked.

"Clay for a building site," Chigi replied. Then he jerked a thumb over his shoulder and added. "So is the wagon behind me."

"Move along," the guard instructed.

Before the wagon started forward, an officer of light infantry addressed the mounted guard.

"The Noricums and Iberians have been dismissed and we're still getting around to scheduling new assignments. Watch your drivers and keep them under control. If they make trouble, you should kill them and save us the bother."

"I'll do just that, sir," the cavalryman responded. "But I've ridden herd over these two for months. I don't expect any trouble from them."

"You've been warned," the Empire Lieutenant stated. "Move them along."

Chigi's eyes narrowed, and he hunched his shoulders. Almost as if he planned to leap from the wagon and run off, the Legionary thought of escape. Without the Noricum's threat to kill everyone if anyone escaped, maybe some of the five hundred could make it to Kelibia and catch a ship home to the Republic. With that in mind, he relaxed his shoulders, snapped the reigns, and guided the mules into the city.

***

Chigi counted five light infantrymen as he urged the mules up the street. Three stood at the gate waiting for the wagons while two more guarded side entrances. His idea of escaping, in the absence of Noricum soldiers, died in his heart. It seemed the Empire had not forgotten to assign light infantrymen to the compound.

"You go ahead, I want to be sure your comrade doesn't run," the mounted guard ordered. Then he added with a laugh. "I don't think you can get away between here and them."

He pointed at the two men opening the gate and the stern-faced NCO who was supervising. Chigi's heart sank, and in his frustration, he viciously snapped the reins. The cavalryman laughed at the Legionary's outburst.

Chigi brought the wagon of clay blocks into the courtyard and walked the mules around until the tailgate came to a stop at the Master of Clay. As always, Remus stood waiting to inspect the quality of the white clay. By the time Chigi settled the mules, the second wagon rolled into the courtyard.

In the open gateway, the mounted guard stopped and asked.

"Will you watch them?" he inquired. "I need a drink."

"What did you say?" the NCO questioned. While marching to the cavalryman, he tapped the side of his helmet. "You'll have to speak up. I caught an Etruscan ax on that side a few years ago. Ever since then, I can't hear out of that ear."

"You caught a what?" the cavalryman demanded.

"I said," the NCO answered. He drew a dagger, reached up, and stabbed the horsemen in the ribs. As the mounted guard curled around the hand and hilt, the acting Optio pulled him off the horse and slammed him to the ground. "I said, "I can't hear out of my left ear."

Two Latians dressed in the uniforms of irregulars rushed up and grabbed the guard's heels.

"Just a moment," the NCO ordered. He reached down and pushed the blade deeper into the wound. Then he twisted the dagger before jerking it from the guard's ribs. "Now you can take him."

While the fatally injured cavalryman was pulled away, two other men raced up and closed the gate. Chigi sat with his mouth open.

"Close your trap, Legionary," Remus directed, "and help us unload the clay."

"Why the rush?" Chigi inquired.

"Because we need these two loaded before any of the other material wagons arrive," the Master of Clay told him.

"Loaded with what?" Chigi questioned. "I usually roll back empty."

"Not this time," Remus assure him. "For your last trip, you'll have a bottom layer of helmets, armor, and gladii. Then a layer of scuta covered with a goatskin tarp. And to hide the war gear, a healthy layer of broken tiles."

"That's only quartermaster stuff," Chigi protested. "What about the men?"

"We're working on that," Alerio Sisera informed the Legionary. "For now, get the clay off and the equipment loaded. And before you ask. Yes, we are going to Kelibia."

"And from there to home?"

"That is the plan."

Act 7

Chapter 19 – Disguised and Undignified

Late in the afternoon, eleven supply wagons rolled from the compound. Each piled high with broken tiles and accompanied by groups of captives. They were dirty and shuffled as if they didn't have the energy to walk. And every wagon had a light infantryman to help the cavalryman guard the Latian prisoners.

The caravan weaved through the streets of Qart Hadasht then left the urban district. As the first group of walking captures approached the gate in the defensive wall, one of the five mounted guards turned on his saddle.

"We've a long way to go," he instructed the guards walking with the wagons. "If any dither on the trail, you have my permission to whip him into motion."

"Yes, Sergeant," an irregular responded.

Just as the convoy reached the gate, a captive fell to his knees. The soldiers on sentry duty laughed as they had just heard the NCO tell the guards not to let any of the prisoners fall behind. But the wagons and men were halted for inspection, so the beating was entertainment.

"Get up, you filthy Latian," the infantryman ordered. Which, to the soldiers, was doubly hilarious as the guard was a Latian mercenary. The guard whacked a length of leather across the captive's back. "I said get up. Or I'll beat you and leave you here bleeding on the ground."

While the drama played out at the front, an Empire Sergeant marched to the first wagon.

"What are you hauling?" he demanded.

"They're cleaning the building side," Chigi responded. He indicated the men to the front and the men and wagons behind. "The work on the building is almost completed. We're disposing of broke tiles."

"What about the prisoners?" the NCO inquired.

From the front of the convoy, the walking guard yelled louder as he lashed the helpless prisoner.

"I said get up. Or I will leave you here broken and bleeding."

Worried his men would have to care for an injured Latian, the Sergeant of the Guard left Chigi and marched to the front. He arrived to see three more prisoners drop to their knees. An equal number of guards rushed forward ready to begin beating them.

The NCO looked from the lifted arms and leather whips of the guards to the pitiful men collapsed on the ground. He visualized an afternoon of watching broken men moan and die. Instead of dealing with dead bodies, he decided to get rid of the caravan.

"Hold those whips. You'll not leave your throwaways at my gate," he stated. "Move this mess along."

"Yes. Sergeant," the mounted guard acknowledged. He waved the convoy forward and directed. "Some of you, help those men to their feet."

Slowly, because they seemed to have as little energy as the man with the lash wounds, the Latians helped each other to their feet.

"Move along," the Sergeant of the Guard insisted with a snap of his hand.

The wagons and groups of weak men struggling to walk moved through the gate.

"Sergeant. I thought that guard was going to kill the man," one of the sentries said. "He was bleeding after the first lash. I wouldn't beat an animal like that."

"When you spend too much time guarding prisoners," the NCO lectured, "you lose some of your humanity. And then you begin to see your charges as less than human."

The sentries watched as the caravan left the city. They didn't pity the prisoners. Those were enemies of the Empire. But they did feel for the guards and their loss of compassion.

***

The eleven wagons and seventy-five men moved through the second gateway without incident. Farther down the road, they left the third defensive wall behind, and the weary men straightened and began marching. After looking around to be sure the area was free of Empire troops, Chigi pulled his wagon to the side of the road. Behind him, the caravan stopped.

"How are you feeling, Naevus?" Didacus asked. He dismounted and put an arm around the man with the lash marks on his back.

"Once on a dig, I was buried under five feet of rock," the Foundation Mole reported. "How do I feel? Undignified is one word."

"I shouldn't have hit you that hard," a Legionary dressed as a guard apologized.

"You just did what needed to be done," Naevus assured him. "You had the gate sentries so worried that they didn't check any of the wagons."

"Sure, but look what I did to you," the Legionary noted.

"Tell you what," Naevus moaned as Didacus poured water on the cuts and dabbed away blood, "when we get to Rome, you can buy me an amphora of vino."

"And a beef dinner," the guard promised.

"Whoa, there money bags. You can spend your coins later," Naevus teased. He indicated the walls and the city they had just left. "First, we have to get the rest of our people out of Qart Hadasht."

***

The sun cast long shadows over the courtyard and the Legionaries remaining in the city.

"We have rope," a Latian assured Alerio while wrapping hemp line around his shoulder. "Our problem, sir, is the length of our ladders."

Alerio peered across the courtyard at his carpenters. Groups of them huddled around stations pegging and tying rungs to rails. One man drew questions and gave answers as he dashed between areas.

"Centurion Tullius. How are we doing with the ladders?" Alerio called over to the Master Carpenter.

"Calling me Centurion is like building a temple to Virbius in a desert," Tullius said. "It just doesn't fit, sir."

"Putting the God of Forest aside, I need officers to command the Centuries," Alerio scolded. "You are one. Act like it. Now, report."

"We can overlap and lash together two ladders," Tullius clarified. He ran a hand down a rail and stopped a few feet from the end. "We lose some length on each, but we'll have a stable ladder of twenty-two feet. When we tied three ladders together, the center sagged and broke."

"How does that help us with a forty-foot wall?" Alerio asked.

"We're going to hang the top ladders and match them to ones on the ground," Tullius boasted. "That'll give us forty-four feet of rungs for climbing down."

"A solution worthy of a Senior Tribune," Alerio remarked.

"Please sir, no more promotions," Tullius requested. Around him, helpers called the Master Carpenter's name, requesting his opinion. "I have as much as I can handle as a combat officer."

From his experience, Alerio understood the man's problems. As a Colonel his job centered around executing the plan, leaving the chore of clubbing the pieces together to his officers.

The Master of Clay walked up to Alerio and saluted.

"It's time we showed our colors, Battle Commander," Remus insisted. "Our five men on the gate won't stand a chance if they get challenged. We need to be ready."

Alerio glanced at the gateway. They would move at sunset and the long shadows were already blending into areas of solid darkness. The Master of Clay was right. To be discovered and ensnarled in a battle at this point, would be disastrous for the escape plan.

"How many Legionaries can we equip, Centurion?" Alerio asked.

"We have war gear here for ten," Remus answered. "Centurion Albin says we can equip fifty more at the warehouse. That leaves us two hundred and forty men in tunics. Sir."

The honorific came late as the Master of Clay still couldn't get his mind around the fact that the draftsman was Battle Commander Sisera.

"Tunics are fine for a banquet," Alerio commented. "Not good for a battle. Pick your ten and gear them up."

***

There were two ways for the Legionaries to travel through the city and not get stopped. One involved sneaking groups from block to block while avoiding patrols all the way to the warehouse. And after a pause to be sure the area was open, shuffle the men down the street to the building next to the wall.

Or, they could be moved all at once, daring a patrol to question the movement.

"Move it, move it," an irregular yelled at the lines of prisoners. "And don't think about running off. If you try, I'll personally chase you down and gut you."

Four lines of sixty Legionaries dressed in tunics lumbered through the streets of Qart Hadasht. Pacing alongside the prisoners were a combination of light and heavy infantrymen providing security.

Three blocks from the courtyard, a five-man patrol came from a side street.

"What's going on here?" the patrol leader inquired.

"Good. You're finally here," Remus greeted them. "Fall in."

"What are you talking about?" the Empire NCO asked.

"Only fifteen of us were sent to move the Latian's to the docks," the Master of Clay answered. "The Lieutenant said the others would catch up. Come on, get into position."

A universal truth across all militaries concerned getting caught up in extra duties beyond the assigned mission. Soldiers hated it. And getting stuck herding prisoners to the docks, in place of walking easy loops around the city, qualified.

"We're a foot patrol not prison guards," the NCO informed him. He studied the men plodding by and asked. "What are they carrying?"

"Ropes and ladders for work on the harbor wall," Remus replied. "Aren't you going to help?"

"They look docile enough," the NCO observed. "We already have a job."

The Empire patrol turned west and marched away. From the dark behind the patrol, Colonel Sisera and two men materialized. They slipped daggers into sheaths as they approached Remus.

"Good call inviting them to help," Alerio complimented the Master of Clay.

"Part of my life is standing around watching kilns bake clay," Remus told him. "Officers always want to question the inactivity. I've found sir, if you ask them for help, they find an excuse to leave."

The end of the files entered the east-west road. Alerio and his pair of scouts jogged back down the way they came. While the Legionaries moved eastward in the direction of the turn towards the warehouse and the building, Colonel Sisera and his killers stalked a parallel route looking for threats.

***

The street between the depository with the war gear and the building at the wall, lay in silence and darkness. Then the foot falls of three hundred men broke the peace. The first fifty entered the warehouse and the remainder of the prisoners continued to the building at the end of the street.

"Centurion Remus, report," Alerio requested.

"We'll soon have sixty-five men under arms, sir," the Master of Clay stated. "If anyone attempts to interfere, they'll be dead before they can sound the alarm."

"I hope to be away before the Empire knows we're gone. Search parties out looking for missing patrols might clash with that idea," Alerio said. "But you do what's necessary to hold the street. I'm going to the roof."

"Yes, sir," Remus acknowledged.

***

Ladders and long boards rested against the side of the three-story building. The collection resembled a giant trellis. At each object, a Legionary waited while Tullius paced back and forth in front of the ladders and boards.

"Why aren't they on the roof?" Alerio asked.

"We're waiting for the ropes to pull them to them up," the Master Carpenter answered. "I don't know what's delaying my line handlers."

Alerio marched to the building and realized the problem. He had to push aside the men queued in the doorway. Inside, the ground floor was packed, and the stairs jammed full.

"Clear the steps," he ordered. "Move up or move down. I don't care which way, just move."

"Who says?" a Legionary scoffed.

"Colonel Sisera," Alerio responded. "I don't have the organization to enforce discipline. Or the time to explain everything we're doing to get us out of Qart Hadasht. Let me say this. If I must sacrifice a few of you to get the rest of us out, I won't lose sleep over the deaths of a few fools."

"It's the Battle Commander from Legion North," someone announced. "Clear the steps."

"And keep them open for the carpenters," Alerio directed.

He climbed the risers to the second floor and the crowd parted. On the third floor, he repeated the speech and cleared the steep ladder. At the roof, he located men with the ropes.

"What's the hold up?"

"Sir, we need space to loop the ropes and tie them together," one of the men said. "And we've lost the men with the weighted sacks and the hooks."

Alerio grabbed five men from those amassed on the roof deck.

"One of you go through the building and bring up the sacks and the hooks," he instructed. "The rest of you, open a space for the rope handlers."

While a void was being created for manipulating the hemp lines, Alerio pushed his way to the back of the roof. Between the building and the defensive wall, an impassible chasm lay before the Battle Commander.

***

Colonel Sisera stared at the obstacles to the escape for several beats. Three stories down meant injury or death for anyone falling from the building. Across the gap and on the far side of the earthen wall, according to the teamsters, the face fell forty feet to a ditch. Their one advantage was the building rested close to where the three defensive walls converged. They only had to descend one wall to reach open ground. But still, the task appeared impossible.

Seeking help, Alerio prayed to Hephaestus for guidance.

"God of Sculptures, Technology, Blacksmiths, and Artisans," he intoned. "Grant us the means and talent to overcome this obstacle."

As if the God answered boards clashed to the deck and ladders rattled as they were hauled up and dropped onto the roof.

"Make a space," Tullius ordered.

Alerio turned to see the Master Carpenter and five men standing with lengths of rope dangling from their right hands and coiled rope clutched in their left. Heavy sacks of sand hung at the ends of the lines.

"I'll go first," Tullius informed a group of men standing behind him. When the coiled rope was handed to them, they held the line as if preparing for a tug-of-war. The Master Carpenters stated. "Colonel Sisera, you'd be advised to move aside."

"May Hephaestus guide your throw," Alerio responded. He moved out of the way, giving the carpenter space before saying. "Proceed."

Tullius swung the sack forward and back. Each forward arc got higher as did the back swing. After several movements, the sack reached the top of an arch before completing a circle. Now with the bag zooming around and around, Tullius rocked and grunted from the effort. But the carpenter continued to spin the rope faster and faster. Finally with a shout, he released the line.

Freed from the constraints of the carpenter's arm and hand, the sandbag sailed away, drawing the rope into the air with it. It reached a peak high in the night sky before falling in a steep dive. While the line of men allowed the rope to slip between their fingers, Tullius and Alerio held their breaths.

On the downward slant, the sandbag vanished over the far edge of the defensive wall. No one could see it due to the height of the barrier. But they knew the throw was successful because the rope, as if tied to a running stallion, began running through the men's hands.

"Hold it," Tullius barked. Still short of breath, he stepped out of the way and directed. "Tie that one off. Next thrower, up."

A big Legionary mimicked the Master Carpenter and completed his throw. With two lines spanning the gap and held taut by the weight of the sandbags, Tullius reached for a pair of bound ladders.

"This is where slow and steady pays off, Colonel," he said while shoving the ladders out onto the ropes.

The forward rung wobbled on the ropes, threatening to topple off. But as Tullius fed more ladder onto the lines, the rails stabilized. But even as the ladder balanced, the weight caused the lines to sag. When most of the conjoined ladders rested on the ropes and the first rung hung below the lip of the wall, the Master Carpenter ceased pushing.

"Stand by the lines," he directed. "Raise your arms."

Behind him, the men holding the ropes lifted the lines over their heads.

"And this, Colonel Sisera, is where it gets dicey," Tullius said. Then he called out. "Stand by to snap the lines."

"Standing by, Centurion," the holders responded.

Tullius cringed at the officer's title, collected himself, and ordered, "Snap the lines."

The men dropped their arms creating slack in the ropes. When they jerked upward, the motion sent a wave along the lines. The oscillation traveled under the ladder, vaulting it off the ropes. Holding the last rung, Tullius shoved with all his might when the front rung lifted. The ladder hovered in the air. But the push from the carpenter sent the rails over the lip. When the front of the ladder dropped, it landed on the defensive barrier.

"Boards," Tullius instructed. Pairs of long boards were slid along the rungs until the ladder became a wobbly bridge. Then the carpenter inquired. "Where is my eagle?"

A slightly built man with pouches of stakes and a hammer crawled onto the ladder. His weight caused the bridge to sag and the far end to slide towards the edge of the wall. Shaking in fear, the Legionary appeared as undignified as a frightened lamb. But he kept his knees and hands moving despite the trembling of his limbs.

The God of Sculptures, Technology, Blacksmiths, and Artisans must have approved because the eagle reached the far side. After pounding in stakes to secure the ladder, men with lengths of coiled rope crossed to the wall. On the far side, they pounded in anchoring stakes for the ropes.

Picking a spot between teams of men hauling ladders, Alerio walked the bridge.

"Will you go down with the first wave, sir," Tullius inquired.

"No, Centurion," Alerio replied. "I'm staying here until the last of our Legionaries are out of Qart Hadasht."

"I'm beginning to understand, Colonel," Tullius commented.

"Understand what?" Alerio questioned.

"What being an officer is about," Tullius told him. "It's not about the power of a Centurion. It's about caring for the Legionaries and being sure at the end of the day, they're safe."

Alerio glanced at the stars before remarking, "We have a long way to go before the end of the day."

"And farther still before we're safe," the Master Carpenter added. "I'll see you on the beach, sir."

Alerio didn't reply. He recrossed the ladder and went to check on the men securing the streets. They, and Battle Commander Sisera, would be the last Legionaries to leave the city.

Chapter 20 – Travel Routes

Alerio hadn't realized the noise level that three hundred men made until the streets were mostly deserted. The quiet that settled over the area was a marked difference.

"Any problem from the neighbors?" Alerio questioned while hiking uphill to the Master of Clay.

"A few people came out to check on the disturbance," Remus responded. The two fell in step and continued towards the warehouse. "I offered them an opportunity to help with the defensive drills to protect their city. But they declined and slinked back into their villas."

Alerio studied several of the homes along the street. Although a little light leaked from around their shutters, every window was boarded up. As Remus described, the residents had no interest in getting involved in the Legionaries escape.

"Fold in your perimeter," Alerio instructed. "And start sending your Century to roof."

"My Century?" Remus repeated. "I never thought I'd be an Optio let along an officer."

"Why's that?" Alerio inquired. "You're a capable Legionary."

"I'd rather mold clay," Remus admitted. He tapped the shoulders of a pair of infantrymen in the center of the street and ordered. "Fall back to the escape building."

The two began the final withdrawal from the city. As if paint peeled from a vase, the Legionaries of the guard Century left their positions and drifted back to the building. Soon, only the entrance to the three-story building had security.

"You know, Remus, training men is a lot like molding clay," Alerio stated. "You shape them into your vision of a successful Legionary."

"But that's the problem, Colonel Sisera," the Master of Clay remarked. "With clay, once I put it in the kiln, the heat sets the shape. And the shape is permanent. With Legionaries, one too many cups of vino and everything falls apart."

"Two hundred years ago the Greek statesman Pericles proposed what you leave behind is not what is engraved in stone monuments, but what is woven into the lives of others."

"Sirs, we are the last ones left," an infantryman notified Remus and Alerio.

Alerio placed a hand on his arm and pushed the Legionary through the doorway. Then he reached for Remus.

"I'm the last one out," Alerio informed the Master of Clay.

"Because you want to demonstrate leadership by example?" Remus guessed.

"Yes," Alerio admitted. "It's my way of weaving duty into the lives of others."

Alerio followed Remus through the doorway, and they found the infantryman waiting inside.

"I thought you'd be up the steps by now," Alerio questioned him.

"Sir, your words touched me," the Legionary commented. "But while you're discussing high concepts, I'm a practical man."

The infantryman closed the door, shoved a beam into place, and secured the entrance. Then he went to the steps and walked to the second floor.

"I forgot about the doorway," Alerio admitted.

"That infantryman's response to your words, helped me understand Pericles' meaning," Remus stated as he mounted the steps. "But, Colonel, I still prefer molding clay to molding men."

***

Alerio followed Remus up the steps, and the two ladders to the roof. On the far side of the bridge, the Master of Clay proceeded to the far edge of the wall. Alerio stopped to talk to a man wearing a tunic and holding a coil of rope.

"Moonrise, sir," the Latian observed. "The night is half over."

"What are you waiting for?" Alerio inquired.

"I'm the chief rigger," he said. "When the last man is over, I'll drop the bridge. After he descends, I'll drop the lines. Then repel down on the last rope."

"I'm the last Legionary out of the city," Alerio informed him.

"Not exactly, sir," the Legionary noted.

Alerio clamped the man's arm and shook it to acknowledge the order of exit. Then, while the rigger reached down to dislodge the ladder bridge, the Battle Commander backed to the edge of the defensive barrier and knelt.

Picking up one of the three ropes that ran between his knees, Alerio scooted backward. Squirming off the ledge, Alerio's legs swung free, and he felt the weight of his body in the muscles of his arms and shoulders. After a few misses, one foot located the rung of the suspended ladder. Held up by the other two ropes, the ladder swayed but hung fast as he descended.

Fear of the unknown and the uncertainty that the ropes would hold the ladder gave Alerio a hint of what the men who had gone before felt. But the knowledge also gave him comfort. Three hundred men had climbed down and escaped Qart Hadasht. When the floating ladder ended, he tapped around until locating the one grounded at the base of the wall. The descent into the dark ended when a hand touched his back.

"Welcome to freedom," a man said. Along with his words, he left his arm extended for support. "Forty feet in the dark is unnerving."

"That it is," Alerio confirmed.

He didn't realize it as he climbed down the last few rungs, but the tension of traversing the wall revealed itself in wobbly knees. Alerio held the arm for a beat until he was steady on his feet.

"You'll find a guide at the top of the ditch," the man informed him. "Follow his directions and you'll catch up with the others. How many more are up there?"

"Just the rigger," Alerio reported.

"Then you better get moving," the Legionary encouraged. "Because once the rigger gets here, we'll be running you down."

Alerio climbed the defensive ditch to find a man kneeling in the dirt.

The guide pointed eastward and directed, "That way."

In the light of the rising moon, Alerio looked back. High above, the rigger released ropes and the top ladder fell. Although he wanted to wait and thank the men who facilitated the movement down the wall, Alerio understood the desire to get away from Qart Hadasht.

Alerio jogged away from the ditch. Although it appeared he was running away, in reality, Battle Commander Sisera ran towards his Legionaries and freedom.

***

Proconsul Marcus Regulus tossed and turned until he was fully awake. At that point in the night, he threw off the light blanket and swung his legs to the floor.

"Can I get you something, sir?" Tutus inquired from the door to the other room.

The aides, as they had done in Qart Hadasht, split the night standing watch over the Proconsul.

"Something bitter to wash away my guilt," Marcus mumbled into his hands. Then, so as not to inflict his self-hate on the Legionary, he answered. "No, thank you. I just need to think."

"In that case, sir, I'll leave you to your contemplations," Tutus told him.

The aide went back to the adjoining room, crossed the floor, and shook his partner awake.

"He's troubled again," he notified Vitus.

The other aide sat up.

"We don't know the mind of a Senator," Vitus said. "It might be nothing that concerns us."

"I've seen befuddled men in the Legions," Tutus informed him. "I'm going to the dock and check on the launch."

"And you want me alert, in case the Proconsul needs company," Vitus stated.

"In case the Proconsul wants to be alone, permanently," Tutus corrected.

He strapped on a gladius, tossed a red Legion cloak over his shoulder, and left the rented rooms.

***

Below the hillside town, the harbor and beach had a few lanterns burning. But most of the illumination came from moonlight reflecting off the water.

It had taken two days for the Egyptian trader to reach Malta. The next leg of the journey would take Proconsul Regulus and his aides to Sicilia. At Syracuse, they'd change vessels and go up the strait to Messina. Regulus would then commandeer space on any Navy vessel sailing for Rome.

Tutus located the trading vessel at the docks. Men moved around the deck and pier positioning carts and amphorae.

"Going somewhere?" he inquired.

"Optio, good morning. We were just organizing the deck," the ship's Captain clarified. "Why don't you go wake the Proconsul and begin packing? My son will be along directly to collect you."

"How far is it to Sicilia?" Tutus asked.

"It'll take us all day to reach Portopalo di Capo," the Egyptian answered.

The captain's twelve-year-old son strolled down the dock with a bag. As he approached, Tutus latched onto the boy's arm and pulled him close.

"You're correct," the Legion NCO said. "We do need your son's help. Come on lad."

Before the skipper could protest, Tutus escorted the young Egyptian back towards town. Tutus hadn't trusted the merchant after watching the man trade with locals along the route. Taking the boy assured that the vessel would be at the dock when the Legion NCOs and the Proconsul returned.

Tutus had no problem with an early start on the day's sailing and he knew Marcus Regulus held the same view.

What none of them knew, sailors and rowers of a Republic fleet on the coast of Sicilia felt differently about a moonlight launch.

***

Consul Servius Nobilior stood on the deck of his flagship examining the Roman fleet.

"Senior Tribune, we seem to be a little sluggish this morning," Servius observed.

"General, you've pushed the fleet hard since we left Ostia," the senior staff office responded. "It might do the men good to rest here for a day."

"I have no intention of remaining at Portopalo di Capo any longer than is necessary," Consul Nobilior told him. "We've fifteen thousand men to pull out of Punic territory. Go ask our rowers what I should do if it was them stranded between the sea and an Empire army."

"We all know the answer to that, Consul."

"Then let's get launched," Servius Nobilior instructed. "It'll be light soon and I want to be far, far north of here before noon."

"Launch the screen," the Senior Tribune instructed the signalmen.

Using lanterns, the Legionaries waved predetermined patterns. In response, five three-bankers slid into the water and rowed out to sea. Another five launched and rowed northward to scout in front of the fleet. The squadron of trireme didn't row far. They couldn't as there were still four hundred and fifty-four warships and transports still at the beach.

***

Battle Commander Sisera finished tying an armored skirt around his waist. He reached for a piece of chest armor and Didacus tapped the armor with a finger.

"Sir, we need you to guide the expedition," he pleaded. "Let someone else lead the attack."

"Craftsmen and builders are good for organizing and finding creative solutions," Alerio told the Foreman. "But in a shield wall, only a combat officer can hold a line together when things get rough."

"Does it have to be you?" Albin demanded.

"Let me see," Alerio remarked. He faked glancing around at the shadowy figures of the men near him. "There's no sign of the God Quirinus in the group. I guess, it'll be me leading the assault."

His mentions of the ancient God of War and Spears brought groans from the craftsmen.

"We could just bypass the hill fort," Tullius recommended.

"On the move, we'd be too loud," Naevus commented. "Besides, tell me carpenter, what commander leaves seventy-five cavalrymen in place to attack the rear of his march."

"Who'll guard my right flank and secure the corral?" Alerio questioned.

"That would be my Century," Remus volunteered. "Ever since your speech at the building, my infantrymen can't talk about anything else except going into battle with Colonel Sisera."

"And how do you feel about that?"

"I'm still not convinced that you wouldn't be better off with an apprentice boy in command," Remus answered. "But I've brought my infantrymen this far, I'll see it to the end. Even though I'm afraid I'll fail them."

"The first and greatest victory is to conquer yourself. To be conquered by yourself is of all things most shameful and vile," Alerio quoted. "That's what Plato said one hundred and thirty years ago. And it's true today."

"How does that apply to this situation?" Didacus asked.

"You don't need to fear the Empire horsemen," Alerio assured them. "In the morning and in the days ahead, hold yourself to a standard of courage and honor. Do that and in every battle, the enemy is already defeated."

"Even the troops on Jellaz Hill?" Naevus asked.

"They just don't know it yet," Alerio guaranteed the Foundation Mole. He glanced at the fading stars in the sky and instructed. "Optio Celso, get us moving forward."

The man who helped Alerio stalk the route of march through the city and during the first phase of the escape, left the commanders meeting. A short way from Alerio, he entered a circle of fifty-five heavy infantrymen.

"Centurion Remus' Century will cover our right flank," Celso told them. "We'll move up the high side of the hill with Colonel Sisera. Let me remind you all. Our first job is to protect the Battle Commander."

"Optio Celso. You do realize you're talking about Sisera, the Battle Commander of North Legion," one of the infantrymen pointed out. "He's not known for avoiding a fight."

"Just be sure he has scuta on either side of him during the actual assault," the NCO advise. "We're moving one hundred paces into the trees. Let's go."

***

Alerio squatted under a tree and allowed his eyes to sweep up the slope to the hill fort. If he had experienced officers and NCOs, he would order a dawn attack while the shadows were long, and the enemy slumbered. As it stood, he couldn't risk the confusion caused by weak leadership.

"Centurion Remus. I'm going to lead the attack up the spine of the hill," Alerio informed the Master of Clay. "I need you to sweep up the lower slope and stop any horsemen from breaking out."

"What about the sentries?" Remus questioned.

"Nothing to be done about them," Alerio said. Then he asked. "Optio Celso, are we ready?"

"Yes, sir," the NCO replied.

Stealth might have been a smart strategy. But Colonel Sisera lacked the scouts to sneak up the ridge. Plus, his Legionaries needed motivation. Thus, he threw out silent-and-deadly, and went full throated. Standing, he drew his gladius, and while springing from the woods, Alerio sang.

Although my feet trip and stumble

Goddess Hybris shows the way

As if a giant spoon had taken a scoop from a lake size platter of lard, the rocky ridge curved around a steep drop off. With his feet dancing along the edge, Alerio powered up the hill.

Attributes to clear the path
Insolence and violence
My blade, my wrath

One advantage to running the crest, the route brought Alerio and his squads in from the high side of the hill fort. The approach allowed the Legionaries to get close as the Empire sentries ignored that direction. But down on the lower slope, Remus' Century came out of the trees in plain sight.

I've got seventy miles of hike
Just to reach the beach
Seventy miles of fight

Alerio leaped from a battlement, sailed into the fort, and landed on a distracted sentry. Before the Colonel could stab the man, two Legionaries appeared on either side of him. One stabbed the downed man before racing ahead of Alerio.

Just to launch a ship
Eight hundred miles to sail
Just to see Ostia
Eight hundred miles of sea
Just to be free

But one dead sentry didn't stop the cries of alarm. Cavalrymen swinging swords rushed from the sleeping bunkers. The ones who stood and fought, posed no problem for the heavy infantrymen. But, a large portion of the nimble horsemen dodged around the big shields and escaped.

While lambs can frolic and play

Pious Priest dismiss her gifts
On our trail behind or ahead
With the enemy closing in
It's Hybris or death

An officer dashed from a tent and Alerio set his guard to duel with the man. Before their blades crossed, two shields slammed together in front of Alerio. When they parted, the officer lay dead from a pair of stab wounds.

I've got seventy miles of hike
Just to reach the beach
Seventy miles of fight
Just to launch a ship

While Alerio's squads fought for the hill fort, down slope, Remus' units defended the corral. Their shield wall stopped any of the Empire horsemen from gaining a mount and getting away. On the road and in the fields around the base of the hill, unarmored Legionaries sealed off Jellaz Hill. They prevented any cavalrymen on foot from breaking out.

Eight hundred miles to sail
Just to see Ostia
Eight hundred miles of sea
Just to be free

By the time the fighting ended, the Legionaries controlled the fort and to Alerio's disappointment, his blade was still clean. As Centurion Didacus had alluded to before, Colonel Sisera was needed to guide the expedition and was too important to be leading a charge into a melee.

Chapter 21 – Counter Ambush

It wasn't the men slowing down the escape. Hiking for Legionnaires went beyond training and conditioning. To qualify as a Legionary, an infantryman needed to march and run for miles and still be able to function. Therefore, it wasn't the men slowing down the escape.

"I've nothing to report," Naevus recounted. His horse pranced to the side while settling down from the run. "No one is on our trail, sir."

The Legion detachment had eighty-five men assigned to captured horses. To coordinate the cavalry units, Alerio appointed the Foundation Mole as the Centurion of Horse. Naevus protested at first saying it wasn't right for a man accustomed to crawling around in the dark of a hole to be that high above ground. But all Legionaries were taught to ride, so the digger had the physical skills. Plus, the talent it took to anticipate a weak wall of soil translated to visualizing the placement of scouts over a broad area.

"We're five hundred strong, Centurion," Alerio pointed out. He continued to walk the path beaten by the men hiking out front. "It's not as if the Empire can dispatch a few squads of irregulars to bring us back."

"Still, Colonel," Naevus observed, "you would think someone would have noticed our disappearance."

"Feeling snubbed?" Alerio teased.

"No, sir, I'm going to check out front."

"Carry on, Centurion," Alerio said, dismissing the Foundation Mole turned cavalry officer.

"Sir, you should be on horseback," Optio Celso recommended. "No one will think less of a mounted Battle Commander."

"Sergeant, putting me on a horse will short our detachment one mounted Legionary," Alerio stated. "I'd rather have that one scout out watching for the Empire's response than to have me resting in a saddle. Besides, I was an infantryman before the Republic made me an officer."

"Yes, sir," the Optio acknowledged. He glanced back at the line of eleven wagons and the teams of mules. "Colonel, we're separating from the baggage train again."

Alerio looked to his left and out over the Punic Gulf. Several merchant ships sailed across the water, but no ships-of-war were in view. In the other direction was the start of a mountain pass. Regulus' couriers had used it to alert Alerio when the Legions were trapped on the coastal road.

If he possessed a few extra Centuries or cavalry troops, Alerio would seal off the mouth of the mountain pass and allow for the detachment to spread out along the line of march. Having neither, he called a halt.

"Get word to Centurion Tullius," he directed the Legionary marching ahead of him. "Hold up short of the pass."

The infantryman called to the man ahead and the men ahead of him passed on the information. Tullius commanded the head of the detachment because that was the least likely element to come under attack. Remus and his sixty infantrymen controlled the rear, where Alerio expected trouble.

"We could move faster if we unloaded the wagons, set the mules free, and had the men carry the goods," Didacus suggested while strutting to Alerio. "The draft animals are holding us up. At this rate, it'll take us four days to reach Fort Kelibia."

The Foreman controlled the center of the detachment which included unarmed Legionaries and the wagon train. Alerio sensed that Didacus wasn't happy dealing with wagon and mule issues.

"When we get into a fight, I don't want our infantrymen to stop and drop food before engaging," Alerio said, laying out his reasoning. "Besides, it'll take us four days in either case."

"Why four days?" Didacus protested. "It's only forty miles to Kelibia."

"We can't reveal our location until we're sure the Legion still holds the fort," Alerio cautioned. "We'll need to scout Kelibia before rushing into town."

Before Didacus could say more about the plan, Naevus and two other scouts rode up.

"Colonel Sisera, there are Empire soldiers in the mountain pass," the Centurion of Horse reported. "I sent these two up to scout the approach."

"Did they see you?" Alerio questioned.

"I'm not sure, Battle Commander," one horseman replied. "They don't have skirmishers out front, and we left quickly. But we saw enough to think they're trying to sneak up on us."

The other scout nodded his agreement. Alerio faced the gulf and let his eyes rest on the far-off horizon.

"They didn't have time to march from Qart Hadasht," Alerio pondered. Then he added what was really bothering him. "Where did they come from?"

"Kelibia," Didacus guessed. "What are you going to do, Battle Commander?"

Alerio raised his arms. With one he pointed at the mountain pass and with the other he indicated a direction to the northeast.

"Centurion Naevus. Pick four scouts and have them ride to Kelibia," he directed. "If it's in Legion hands, the survivors can make a run for it."

"Survivors? Survivors of what?" Tullius asked while marching to Alerio and saluting. "We stopped short of the entrance as you instructed. But the scouts report the road ahead is clear. What's the hold up, sir?"

"Mules, wagons, and the Goddess Nerio," the Battle Commander replied.

"But we don't have any spoils from battle to dedicate to the warrior Goddess," Didacus proposed.

"But we do have an enemy force sent to murder us," Alerio responded. "We can't outrun them, go around, or hide. That means we fight which means survivors. Naevus get your scouts off to Kelibia then go back and bring Centurion Remus and his Century up."

"Are you suggesting we'll have battle loot to offer to the Goddess Nerio?" Tullius speculated.

"Either us or the Empire," Alerio remarked. "If you'll excuse me, I need to make a sacrifice."

Alerio marched away from the command staff. After a hundred feet, he opened the cork on a wineskin and poured a healthy dose on the ground.

"Goddess Nenia accept this to sate your thirst before blood flows and men die," Alerio prayed to his personal Goddess. "I want to ask nothing for me. My death after all these years of war is long overdue. However, I would like to see the face of my child before you carry my soul away from this body. If not, well, we'll meet before sundown."

Alerio poured another offering on the ground. Then he lifted the wineskin and his face to the sky and drank a toast to his wife and his child.

"Gabriella, forgive me," he uttered before capping the wineskin and marching back to his detachment.

***

The wagon rattled, sending sounds up into the hills on both sides. Pans and pots hanging from the side boards clanged and one wheel wobbled. But the mules paid no mind to the disturbances as they pulled the wagon into the mountain pass.

"This is a bad idea, Colonel," Celso whispered from the back of the wagon.

"Getting lonely back there?" Alerio asked. He snapped the reins, encouraging the mules to pull harder as the wagon encountered a slight incline. "You could be up here and a target for arrow practice."

"I should be driving," the Optio confirmed from under the tarp. "But the truth is, we should not be here in the first place. At least not without our scuta and a Century of heavy infantry."

"Where's the fun in that?" Alerio asked.

"You call this fun, sir?" Celso questioned.

"Quiet back there. We have company," Alerio alerted the Sergeant. Then he spoke to the four soldiers who stepped out from behind a mound. "Good day gentlemen. Pots, pans, or sundry other household goods. But wait. You're military men. I have what you need. Wine?"

Alerio reach behind him and lifted three wineskins from the wagon. Resting two on the driver's bench, he hoisted one and took a long stream into his mouth.

"Try this stuff. It's excellent," Alerio slurred. Selecting one of the wineskins from the bench, he tossed it at the Empire NCO. "That should be enough for you and your three comrades. Let's call it a toll."

After catching the full wineskin, the Sergeant inquired, "Where are you going?"

"To Cité Seltenne," Alerio said slowly as if his lips were numb. He stood, took another drink, then toppled from the wagon.

The Sergeant and his unit bent and looked down at the drunken tradesman.

"Cité Seltenne is back the way you came," the NCO informed the trader.

From his back, Alerio appeared to be confused. His eyes jerked from man to man, blinking as he tried to clear his vision.

"Back the other way? Stupid mules," he cursed while waving his arms in frustration. Then Alerio rolled over, gathered his hands under his shoulders, and prepared to push off the ground. Turning his face, he asked the NCO. "Can I interest you in a pair of old mules? Not bright, but they pull hard."

The soldiers laughed at the antics of the inebriated peddler. But movement from the wagon bed pulled their focus from Alerio. The goatskin tarp flew aside and Optio Celso came up in a crouch. Leveling their spears, the four Empire soldiers stood ready to defend themselves.

Alerio came up from under the shafts with two daggers. He slashed the Empire Sergeant with one blade. With the other, he stabbed the underarm of a spearman.

Short blades had a flaw in an uneven fight. Neither soldier was totally disabled. The two healthy spearmen swung their spear tips in Alerio's direction, and the wounded men drew their own swords.

With the shafts swinging towards Colonel Sisera, Celso leaped from the wagon. Hooking an arm around both men, he let his bodyweight press them to the ground.

From his knees, the Legion NCO asked, "Can we go now, sir?"

Alerio parried one sword while snaking his other blade around the Empire NCO's wrist. When the Sergeant cursed and hopped back to nurse the deep cut, Alerio caught the sword with his small guard and kicked the soldier in the chest.

"Yes, definitely," Alerio replied.

The two sprinted down the pass.

"You call this fun, sir?" Celso asked while they ran.

Alerio glanced at the bloody daggers and responded, "The most I've had in days."

***

Alerio and Celso slowed when they passed two pair of scuta. Beyond the Legionaries positioned to stop any pursuit, they halted. Centurion Remus stepped from behind a tree.

"Was it worth it, Battle Commander?" his tone showed it wasn't a question. There was more sarcasm, then inquiry in the statement.

"They have one hundred soldiers," Alerio reported. "Fifty on each side of the pass."

"How can you know that, Colonel?" Didacus asked.

"Infantrymen enjoy being entertained," Alerio replied. "When the drunk fell from the wagon, every one of them stood up to watch. While on my back, I counted one hundred. Give or take a few."

"They don't have enough to attack us directly," Tullus stated. "Why are they here?"

"We're back to the question, where did they come from?" Alerio ventured. "Besides that, I'd guess they're supposed to keep an eye on us and maybe do some damage, given an opportunity."

"What are we going to do about them?" Remus inquired.

"We're going to remove the threat," Alerio remarked. "If the Empire is going to feed us bite sized pieces of their reaction force, who are we to turn down the meal."

***

Later, the infantrymen scoffed their boots, talked, and grew agitated. The newly appointed Centurions stood with, but not looking at, their Battle Commander. They had for a period, but it became uncomfortable staring at him.

"We should attack now, Colonel," Remus blustered. He looked at the early afternoon sun. "Waiting only allows them time to get organized."

"Observe due measure, for right timing is in all things, the most important factor," Alerio recited. "That's from Hesiod, an ancient Greek poet."

"I'm a simple carpenter," Tullius argued. "Due measure to me means cutting the lumber to the right length."

"And to me it means we wait," Alerio responded.

A few moments later, Naevus rode in from the rear with a horse in tow. Shortly after the Centurion arrived, another scout came from the east. Both reported no enemy sightings for miles around.

"We have one hundred and fifteen heavy and forty light infantrymen," Alerio said. "If we pour them all into the attack, we will win. However, our wagons and unarmored men will only have sticks and a few cavalrymen to defend them."

"Defend them from what?" Remus asked. "There are no other Empire forces for miles around."

"Exactly," Alerio agreed. "And that, gentleman, is due measure. March your Centuries forward."

Naevus extended the reins for an extra horse. Alerio took them, mounted, and moved the animal behind the Legionaries. A pair of infantrymen marched beside Alerio.

"Who are you two?" he inquired.

"We're First Century," one replied. "Assigned by Optio Celso."

"And where is Optio Celso?"

"Sir, he is commanding Centurion Tullius' left side," the other bodyguard answered.

In front of Alerio, the Legionaries of Tullius Century formed two ranks of twenty-five. Close behind, marched fifteen infantrymen and then two lines of twenty-five from Remus Century. Following the heavy infantry, forty skirmishers shuffled forward in two rows under the direction of Albin, the tool maker. For an undersized, clubbed together detachment, Colonel Sisera was pleased with the ordered movement.

***

A mile into the pass, rows of Empire mercenaries blocked the way. Unlike the lines of Legion infantrymen, the Hoplites were grouped together.

"Think they'll go phalanx, sir?" Albin asked.

"I don't know the men, but I recognize their Captain as a Macedonian," Alerio replied. "Those Tail-Leaders are harnessed to the phalanx. He will keep them bunched together and moving straight forward. Until he finds the weakness in our formation. Then he'll shift the phalanx to take advantage of it."

Albin scanned the double, straight rows of Legionaries.

"Sir, I don't see any weakness in our ranks," the tool maker noted.

"You're right," Alerio acknowledged. "I'll have to do something about that."

Putting heels to the beast's flanks, Alerio rode through the ranks and approached Sergeant Celso. Bending down, he addressed the NCO.

"Optio, I need your side to give ground after the initial contact," Alerio instructed. "I don't mean bowed either, I want a collapse of the left side."

"Sir, we can hold the barbarians while breaking up their formation," Celso guaranteed the Battle Commander.

"I'm sure you can," Alerio confirmed. "But we'll take too many casualties against a phalanx. I need you to draw them out of the formation, and yes, suffer the humiliation. Afterward, and you'll know when, you'll need to collect your section of the maniple. And then, Optio, you can pay them back for their rudeness."

"As you wish, sir," Celso commented without enthusiasm.

At the center of the line, Alerio's instructions to Centurion Tullius were the exact opposite.

"Stop the phalanx and hold them stationary," Alerio ordered the carpenter. "No matter the cost, hold them."

After orchestrating the first few moves of the battle, Alerio rode to the rear of the detachment.

He reined in next to Albin and remarked, "That's settled."

"What's settled, Colonel?" Albin asked.

"What direction their formation will go," Alerio said, "when the Macedonian spots our weakness."

Act 8

Chapter 22 – Thracian Barricade

The Mercenaries stepped inward and linked shields. Using small steps to maintain order, the phalanx shuffled forward. Densely compacted, the shields covered a formation composed of ten hoplites across in columns ten deep.

"Brace, brace," Tullius ordered.

Echoing his instructions, a Corporal on the right and Celso on the left notified the Legion lines.

"Brace," the Sergeant repeated before adding. "Standby for a change of orders."

"Standing by, Optio," the twenty Legionaries in his double rank responded.

With a burst of blade strikes by the Legionaries, most of the long spears of the phalanx were shoved up or down. In the flurry, three Legionaries on the front line caught spearheads. Men from the second rank pulled them from harm's way and others stepped up to fill the gaps. But the forward spears were not the primary weapon of a phalanx.

The Legionaries allowed three steps of give when the two sides smashed together. Then the Legion lines hardened as muscle and bone shoved back.

The phalanx stopped momentarily. Soil under the grass turned to dirt and after more grinding, the earth turned to dust. Finally, as designed, the Greek formation began pushing the Legionaries backwards.

"Step back," Celso shouted. "Shields up, step back. Step back."

And the Legion line curled and crested over as if it was a plowed row on a farm. Centurion Tullius and the Corporal held the center and the right, but the left side crumbled.

Dealing with an uneven front, a third of the phalanx faced no resistance. In theory the situation should have been optimal. Except, only part of the mercenary force had resistance to their drive forward. The rest slackened without adversity and had to stood still in order maintain the phalanx formation.

The Macedonian Tail-Leader noticed the tension slip from his right side. As if a plague running rampant through a village, more and more of his best hoplites relaxed. Placed on the right side to face an enemies weaker left, the quality soldiers should be crashing through the enemy's lines, guiding the rest of the ten-hoplite front. But they weren't.

Behind the Legion line, Naevus placed his fists on the saddle and hoisted himself on his arms.

"We're lost, Colonel," the Foundation Mole declared.

Remus jogged to Alerio.

"Sir, I can stop the hemorrhaging," he submitted. "Let me take my Century forward."

"Hold your Legionaries where they are, Centurion," Alerio instructed. He didn't look down at the Master of Clay. Instead, his eyes were fixed on the Macedonian Tail-Leader. From the side of his mouth, he called to the tool maker. "Albin, come closer."

The commander of Alerio's light infantry walked to the Battle Commander.

"Colonel Sisera, we can cover the retreat," Albin assured him.

"Glad to hear it," Alerio acknowledged. "But I'm afraid your skirmishers won't be in a position to do that task."

"We won't?" Albin questioned. He looked at the broken assault line and the struggle going on at the center and on the right. Then he asked. "Where will we be, Battle Commander?"

***

The Macedonian shifted his eyes as rapidly as he changed his mind. His best languished on the right flank while his weaker hoplites fought to gain ground. In a battle of attrition, his phalanx would prove superior given a few days of fighting. But his Thracians would suffer casualties. Or, he could break the formation and set battle lines. By dark, the Legion commander would withdraw. Between the big shields on both sides, neither opponent would suffer many deaths.

After weighting his choices, he decided to take advantage of the weakness.

"Phalanx, prepare for a right diagonal march," the Tail-Leader ordered.

File-Leaders repeated his command and the instructions filtered from the back to the men fighting at the front.

The diagonal move would get his right side back into the fight. Then they would punch through the disorganized sector of the Republic line. After chewing up the right side, he'd turn the phalanx and claw apart the main body of Legionaries.

***

"Centurion Albin, take your light infantrymen through the gap," Alerio told the tool maker. "Once through, secure their escape route."

"Sir, I don't see any gaps," Albin protested.

"Get them moving to our right side," Alerio instructed. "The gap will be there momentarily."

He had watched the Macedonian's eyes shift under the Greek helmet. When they locked right, Alerio made the call.

"Centurion Remus. When the enemy formation shifts left," Alerio said, "I need your Century to fill the gap and collapse the side of the phalanx."

Like Albin, Remus studied the fighting and couldn't identify an opening. But he heard Alerio's promise of a gap and acknowledged.

"Yes, sir," the Master of Clay stated.

***

"Let's teach those Republic dogs to fear Thracian bears," the Macedonian Tail-Leader instructed. "Execute the diagonal march."

As if a great beast quaking before a fight, the shields of the phalanx rippled to the right. And the corner facing the Legion's left side stepped forward.

Lost to the men in the cocoon of Thracian shields, Optio Celso's voice across the combat line bellowed, "About time. Legionaries, form your assault line and brace."

The Macedonian expected his formation to surge forward as a single entity. When his two right files shuffled ahead of the other columns, not once but twice, he knew something was wrong. It was. Four Hoplites in the right corner had fallen to Optio Celso and his Legionaries.

But the dust blocked the Tail-Leader's vision. He reconsidered shifting to a combat line to cover a wider front. Before he could issue the order, the right flank of the formation caved in followed closely by the center of the phalanx collapsing.

One disadvantage of a phalanx concerned retreating. Because the front fought way ahead of the commander, the order to withdraw took long heartbeats to reach the combatants. And for an emergency evacuation, those moments proved deadly.

"Retreat," the Macedonian ordered.

Even while passing on the instructions, his File-Leaders backed away from their columns. And the men engaged in the fighting at the front didn't hear until the men behind them yelled the order to withdraw before they ran. Between the fighting in the center of the phalanx and the abandonment at the front, a dozen Thracian Hoplites died on Legion blades. Eventually, the ones trapped near the front backed into a cluster while the rest of the phalanx ran.

***

"Naevus take what riders you have and go support Centurion Albin," Alerio instructed.

The Centurion of Horse took six riders and galloped to the other side of the enemy formation. Remus noted the fighting and direction of the Legion horsemen. He sent two squads of heavy infantrymen to support the skirmishers and the cavalry.

The battle ended when the Macedonian took off his helmet and waved it in Alerio's direction.

"Centurion Tullius, kindly go pull Optio Celso and his Legionaries off the poor Hoplites," Alerio told the carpenter as he nudged his horse forward. "I believe, they've been punished enough."

Alerio trotted into the middle of the battle zone. Legionaries stopped in mid slash or stab. Taking the hint from their adversaries, the Hoplites also ceased fighting.

"I am Battle Commanders Sisera. Lay down your arms and live," Alerio shouted. "Or not. We don't care which."

A roar of 'Rah' came from the Legionaries, letting the Empire mercenaries know the infantrymen agreed with their Colonel.

The Macedonian lifted his xiphos over his head, then with a bow, he placed it on the ground.

"You have won, Battle Commander Sisera," the Tail-Leader announced. "What are your orders?"

"Where did you come from?" Alerio questioned.

"I am Macedonian, and these fighting men are Thracians," the phalanx officer responded. "The Thracians are allies of Macedonia going back to King Alexander's time."

"Thank you for the history lesson, Hektor would have enjoyed it," Alerio stated. "But what I want to know is, how did you come to be in this mountain pass?"

"We left Kelibia soon after the messenger from Qart Hadasht brought the news about your escape," he replied. "We were delayed because I had to reorganize the siege lines. But we forced marched for a day and got here quickly."

Alerio peered in the direction of Tullius, then Remus, over at Naevus, Albin, and lastly, to where Optio Celso stood holding a blade covered in the blood of his enemies. A smile crossed the Battle Commander's face. They would all make it to Fort Kelibia. And once the Republic Navy came, they would escape Punic Territory and return home.

"Orders?" the Macedonian officer asked.

"Strip naked, leave your armor and weapons on the ground," Alerio instructed. "Then pick up your wounded and run northward. Don't stop or come back this way. For this, I grant you and your Thracians life."

***

Two days later, cheers rose from the siege line which conflicted with jeers floating down the hill from Fort Kelibia. Both came in response to the approaching caravan.

"You're not very popular with the Legion, Battle Commander," Celso commented.

"The Thracians seem to approve," Alerio protested. "You have to admit, I look like a Greek God in this Macedonian armor."

"Sir, that armor is pitted from wear and smoothed with rough grains of sand," the NCO observed. "No self-respecting Greek hero would be caught dead in that armor."

"I guess the Macedonian and his phalanx weren't very successful mercenaries," Alerio guessed. He looked back at the men in Thracian armor. The fake guards shoved and thumped the Latian captives, crowding them into lines beside the seven supply wagons. Then, while waving his arm, he shouted. "Close the gaps. We want to make a good impression."

In response, the captives gathered behind the wagons and began pushing them. With less load, the mules obliged and picked up their pace. By the time they neared the barricade, the entire caravan traveled at the speed of a Legion jog.

"So, you caught them," an officer shouted from a barrier.

Behind him, six soldiers manned a log blockade, obstructing the trail leading up to the fort.

Alerio extended both arms and raised them, palms up, as if hoisting a log. The Thracian officer's smile vanished when the Latian captives stepped away from the tailgates of the wagons with gladii and shields.

"I believe Colonel, you are off his winter solstice gift list," Celso informed Alerio.

Ignoring the jest, Alerio asserted, "Everybody gets through."

Battle Commander Sisera kicked his horse, sending the animal racing ahead. The Thracian officer, who a heartbeat before had been gloating at the victory, jumped out of the way, and crashed to the ground. Even with the way clear, Alerio didn't ride around the barrier and up the hill. He hopped off the horse, slapped its rump to keep the beast moving, and drew a xiphos.

Optio Celso sprinted up and put his back to Alerio's.

"You could have waited until everyone was closer, sir," the Legion NCO remarked as he slashed a spearman and blocked a shaft.

"In two heartbeats, he would have seen I wasn't the man he was expecting," Alerio said defending his one-man assault. He ducked, stepped out, and stabbed a spearman in the ribs before saying. "It was now or wait until they flooded the barricade with reinforcements."

"It's pretty crowded as it is," Celso observed while smashing his scutum from side to side to keep the soldiers away.

Thracians raced for the barricade, adding to the soldiers facing Alerio and Celso. The two Legionnaires assigned as Alerio's bodyguards sprinted forward and waded into the melee. Blocking strikes, they battled to open a passage through to Alerio.

"We thought you'd need this, Colonel," one stated as he and his partner slammed their shields together.

Behind the tiny shield wall, Alerio took the scutum from the infantryman and strapped it to his left arm.

"One of you work with Celso," he instructed while shoving between the two. "We need to keep the pathway open for the wagons."

Six more Legionaries plus Centurion Remus reached the blockade of logs.

"Remus, form a corridor," Alerio shouted.

"Yes, sir," the Master of Clay acknowledged.

As more infantrymen, both those in Legion gear and those in Thracian armor joined the fighting, Remus directed them into two outboard facing lines. The cavalry trotted down the lane accompanied by light infantrymen running alongside the horses.

"Remove the logs," Albin instructed his skirmishers.

By the time the first wagon reached the path leading up to the fort, the trail was open.

The seven wagons rolled through, and Centurion Remus began collapsing the corridor. Soon, Alerio's Centuries changed from a force maintaining an open lane, to a combat line. Spread in a wide formation, the Legionaries backed up the trail towards Fort Kelibia.

"Have you noted something strange?" Alerio asked Albin.

"That the Legion commander hasn't sent down a Century to help us," Albin responded. Seeing the wagons slow down on the hill, the tool maker directed his light infantrymen. "If we leave it up to the mules, it'll take all day to reach the top. Get on the wagons and push."

Behind the tool maker and the Battle Commander, Centurions Tullius and Remus commanded a double line of heavy infantrymen. Their solid wall of scuta blocked the Thracians while the Legionaries retreated up the hill.

***

Alerio's cavalry, the wagons, and his light infantrymen reached the fort.

"Open the gates," Naevus shouted.

Downhill, the Legionaries held back the soldiers. But as the Foundation Mole could make out, more moved through the trees. Soon they would be in positions to get around the ends of the Legion lines. If the fighting reached the wagons, a stationary fight spelled doom for Colonel Sisera's outnumbered detachment.

"Open the gates," Naevus yelled again.

A head appeared from one of the twin platforms that bracketed the entrance.

"Do you think you could stage a play and I would open the gates for you?" a Legion NCO demanded. "Go away Thracian."

The cavalrymen wore Empire gear and the only armor on the men fighting was Thracian. All the other infantrymen had only a scutum and a gladius to identify them as Republic Legionaries.

"I'm Legionary Naevus of the Twenty-Third Century, 2nd maniple, Legion East," the Mole stated. "We've just escaped from Qart Hadasht. Now, open the gates."

"Colonel Balint said no one survived Tunis," the Optio replied.

"We were taken captive," Naevus informed him. Behind the Mole, the battle drew closer. Shortly, it would engulf the wagons and carry the fighting to the gates of the fort. "We fought our way here. Don't make us fight our way in."

"Even if I believed you, Colonel Balint said we don't have enough food for strays," the Sergeant revealed.

Naevus nudged his horse to the first wagon. Bending down, he untied the goatskin tarp and tossed it back. Dried fish peeked out from between straw packing.

"We bring food," he called to the top of the wall. "Think of us as a resupply caravan."

Alerio trotted up, stopped beside Naevus, and addressed the Sergeant.

"Open the gate, Optio," he instructed. Taking off the Greek helmet, he added. "By order of Colonel Alerio Sisera, Battle Commander of Legion North."

Shortly after he spoke, the gates swung open, and a Century of infantrymen raced through. Spreading to either side, they set a shield barrier, defending the gate. Alerio stood beside the entrance while his detachment entered Fort Kelibia. Not until the Fort's Century folded back did Alerio march in to find the Battle Commander for Legion West scowling at him.

"Look here, Sisera," Balint informed Alerio. "Fort Kelibia can only have one commander and that's me."

Alerio studied the set of the man's face trying to figure out what caused the hostility. With fifteen thousand men and their officers' dead, he expected a welcome from the only other senior officer to survive. Then it came to him, Battle Commander Balint felt guilty for living and needed to justify his existence.

"Yes, sir," Alerio acknowledged with a salute. "I just want to get home."

Chapter 23 - Getting Home

Marcus Regulus braced on the deck boards as the merchant vessel fought the current along the shoreline. Once out of the flow and into the calm waters of Messina Harbor, he relaxed.

"Another week and we'll be in Rome, sir," Vitus noted.

"We'll be home in a matter of days," Regulus corrected before explaining. "I plan to commandeer the next Republic warship to beach here."

"An excellent idea, sir," Tutus chimed in. "What's the first thing you'll do when we get there, Proconsul?"

The two aides expected Marcus to describe a glorious homecoming. Instead, he stared across the harbor at Messina Beach. Thinking it might be another bout of melancholy, they exchanged glances. One would need to talk first and try to lift Marcus Regulus out of his fog. But the words and topic had to be chosen carefully to prevent insulting the General.

"Sir, how long will we be in Messina?" Vitus inquired.

"What? Oh, until a warship arrives," Marcus replied. But he answered without taking his eyes from the sand at the end of the harbor. Indicating a mount, he asked. "Do you recognize that horse?"

Vitus and Tutus gawked at a big stallion on the beach. A youth sitting in the sand with his head hung between his knees held the reins. Both appeared to be abandoned.

"No, sir," his aides admitted. "Should we?"

"After we dock, one of you go find out the boy's name," Regulus instructed. "If it's Hektor, bring him to me. I'll be at the Sicilia commander's villa."

"If it's Medic Nicanor, we'll carry him to you," the two Friends of Hektor responded.

***

A short time later, Marcus Regulus sprawled on a patio sofa. For the first time since they were assigned to him, Vitus and Tutus noticed the tension leave the General's body.

"So, where is the boy and the stallion?" Marcus inquired.

"Hektor wouldn't leave the horse until it was brushed down and fed," Tutus responded. "I realized why when the beast attacked the stablemen. They gladly turned the stable work over to the Medic."

Marcus took a sip of vino, raised his glass, and announced, "that's Phobos, all right. To Alerio Sisera's horse."

He took another sip and allowed a smile to touch his lips at the memory of Alerio Sisera. Footfalls from beyond the patio drew his attention and a few steps later Hektor Nicanor appeared from the garden. The Greek boy marched across the granite flooring.

"General Regulus, it's good to see you alive, sir," Hektor greeted Marcus with a salute. "If I may, I have a favor to ask."

"Certainly, Medic Nicanor. What do you need?"

"I was divested of my funds and my medical kit. Without the kit, I'm unable to earn passage for myself and Phobos. Can I impose on you for the funds necessary to transport us to the Sisera Villa?" Hektor requested. "I'm positive Colonel Sisera will repay you when he gets home."

The light heartedness that surrounded Marcus faded at the request. His face fell and the hint of a smile was replaced by a tight grimace. Seeing the General pale, Hektor and the aides assumed the request exceeded civility.

"I'm sorry to disturb you, sir," Hektor begged as he walked backward.

Vitus and Tutus grabbed the boy's arms and pulled as if Hektor's departure lacked urgency.

"Hold," Marcus ordered. "I am sorry to tell you, Hektor, but Colonel Sisera died at Tunis."

Hektor Nicanor's fists shot down by his sides and he stiffened as if strapped to a board. Then tremors racked his body and his mouth quivered. Seeing the stress, Marcus stood, walked to the boy, and rested a comforting hand on his shoulder.

"I understand. Alerio Sisera was a unique Legionary, a brave officer, and a good man," Marcus commiserated. "I'm sure he and his Goddess had a nice long talk on his journey to Hades."

"No. No sir," Hektor whispered.

"No what?" Marcus requested. "He talked to Nenia the Goddess of Death often enough. You don't think they conversed on the way to Hades?"

"No, sir," Hektor responded. "I don't believe Colonel Sisera is dead, sir."

The statement challenged the General, and delusional or not, Tutus feared it would upset Regulus. He stepped forward to change the subject.

"How did you lose your money?" the NCO inquired.

"I'd rather not say, Optio," Hektor pleaded.

Marcus sat, picked up his glass, and used it to point at Hektor.

"If you want my coins," he stated, "you'll explain yourself."

"Sir, there's been enough bad blood," Hektor warned. "I don't want to add to the carnage."

"I don't see how a few drops from you will make a difference," Marcus said. "Tell me how you came to be stranded on the beach at Messina."

***

"Centurion Palle took the First Century to the Medjerda River. He made sure I crossed over with them," Hektor related. "But, the farther from Colonel Sisera we got, the more unmanageable Phobos became. The stallion got so bad the Centurion sent me running ahead trying to exhaust the mount."

"I don't know why but Sisera loved that horse," Marcus stated.

Hektor dropped his eyes as if in prayer before lifting them.

"On the far side of the river, the Centurion set up set up a defensive position with his infantrymen and Cavalry from Legion North. He sent me off with a few wagons," the boy described. "We had gone several miles when cavalrymen came from the direction of Tunis. I didn't learn until I reached Fort Kelibia that the riders were your mounted messengers and cavalrymen from Legion West."

"At least some of the noblemen got out," Marcus growled. "Go on."

"Sir, I'd rather not," Hektor requested. "It's better forgotten."

"Nonsense. You've created an intriguing situation. You can't stop now. Continue."

Hektor squared his shoulders as if delivering the news that a farmer's prized oxen had been stolen.

"Centurion Palle arrived at the hill fort with Colonel Balint and two thousand survivors," Hektor told the Proconsul. "Unfortunately, there were only three transports anchored offshore and a three-banker warship on the beach. The cavalrymen claimed the merchantmen for themselves and their horses."

"Didn't Balint use the boats for his troops?" Marcus asked.

"He wanted to. But one of the Patricians threatened to ruin Colonel Balint's businesses and his social standing when he returned to Rome. The Battle Commander relinquished the boats and allowed the cavalrymen to load their horses," Hektor responded. "General Regulus, there weren't enough ships to carry all the Legionaries from the Punic coast."

Marcus fell silent and his hands shook. Seeing the stress on the Proconsul from the aftermath of the disaster at Tunis, Vitus stepped forward.

"How did you get away?" the Sergeant asked Hektor.

"Centurion Palle argued with Tribune Colonna about putting Phobos on a boat," Hektor said then he covered his mouth with a hand. "Sir, I didn't mean to name him."

"You mean it was Ostentus Colonna who threatened Balint with social ruin?" Marcus demanded.

"Yes, sir. Centurion Palle said he would march his Century to the beach and remove all the horses and cavalrymen if Phobos and I weren't granted passage," Hektor replied. "We loaded and rowed away from shore. As we rowed into deep water, ten Empire ships-of-war came around

Cape Bon. We sailed clear because the ships-of-war seemed more interested in patrolling the coastline than in chasing us."

"But how did you get to Messina?" Marcus questioned. "And where is Tribune Colonna and the other horsemen?"

"The transports were Greek, and their Captains wanted to go home," Hektor told him. "They dropped us at Messina before rowing back down the strait. After they left, Tribune Colonna said we needed to pool our coins to secure transportation for the rest of the trip to Rome. He took all my coins and my medical bag, explaining that he could barter with the medical supplies. Then he sent me and Phobos into Messina to locate a corral for the cavalry horses."

"Let me guess," Marcus said while rubbing his forehead, "when you got back to the docks, the cavalrymen were gone."

"Yes sir, along with my coins and my medical bag," Hektor confirmed. "They rowed out without me."

"Alerio didn't like Colonna very much," Marcus Regulus stated.

"Still doesn't," Hektor mumbled.

"What did you say?"

"I said, General Regulus, Colonel Sisera still doesn't like or respect Tribune Colonna," Hektor blurted out. Then he lowered his eyes for a beat before lifting them. "Alerio Carvilius Sisera said he would return for the things he loves. And I believe him. He's not dead sir."

Marcus Regulus pulled the coin pouch he received from the Messina commander and handed it to the poor, delusional boy. It was more than enough to buy transportation home for Hektor and the stallion.

"It's the least I can do for Alerio's valet and his favorite horse," Marcus announced. "Optio Tutus take Hektor to the cook and get him fed."

"Follow me Medic Nicanor," Tutus invited.

"How is your wound?" Hektor inquired.

The two walked from the patio and soon vanished around the corner of the Villa.

"Some people can't accept reality," Marcus remarked.

"Yes, General," Vitus agreed.

He wanted to add, 'and some people embrace reality to closely.' But he kept his opinion to himself and refilled Marcus' cup.

***

Several days later, a five-banker cut a half circle in the water before backstroking onto the beach at Ostia. Vitus and Tutus tossed Regulus' bags off the warship and climbed down.

"Thank you for getting me home, Centurion," Marcus stated to the ship's senior officer. "I hope I didn't bring too much shame to your crew."

"Shame, Proconsul? No sir, it was an honor to have the hero of Tunis on board," the Centurion replied.

Marcus Regulus climbed down to the sand and marched for the naval headquarters. When he arrived, a Senior Tribune met him outside the building.

"General Regulus. We can arrange immediate transportation," the senior staff officer informed him. "Or if you prefer, we have a bath and a bed for you. After a night's rest, you can leave fresh in the morning."

"I've been gone a long time," Marcus said. His voice caught in his throat as he choked up from emotion. "I think

I'll leave for home right away. Marcia would be angry if she knew I lingered in Ostia."

"I'll have horses brought around and a wagon," the Tribune listed. "The honor guard will be along by the time your aides have the wagon loaded."

The Tribune in command of the ten-man cavalry escort placed the General and his Optios in the middle of the formation. He assigned two riders to the wagon and directed them to stay with the wagon even as the horsemen rode ahead.

By twilight, the riders trotted into the city of Rome. By full dark, on the steps of his villa, Marcus Regulus held Marcia Regulus in his arms. As the husband and wife hugged, they both wept tears of joy at the homecoming.

***

Eight days after returning to Rome, Marcus Regulus rode to another villa for another uncomfortable visit.

The knock on the front door had authority but wasn't insistent. A house servant peered out. After seeing the caller, he ran to fetch Senator Spurius Maximus' secretary.

"I didn't know if I should open the door," the servant told Belen.

"You can't listen to household rumors," Belen instructed. "But I'm glad you came to me. Please have the Senator meet us in his study and arrange for refreshments for his guest."

After issuing the orders, the secretary briskly walked to the front door and flung it open.

"General Regulus, please come in," Belen announced. "Senator Maximus has been expecting you."

"Belen, I feared I would be greeted by spear tips," Marcus admitted while sliding off the saddle. "At some of the villas, weapons would have been welcomed over the wailing."

"Not at Villa Maximus," Belen assured him. "Your aides can go to the cook shed for snacks. Master Sisera always enjoyed that..."

For a heartbeat, darkness flashed across the secretary's face. But it passed when he got control of his emotions. Belen bowed then led Marcus down a hallway to the office of Alerio's adopted father.

"Marcus Regulus, welcome home," Spurius Maximus greeted the Proconsul. The two men shook and Spurius waved his guest into a chair. "You've had a trying year and a half."

"I want to say it's good to be home," Marcus reflected. "But visiting the villas' of my dead officers has taken all the joy of it."

"When I returned from the Samnites conflict, I only had a handful of visits to make," Spurius recalled. "Nothing on the scale that you face. Refreshments?"

A servant walked in with a pitcher of vino and two mugs. Belen stood in the doorway watching to be sure the beverages were delivered without incident. Once Marcus and Spurius held full mugs, the servant left. The secretary remained at his post.

"Alerio was my best Battle Commander. He took Tunis with one Legion," Marcus reported. "I often wonder if I had kept him in the center instead of holding Legion North in reserve, would I have murdered fifteen thousand Legionaries."

"You can't carry the guilt," Spurius assured him. "In war, Generals set the best plan they can. But no matter how excellent the strategy, men die. You can't blame yourself. What you should feel bad about is not appearing before the Senate. You've been home a week."

"I have demands from Qart Hadasht," Marcus informed Spurius. "But I'm not ready to present them to the Senate. It's why I held off on seeing you."

"Are they that terrible?"

"No, Senator Maximus. The items are fair," Marcus confessed. "And the terms of my release are to convince the Senate to agree to them."

"If they're not too harsh and your peace of mind rests with the demands," Spurius coached, "come before the Senate and propose them. I will do everything in my power to pass the resolution."

"There is a problem," Marcus stated. "I don't know how I feel about the Empire's demands."

***

Across the Capital, in a neighborhood of newer villas, a servant peered through the main gate.

"Go away," he ordered. "Take the stolen horse and leave. The Lady DeMarco is not interested. The villa is in mourning."

Tall iron bars set in a heavy wooden frame gave visibility to the world beyond the walls of the villa. Outside the compound, a Greek boy holding the reins of a horse peered back at the servant.

"Please, just tell her that Hektor Nicanor is here with Phobos," Hektor begged. "I don't have the means to take care of the stallion until Master Sisera returns."

"Master Sisera is dead you scoundrel," the servant scolded. "Take your confidence game elsewhere before I have the household guards thrash you."

"Then bring them out, if they dare," Hektor challenged. He hoped the household guards would recognize him even if the new servant didn't. "If they can in fact beat me, I'll give them this horse."

On the far side of the courtyard, the door to the villa opened, and a woman glanced at the gate. Her balanced yet strong features blended into a beautiful face, befitting a Goddess. And although her visage projected loveliness, her eyes were red rimmed, and her cheeks stained with tears.

"What's going on out there?" Gabriella DeMarco Sisera demanded.

"Nothing for you to be concerned about, Lady," the servant assured her.

Blinking, she cleared her eyes and stared beyond the iron bars.

"Hektor. Oh Hektor, is that you?" she shouted while running towards the gate. Before reaching the iron bars, she demanded. "Open it, this instant."

Hektor was halfway through the entrance when Gabriella crashed into him. Squeezing him to her breasts, she cried softly.

"You brought Phobos home, thank you," Gabriella whispered. "He's gone Hektor. By the Goddess Algea, and her gift of pain, I miss him so."

"Lady DeMarco, I can't accept that he's dead," Hektor stated.

She pushed him back to the limit of her arms, stooped forward, and gazed into his eyes.

"Of course, Alerio is dead. Everyone, every report says it," Gabriella uttered. "How can you believe differently?"

"Before he sent me away, he made a Tribune's Oath," Hektor explained. From under his shirt, he lifted the chain with the Helios pendant and displayed it on the palm of his hand. "Alerio Sisera, as a senior officer of the Legion, swore to me that he would return home for all the things he loves. You, Lady DeMarco, Senator Spurius Maximus, Lady Aquila Carvilius, his birth family, and his new offspring. I am positive that he will present this necklace to his child when he returns."

Gabriella blinked away her tears, straightened her shoulders, and released the boy.

"Put Phobos in the stable, then come into the villa," Gabriella directed. "There's something about Alerio Sisera's son that you should know."

Chapter 24 – Off the Punic Coast

Alerio stood on the east wall peering out at the blue-green water.

"Your supplies were timely," Colonel Balint admitted. He walked from the ladder positioned at the nearest lookout tower. "If you were prisoners, how did you accumulate that much meat?"

"I convinced the building's owner that we needed work crews outside the city," Alerio answered. "We assigned more workers than the job required. The extra men hunted and fished."

"You're telling me your escape was planned?" Balint asked.

"From the first day," Alerio confirmed. "But we couldn't have completed the plan without the help from the Noricum infantry."

Balint's face sagged as he tried to comprehend how an Empire mercenary force aided in the Legionaries escape.

"It's a lesson in honoring commitments to auxiliary units," Alerio commented. "And in treating them with respect."

"Colonel, warships on the horizon," a lookout called down from the top of the tower. "They're coming from the east."

Balint and Alerio strained their eyes, but neither had the blessing of Theia, the Goddess of Sight, or the elevation of the tower.

"How did Centurion Palle die?" Alerio inquired.

"The Thracians came at us in the dark," Balint replied. "They got men over the wall and were attempting to open the gates. Palle led the attack that stopped them. During the skirmish, he took a sword strike to the neck. I was holding the inner drill field in case they broke through. One moment he was bellowing and encouraging his Legionaries. An instant later, the clash became surprisingly quiet."

"It appears Nenia took him quickly," Alerio remarked. With a glance at the morning sky, he uttered. "Thank you for that."

"Excuse me?" Balint inquired.

"It's nothing," Alerio said deflecting any conversation about his prayer.

"Empire ships-of-war rowing from the north," the lookout announced.

"I hope the Republic brought more than a few merchant vessels," Balint commented.

The coastal waters filled with Empire ships-of-war. They rowed by Fort Kelibia, heading south. Enough went south that a second line was formed from the ships-of-war heading north on their way back. The two columns slid by each other in unbroken lines of Empire ships.

"Lookout, give me a count," Balint instructed.

"Sir, we're guessing at two hundred and ten Qart Hadasht ships-of-war," the Legionary reported.

"That's trouble," Alerio remarked. He waved at three NCOs positioned in the center of the fort. In response, two signaled in the negative and Alerio reported it to Balint. "The Thracians haven't mobilized, Colonel."

"As long as they remain stagnant, we'll be able to watch the developments at sea," Balint noted. "If not, we'll be busy fending off an assault."

"More ships on the eastern horizon," the second lookout announced.

"Can you get a count?" Balint asked.

A few moments went by before the lookout reported.

"Sir, we estimate ten squadrons."

"Only one hundred warships," Balint said. "They'll be sunk during the first assault."

"Legionary, what's happening in the direction of Cape Bon?" Alerio asked.

"Sir, the Cape is sixteen miles to the north," the infantryman responded. "Even from the tower we can't…"

The men on the platform fell silent.

"What's the delay?" Balint demanded.

"Sir, there are Republic warships closing in from the north," the lookout answered. "It appears to be fifteen squadrons."

"Two hundred and fifty warships against the Empire's two hundred. Those are far better odds," Alerio stated. Turning, he waved at the men on the drill field. This time, three pointed at three sides of the fort. He reported to Balint. "Colonel, the Thracians are forming for assaults at the base of the hill."

"Are you all right taking orders from me?" Balint asked.

"Colonel, as I said before, I just want to get home," Alerio reminded him. "And to get my five hundred men off the Punic coast. Fighting for you to defend our position isn't a problem."

"I'll take the main gate," Balint directed. "You cover the other walls."

"Yes, sir," Alerio acknowledged. Then he shouted at the tower. "Study the sea battle. Later we'll need reports on the locations of the transports."

"Yes, sir," the watchers on the tower responded.

***

Alerio sprinted from one side of the fort to the south wall. As demonstrated the year before by his Legion Marines, the vulnerable blind spot required extra attention.

"Sir, you're wanted at the east wall," Remus alerted him.

After noting the Legionary in the tower waving frantically, Colonel Sisera ran back across the drill field.

"Sir, the transports are closer to shore," a watcher reported when Alerio reached the top of the ladder. "Some are full of light infantry, but others are empty. What do we do?"

"We imitate the God Mercury and speed from the fort to the beach," Alerio replied. As if he was the wing-footed messenger of the gods, he descended the ladder and raced to Colonel Balint at the front gate.

"We need an exit strategy," Balint responded when he learned of the transports. "I'll lead the vanguard."

"I'll take my five hundred men and guard your rear," Alerio told Balint. "I'll see you in Rome, sir."

"Yes, Colonel Sisera, you will," Balint promised.

The two Battle Commanders separated. Both held hope for the future in their attitudes and their optimism translated to their twenty-five hundred Legionaries. Soon fire consumed extra gear, creating a column of smoke rising above Fort Kelibia. In the smog that settled over the drill field, Balint waited with a Century of veterans tasked with punching a hole in the Thracian siege line. He couldn't see the gates through the fog but knew Sisera's five hundred crowded around them. The only elements missing were Colonel Sisera and the go signal. Those were at the top of the east tower.

"What do you think?" Alerio asked the watchers.

"The transports rowed in behind a line of warships then stopped," one answered. "They're still staged out there, Colonel."

"Who can blame them with so many ships-of-war present," the other Legionary added.

Signals, unseen by the Legionaries, changed the trajectory of the Empire ships. Those near the coastline pivoted and joined the other column racing north. In moments, the water along Kelibia beach cleared of enemy ships.

"There's the opportunity we've been waiting for," the watchers announced.

Alerio glanced northward and wondered how the Republic Navy was fairing at Cape Bon. But it wasn't his fight. He and Balint needed to get their men on the transports, and away from the Punic coast. If they moved fast enough, the outcome of the sea battle would have no effect on them. If they bogged down in a slug fest with the Thracians, a lost naval struggle would mean doom.

"God Mercury, lend swiftness to our feet," Alerio prayed before instructing the lookouts. "Abandon the tower and find your Centuries. This detachment is leaving Kelibia, one way or another."

He jumped on the ladder, placed his hobnailed boots on the outside of the rails, and slid to the ground. The dirt billowed around his feet when he landed. But none of the dust had time to settle on his boots as Alerio sprinted for his Centuries.

***

Smoke rolled from the fort when the gates swung open. Empire commanders noted the smog on the hilltop, but the gray haze hid the reason for the movement of the gates. They were puzzled until rows of shields appeared at the edge of the smoke on the western crest.

"Finally, they come out to do battle," an Empire Captain declared. "Bring reinforcements from the other positions."

Soon Thracians gathered at the western base preparing to prevent a breakout. Pulled from around the siege lines, the clustering left half the campsites of the siege line with only a couple of soldiers.

"Naevus, uncork the bottle," Alerio instructed.

The Foundation Mole kicked his horse and vanished into the fort. Moments later, a Century of heavy infantrymen with

Colonel Balint in the center jogged through the gateway. Making a sharp turn towards the beach, the Legionaries left the smoke and descended the hill.

"Do you think it'll work, Colonel?" Tullius asked Alerio.

"We got a nice size contingent waiting for us down there," Alerio remarked. "Did we draw many from the east side? I don't know. But we did pull them from the north and south of the siege line."

Following Colonel Balint and the veterans, the rest of the two thousand who survived Tunis emerged from the fort and fled towards the beach.

"Ten steps forward," Alerio ordered his detachment of five hundred. "Make it look good."

"Are we going to attack the Thracians, sir?" a Legionary asked.

"No. We're showing movement to hold them in place," Alerio told him.

After Tullius, Remus, and Albin issued the order, Alerio called them over. Naevus walked his horse to the meeting and Didacus, who had been relieved of his wagon duties by Centurion Gratian, the fort's supply officer, joined the group.

"We're going to be the last ones off the beach," Alerio informed them. As he talked, he unstrapped the armored skirt and let it drop to the ground. "Loosen the bindings on your shields and boots and lose your armor. In short, get as light as you can."

"It sounds as if you intend to swim to the Capital," Didacus challenged. Then he added. "The idea is absurd."

Before Alerio had a chance to respond, Remus put his hands on his hips and stated, "A combat officer's primary job is to kill the enemies of the Republic. Close behind it is the task of protecting his Legionaries. This much I learned even if you haven't."

Tullius nodded his head at the Master of Clay's remarks before poking a finger at the foreman.

"There's little opportunity for a Legionary craftsman to advance to Centurion," the Master Carpenter explained. "For one, our skills are too valuable. And two, we know it and behave accordingly. But what we miss are the moments when infantrymen put their lives into the hands of their officers. In those situations, you feel the weight and the pride of the position. Or, as you've demonstrated, you don't."

"I believe, Legionary Didacus, that the officers of my detachment have dismissed you," Alerio instructed. "You can fall in with the others."

He waved in the direction of the men jogging from the fort.

"Pure insanity," the foreman snarled. "You are Master Craftsmen, not combat officers. No matter what your Colonel says."

Naevus used his horse to separate the foreman from the others.

"Move along," the Foundation Mole directed. "This is a meeting for Centurions."

Didacus spun on his heels and briskly walked to the lines streaming from the fort. He blended in and was soon lost to sight.

"Are we swimming off the beach?" Albin inquired.

"Unavoidably, yes," Alerio responded.

***

The merchant vessels were almost uniformly mid-size traders. Sixty feet long with a fat belly that swelled to fifteen feet at mid-ship. And the most important measurement, they only required seven feet of draft at the keel, meaning the stern could reach chest deep water.

A wave of eleven merchantmen backed towards shore. Once their center beams touched the bottom, ramps were dropped into the surf, and fluttering oars held the vessels stationary.

Alerio observed the landings before turning back to the assault line.

"Hold the right," he yelled. "Don't let them come around you."

Uphill, soldiers batted at the retreating shields with spears and hoplite swords. While the Legionaries fought back sporadically, mostly they stepped back towards Colonel Balint's veterans. The rear ranks of the Thracians had long since given up on trying to inflict damage on the withdrawing shields.

At twenty feet from the beach, Alerio shouted, "Centuries, stand by to advance."

The warning order filtered through his ranks in four breaths.

"Brace. Advance, advance," he bellowed.

The retreating shields locked in place for a beat. Then a wall of flying scuta smashed the leading soldiers. They tumbled backwards into the relaxed ranks of their comrades. Tripped at the knees, none were ready when the plywood shields were pulled back and replaced by steel blades. While the first advance stopped the pursuit, the second killed an entire line of soldiers throwing the Thracians into disarray.

"Step back," Alerio ordered. "Step back."

The Legion assault line resumed its withdrawal. But this time, there was no pressure on their shields.

"Colonel Sisera, compliments from Colonel Balint," a Centurion greeted Alerio. "We have the soldiers pushed off the beach. Orders, sir?"

Alerio studied the shore and the second wave of transports that were loading Legionaries.

"How many more to get off?" Alerio questioned.

"I have two Centuries and your group for the third wave," the combat officer reported.

"We've got the beach," Alerio assured him. "Get your people staged for extraction."

The veteran Centurion cocked his head and paused. Then after a short period, he stated, "Thank you Colonel. I didn't expect to be relieved."

"I do need a favor," Alerio told him. "After the last merchant ship leaves, I need a three-banker to make a pass along the shoreline."

"Why's that, Colonel?"

"To pick me up," Alerio answered.

***

When the next rush of transports backed to the shallows, the veterans splashed to the ramps and climbed to the decks. On one, the Centurion spoke to the merchant Captain. Soon, flags flashed to a five-banker, playing sentry to the merchant vessels. The quinquereme passed the message to a trireme patrolling deep in the fleet of civilian boats.

"Why do they want us parading along the coast?" the ship's First Principale protested. "We should be getting away from the Punic coast as fast as we can row."

"Must be a final insult to the Empire by a Senior Tribune," the three-banker's Centurion said. Then a wicked expression crossed his face. "He wants us along the shoreline. Then we'll give him a show."

"Sir, what do you have in mind?"

"I want the tips of our starboard oars stirring up sand," the ship's senior officer replied. "Command wants us to make a pass. We'll make it the best triumphant display they've ever seen."

The signalmen had directions and a location but lacked any way to transmit specific details. Therefore, the command staff of the three-banker didn't know they were picking up and extracting a Colonel and his Centurions from the water.

***

On the beach, the Legion lines contracted as men streamed from the fighting to the waiting transports.

"Collapse your lines again, gentlemen," Alerio told his officers. Stopping one of the squad leaders heading for the extraction ramp, Alerio instructed. "Tell the merchant Captain to keep one vessel in place for our last row of infantrymen. But once they load, get the boat out of here."

"Sir, what about you?" the Lance Corporal asked.

"That's a question I've been asking myself all morning," Alerio admitted. "Go. Deliver the message."

The last row of shields had started ankle deep in the tide. Now they battled in thigh high water.

"Tullius, Remus, Naevus, Albin, on me," Alerio directed. Shifting to almost waist deep water, he guided the Master Craftsmen to a position in front of the last ramp. Then Colonel Sisera gave what might be his final order. "Legionaries, fall out and fall back to the transport."

Fifteen heavy infantrymen splashed by the five officers. A few saluted as they rushed for the ramp and safety. Other couldn't make eye contact with the Battle Commander and his Centurions.

In every engagement, breaking off while in contact proved to be the hardest maneuver of all. With the absence of three squads, the Thracians had no one to fight but they did have a target. A ramp filled with retreating Legionaries, defended by five shields held by unarmored men.

"This, sir, was a stupid idea," Naevus growled.

He dodged a spear tip and parried a sword thrust. Beside him, Remus hammered his scutum into a bold soldier, driving the man off his feet and under water.

"Too late to complain now, Mole," the Clay Master told him. "The transport is gone."

The deeper water did prevent the Thracians from surrounding the Legion officers. But their bodily movements were restricted by the water and the lack of balance reduced the effectiveness of their strikes. The redeeming feature was the Thracians had the same problems.

"What say you, Colonel?" Albin questioned. "Should we go for a swim?"

"I'm not ready to give up my shield yet," Remus answered. A spear thrown from shore where the soldier had good footing, jammed into the Master of Clay's scutum. "They have missiles and we have nowhere to go."

Noises of swish, splash, swish, splash came from Alerio's right. Resembling a multi clawed monster smacking the surface of the water, the sound didn't register. The four soldiers attempting to batter down his shield had the Battle Commander's full attention.

"Oh, oh, dip me in Hades," Tullius cursed. "Brace, Advance. And swim for your life."

It started in Legion training. Instant adherence to commands saved recruits from punishment. Later in their careers as Legionaries, they learned obedience saved lives. All Legion infantrymen embraced the idea.

Without questioning the Carpenter, the five men braced then shot their shields forward, driving the Thracians back for a moment. In that instance, they used their gladii to slice the bindings on their scuta. Abandoning the shields and their swords, they turned and dove below the surf.

The weight of their helmets pulled them to the bottom just as the keel of a three-banker passed over their heads.

Act 9

Chapter 25 – Before Dawn

"Hold water," the Third Principale yelled from the bow platform.

Below deck, the Second Principale picked up on the panic of the bow watch. Thinking it might be another ship or a submerged rock in their path, the trireme's second deck officer roared, "Hold water."

His one hundred and seventy oarsmen plunged their oar blades into the sea and held on against the strong current.

Moments before, the 3-banker flew along the coastline. On the foredeck, the third officer watched the features on shore zip by. The scene reminded him of a rope swing on his father's farm. As he swung the world blurred, just as it did when he attempted to focus on the Punic coast. Then a hill with fortress walls rose from beyond the beach.

He took in the smoke wafting from the structure, and the men standing on the walls. At the base of the hill, mounted officers posed stately on their steeds while their soldiers spread from the land to the beach and into the water. Oddly enough, the soldiers in the water formed a wedge pointing at five Legion shields.

"Hold water," he had bellowed.

One hundred and thirty feet of watertight oak, pine, and cedar simply did not stop immediately. The forward momentum buffeted the oarsmen as if their oars were thrust into a mountain stream. Even with all the oars in the water, the three-banker required two lengths of the warship to transition from full stroke to docking speed.

Running along the rails, the Third Principale searched the water for any sign of the five men with the Legion scuta. On the starboard side, a sailor performed the same task. Only he ducked spears and ran in a tucked position to avoid arrows.

"Third officer," the ship's Centurion challenged from behind a shield held by a Legion Marine. "You've exceeded your authority and stopped us within reach of Empire missiles. Can you explain yourself?"

"There are five Legionaries in the water, sir," the Principale answered.

Almost as a response to the pronouncement, five heads bobbed to the surface.

One spit out seawater and shouted up, "Took your own sweet time getting here."

"You can have that discussion later," another scolded. "Trireme, how about a couple of lines?"

Sailor tossed ropes over the side and the five men grabbed on and began climbing the hull.

When the men reached the rail, the Third Principale instructed, "Musician, set a rapid pace. Second officer set a rapid stroke rate."

From drifting within range of Qart Hadasht arrows and spears, the warship leaped forward.

***

Alerio walked his feet up the side boards while pulling hand over hand on the rope. Between the fight down the hill, the swim, and the climb, when he reached the rail, he fell to the deck exhausted, yet relieved. Lifting his head, he counted to be sure all his men made it out of the water.

"Centurion Remus, now you can chastise the ship's officers for being tardy," Alerio suggested.

"Colonel Sisera, I might kiss their feet in worship," the Master of Clay responded. "Other than that, they'll get nothing from me except my undying gratitude."

A pair of expensive sandals appeared in Alerio's peripheral vision.

"Who are you and why were you languishing in front of my ship?" a voice demanded.

Alerio pushed to his knees and wiped seawater from his hair before jumping to his feet.

"Colonel Alerio Sisera, Battle Commander for Legion North," he rattled off. "What's your name Centurion, and the name of your vessel?"

The ship's senior officer swallowed and hesitated for a moment to adjust his attitude.

"Sir, Centurion Marianus, senior officer for Occasio's Plight," the officer replied. "Welcome aboard."

"It seems appropriate that a ship named for the God of Luck would show up in my moment of need," Alerio stated. "I'll offer a sacrifice at the first opportunity. But right now, I'd like to watch the Punic coast fade into my past."

"Come to the steering deck, Colonel," Marianus invited. "I believe we can find dry clothing for you and your men."

"And vino, sir?" Albin inquired.

"First Principale, see to their needs," Marianus instructed.

He and Alerio strolled to the steering platform. The ships' officer consulted with his navigators while Alerio went to the rail between the steering oars. From the aft of Occasio's

Plight, he watched the Punic Coastline and Fort Kelibia sink below the horizon.

***

When Occasio's Plight caught up to the transports, the warship began patrolling at the rear of the fleet.

"Were you part of the original expedition, sir?" Marianus asked.

A sailor held a bucket of fresh water, a rag, a clean tunic, and a pair of sandals.

"We were," Alerio confirmed while rinsing the saltwater from his skin. In the breeze blowing across the deck, the water dried quickly, and he slipped on the garment. "At Tunis, thanks to the Goddess Clementia, we were taken captive."

"How does the Goddess of Mercy harmonize with being taken prisoner?" Marianus questioned.

Alerio hung his head and took a few breaths to calm his nerves. Once his heart rate returned to normal, he replied.

"Thousands of Legionaries were not taken," he informed the ship's officer. "They were butchered by the Empire after General Regulus surrendered."

"That explains the shifting expressions on your face as we rowed away," Marianus reported. "You seemed to alternate between a state of grace to one of fierce determination. Do you plan on returning to Qart Hadasht for unfinished business?"

"I have one goal, Centurion," Alerio stated. "And that is to get home to my wife and my child as quickly as possible."

"Consul Paullus agrees with you, despite arguments to the contrary."

"Who would argue against getting home as soon as possible?" Alerio asked.

"Our civilian transport Captains are worried about summer storms that blow off the Punic coast. They want a straight route to the beach at Agrigento," Marianus reported. "But the Consul has ordered a faster and more direct route to southern Sicilia. It'll force the fleet to sail overnight."

"When will we depart Pantelleria Island?" Alerio inquired.

"To make landfall in daylight," Marianus answered, "the fleet will launch before dawn."

***

Shortly before dawn, torches illuminated the steps of the senate building. City guardsmen from the Central Legion stood sentry as Senators and their retainers arrived.

"Spurius, I understand Marcus Regulus is finally going to address us this morning," Senator Lucius Longus mentioned to Spurius Maximus.

To avoid the crowd waiting for admittance to the visitor's gallery, the Senators and aides took the side steps up to the porch.

"That's the rumor," Maximus responded. "But Marcus went through quite the ordeal as you know. I wouldn't be surprised if he took a few more days before delivering his report."

Belen rushed ahead of the legislators and opened the door to the building.

"I, for one, am curious about what the Empire wants. Maybe we can end this frivolous war with a few buckets of gold," Senator Longus remarked. Then he gripped Spurius' elbow, halted their progress, and spoke softly. "Spurius. I forgot about Alerio's death. Please accept my apology for referring to the war as frivolous."

The two men stood silently a couple of feet from the open door. Finally, Senator Maximus spoke.

"Think nothing of it," he assured the other Senator. "You go ahead. I want to take in the morning air and clear my head."

"That's totally understandable," Longus allowed.

After Longus and his aide went through the doorway, Maximus stepped forward and whispered in his secretary's ear.

"Find out what bill or accord Lucius Longus holds dear," Maximus directed. "Then find a way for me to crush it."

"Yes, Senator," Belen acknowledged.

***

At dawn, the Senate began the session with a sacrifice of herbs, grain, and bees' wax in the form of a candle.

"God Aeneas, pious father of the Republic, hear us," the chairman of the Senate prayed. "Guide the Senate in our quest to be worthy custodians of the Roman State and wise architects of its citizens' prosperity."

A priest sprinkled herbs and grain on the altar. Then he lifted a burning brand from a clay fire box and touched it to the wick. When the candle blazed to life, the chairman banged his gavel.

"In the absence of Consul Paullus and Consul Nobilior, who sail with our fleet to save the remainder of our Legions, I announce the beginning of this session," the chairman pronounced. "Are there any objections?"

None of the Senators staged a protest. With silence as his confirmation, the chairman opened the session by indicating a man slumped in his seat on the second tier.

"The Senate recognizes Senator Regulus, a Proconsul, a General, a Consul, and an honored Citizen of the Republic," he proclaimed. "Please come forward and address the Senate and the people of Rome, Marcus Regulus."

Marcus uncurled from his seat. But one hand lingered on the backrest as if unwilling to lose touch with the solid travertine of his Senator's seat. After a pause, he lifted the hand and used the arm to brush back the hem of his robe, placing the appendage behind his back. Although a scholarly pose used by philosophers while expounding on universal truths, in the case of Marcus Regulus, it symbolized his putting the position of Roman Senator behind him.

***

"Citizens of the Republic, I come before you to plead the case for peace with the Qart Hadasht Empire," Marcus Regulus began once he reached the lectern. Several Senators shifted uncomfortably while others leaned forward in anticipation. Senator Maximus and his faction sat unmoving. Marcus continued. "During the Battle of Cape Ecnomus, the Republic's Navy captured sixty-four Empire ships-of-war. Each had a Captain and a First Officer from the noblest households in Qart Hadasht. These sons of the Empire and fathers of future generations were sent to Rome as captives."

Several Senators verbally confirmed the statement. They had the prisoners laboring in business ventures, having discovered the Qart Hadasht men were excellent with numbers and supreme organizers. Marcus let the voices pass on the facts before clearing his throat.

"They are the heartthrobs of their betrothed, the joy in their mother's breasts, and the pride of their sires," Marcus stated loudly enough to echo off the back wall of the Senate chamber. "The Empire misses its sons and will exchange peace for their return."

The reaction to the demand for the prisoners seemed reasonable to some. To the expansionist factions, peace wasn't a satisfying outcome to the war at any cost. For the financially minded, the exchange didn't compensate the Republic for the expense of the fleet or the Punic expedition.

"What else do the devils want?" Senator Colonna shouted from the third tier. He jumped to his feet and waved a fist in the air. "My son was there as a Tribune of Cavalry. He served with honor in Longus Legion North and later he was assigned to General Regulus' staff. At no time during the expedition did Tribune Ostentus Colonna witness any mercy by the Empire for our sons or our citizens."

"Does Senator Colonna wish the floor when Senator Regulus concludes?" the chairman asked.

"No, I'm just saying, they're asking for something they haven't shown," Colonna stated before sitting down.

The chairman waited until a few side discussions subsided. Then he encouraged, "Please, Senator Regulus, continue."

Marcus Regulus had a sour expression on his face as he glared in Colonna's direction. Those who noticed assumed Marcus was upset at the Senator voicing a position running contrary to the proposal. But Spurius Maximus wasn't sure.

"Belen, ask Hektor Nicanor to come over tonight," Maximus instructed. "I want to know what he remembers about Tribune Ostentus Colonna's service in Legion North."

"Yes, sir," the secretary assured him.

At the dais, Marcus ceased scowling and reclaimed his parliamentary face.

"Besides the return of their sons, the Empire asked for peaceful coexistence at specific towns on the west coast of Sicilia," Marcus explained. "They feel this is far enough removed from Republic territory to be of no threat to Rome's heartland."

"What about the islands of Sardinia and Corsica?" a Senator exclaimed. "They're both closer to our heartland than Sicilia."

His observation caused an outburst in the chamber. Scores of Senators attempted to talk over one another.

"The proposal didn't mention those islands," Marcus said in a small voice as if apologizing for the omission.

Most didn't hear him.

"They are staging areas for the invasion of Rome," another Senator thundered. "With Qart Hadasht bases there, this entire presentation is a waste of time."

"Please, Senator, if you'll allow me to finish," Marcus begged. The Senate chamber fell silent, allowing Regulus to speak. "And the third term for peace is a payment of gold as compensation for the damages our expedition visited on the Punic Coast."

Two thirds of the chamber erupted in anger with most suggesting retribution for the insolence of the Empire. Those against the war nodded agreement but remain silent for fear of being attacked by the other Senators.

During the tirade, Marcus Regulus stood stiffly at the podium waiting for the noise to die off. When it did, he began to speak but was interrupted.

"Save your breath, Regulus," Lucius Longus challenged. "I think we all know where you stand."

The chamber hushed and not even the eldest of Senators dared wheeze too loud. Longus had been Regulus' co-consul. And while Regulus languished on the Punic Coast, Longus came home early. In the tense silence, Spurius Maximus stood, raised his arm, and asked, "Chairman, a point of order."

"The chair recognizes Senator Maximus."

"Thank you. I have commanded Legions in war," Maximus stated in a soft voice. But as he spoke, the volume climbed until the visitors in the gallery leaned back from the force of his words. "Some of you have carried the mantle of General and have taken Legions into combat. But none of us have been as far, or as removed from Rome and the Senate as Marcus Regulus. Nor did we served a day longer than was proscribed by the rules of the Republic. General Regulus has done both. Plus, when he asked for a replacement, we denied him. Not just a Consul General but we ignored the end of his term and bestowed the Proconsul title on him. For these transgressions, I, the father of the dead Battle Commander Alerio Sisera, demand silence until the honorable General Marcus Regulus has his say."

"Point of order," the chairman called out. "All those in favor of ejecting anyone who disrupts Marcus Regulus vote now."

There was no need for a count. After the Senate's treatment of Marcus, the Senators were too embarrassed to vote against the motion.

"General Regulus, the floor is yours without interruption until you vacate the position," the chairman promised.

Marcus bowed in Senator Maximus' direction as a thank you for ending further interruptions.

"As I've stated, Qart Hadasht wants her sons back. They want the west coast of Sicilia," Marcus repeated the terms. "And they want compensation for damages. None of these are too much of a cost to end a war that bleeds our Republic of citizens and our temples of coins."

Marcus stopped and looked around the Senate chamber. Those in favor of peace nodded at his conclusion. And while many disagreed, none dared voice a response.

"The conditions of my release involved delivering these three terms to the Senate of the Republic," Marcus admitted. "I have done so with honor. Now I say to my fellow Senators, reject the items. Each will embolden and enrich the Qart Hadasht Empire."

The sounds of low growls raced around the chamber as Senators fought the urge to call out. Whether in support of or against the proposal didn't matter, for none could speak for fear of ejection.

"When I surrendered, I stood with three thousand of the best men Rome had to offer," Marcus boasted. "When I gave myself up, I believed we had an agreement. But alas, we had not. And before my eyes, the barbarians murdered almost an entire Legion of my men. But along with me, they took five hundred captives. The Senate can vote how it wants. As for me, at dawn, I sail for Qart Hadasht. There, I'll beg for the release of the last of my command. Thank you for allowing me to speak. I yield the floor."

Marcus Regulus marched from the dais to the exit, pushed open the door, and left the Senate Chamber.

Chapter 26 – Punta Secca Beach

Almost four hundred warships and over two hundred transports sailed throughout the day and into the dark of a second day. On Occasio's Plight, five passengers lounged around the foredeck. Two straddled water casks roped to the deck frame. The others sat on the edge of the forward platform.

"If we're in your way, let us know," acting Centurion Naevus told the deck officer.

"I'm perched here like a figurehead on an Egyptian trader," the Third Principale replied. "I'm mounted in place and just as blind. Take as much room as you want."

Out front of the three-banker, lanterns blinked across a wide vista. Each marked the location of a transport bobbing in the waves. The black water was separated from the starry night by an invisible horizon. Far away and out of sight even in daylight, the Consuls' flagships and the Republic's warships traveled out front. Left to herd the merchant vessels from behind were half a squadron of triremes and another five quinqueremes.

Tullius passed a wineskin to Alerio.

"You did it, sir," the Carpenter boasted. "All five hundred captives escaped. Congratulations."

"It wasn't all me," Alerio protested. "You four and the Goddess Athena made it possible."

"What does a Greek Goddess have to do with our escape?" Naevus inquired.

"Among her other blessings," Alerio informed the craftsmen, "Athena watches over heroic endeavors."

"Say no more, sir," Remus stated. He took the wineskin, hoisted it above his head, and proclaimed. "To the Goddess

Athena, because if there ever was a heroic endeavor, the last few weeks should be etched in stone for posterity."

"Or on clay tablets?" Albin teased the Master of Clay.

"Centurions, saving lives is difficult work," Alerio announced. "I'm going to roll up in this blanket and go to sleep."

"Good night, sir," the group responded.

Alerio located an empty spot on the top deck and lay down to the gentle flapping of the sails. Above, the stars twinkled. As he closed his eyes, he allowed a tiny bit of pride to swell his chest. Five hundred souls, as he promised, had left the Punic Coast and were on the way home. General Regulus' departing freed him from the oath and now he was heading home. With those pleasant thoughts, Alerio Sisera touched the Helios pendant under his tunic before falling asleep.

***

Flowing robes fluttered in the sky, but the Goddess was backlit by a blinding light. Alerio squinted trying to get a glimpse of her face. But the bright light and her hovering just out of reach prevented him from recognizing her.

Despite the distance, he felt a familiar pressure on his back.

"Nenia?" he asked while reaching out with both arms. "Is it my time?"

"No, Alerio Sisera. Your time has yet to come," her ethereal voice replied.

"Then why are you here?" he questioned.

She drifted closer until one hand caressed his cheek. Then the fingers traced down to his jawline before wrapping around his throat.

While squeezing his windpipe, the Goddess of Death whispered, "I'm here for the others."

***

Alerio sat upright and threw the blanket off. Gingerly, he touched his neck to see if there were any tender spots. To his surprise, there was no pain. Then he swallowed and his throat felt dry and raw.

A sudden thirst came over him and he climbed to his feet. The brisk flapping of the sails was absent as were the stars that dotted the sky. Staggering to the foredeck, he located the sailor on watch.

"What's with the weather?" he asked.

"I think it's the calm before a storm, sir," the crewman replied.

Alerio peered beyond the bow of Occasio's Plight. Where the lanterns on the transports had bobbed up and down, now they floated steadily on a black plateau.

"Do you have any water?" he asked the sailor. "I don't care to dodge sleeping figures by walking to the steering deck."

"You'll find a couple of casts tied to the deck supports, sir. We keep some water in them to plump up the barrel staves. But it's fresh rainwater," the man assured him. "The only problem, you'll need to uncoil the rope to free the barrel."

"I've never minded working for my food," Alerio told him.

On his knees, Alerio began uncoiling rope from around the cast. Obviously, the sailors on the Plight used the empty barrels as places to store extra lines. A mark of good seamanship, but it made for a lot of work. Alerio's thirst grew with each uncoiled length. Finally, the cast came loose from the support.

Alerio sat in the middle of the folds of rope, located the bung plug, pulled it, and lifted the caste above his head. Oak flavored, water ran down his throat. After three healthy swallows, he plugged the barrel and set it on the ropes next to his leg.

Then the wind howled. The sails snapped taut, the masts, both midship and fore, screeched in protest before snapping in half. Caught in the wind screaming across the deck, the barrel bounced to the rail, broke through, and fell.

Alerio reached for the foredeck platform to steady himself. But a coil of rope tightened around his ankle and pulled him across the deck boards. Before he could react, Alerio Sisera followed the barrel over the side and into the sea.

***

The wind, rather than gusting, rolled in as a physical mass. On land, a person encountering that type of wind would face the gale, hold their arms out from their sides, and feel as if they could lift off the ground. Unfortunately, the upper deck of Occasio's Plight had far more surface than a human body.

When the wind slipped under the boards, the decking acted as a giant sail. All one hundred plus feet of the deck caught air. In a mess of twisting and separating joints, the upper deck lifted, rocked over, and rotated the hull forty-five degrees.

A survivable happenstance for a sturdy trireme with a stout hypozomata. Except, the twisted hemp cable holding tension between the stern and bow sections of the keel had a frayed spot. When the deck separated, the sharp end of a cedar beam slammed into the broken fibers. The fibers split, unspooled, and the tension holding the three-banker together, vanished.

As if a basket was over filled with grain, the hull flattened, and the side boards exploded off the ship. The husk of the warship named for the God of Luck and Favorable Moments, her crew, officers, and Alerio's craftsmen settled below the surface. Then an enormous set of waves pounded Occasio's Plight into the depths.

Master Carpenter Tullius, Master of Clay Remus, Naevus the Foundation Mole, and Albin the Tool Maker had survived the battle of Tunis, escaped from Qart Hadasht, and fought their way off the Punic Coast. Fate, however, deemed that the four craftsmen would never reach home.

***

Alerio's first response was to untangle the rope and free his leg. Yet, when he reached down to his ankle, waves flipped him over in the dark soup. Dizzy from being tossed around, he focused on keeping his head up and catching breaths between troughs.

In a swordfight or a shield wall, no matter the intensity, there existed moments to ease off, to breathe, and to sort out events. A tempest allowed for no such luxury. A wave washed over Alerio's head, his mouth filled with saltwater, and the next lifted him. After spitting out the seawater, but too soon to catch a full breath, another crested over his head.

If he only had a chance to rest and collect his scattered thoughts.

The water cascading over his head drove him under. Then once again, he kicked with his legs, reaching for the surface and a taste of precious air. Rocked and rolled by the gale, Alerio lost track of the times he barely made it to the surface. One wave flowed into another as exhaustion stiffened his limbs. And his lungs sought deep breaths while only receiving grasps of air between wet punches. In a few more rolls and dips, he would inhale enough seawater to end the struggle.

If he only had a moment to collect his scattered thoughts.

No mortal could battle the ferocity of the Goddess Tempestas while resisting the peace of Neptune's watery grave. Befuddled by the threshing, Alerio did what people in stressful situations do, he returned to his original task. In this case, the removal of the rope from his leg. Dopey from the constant agitation, Alerio doubled over and reached for the hemp line.

Then, as if his arms had a mind of their own, he began reeling in the rope. For no reason he could fathom, the rope became more important than breathing. Hand-over-hand he pulled until his arm slapped the oak barrel. In a flash, he knew why he didn't untangle the rope from his ankle.

Gripping the belly of the cast, he clung to the wood. And even when a wave slammed Alerio and the barrel below the surface, it popped back up. High enough each time to reach the top of the waves where the air was clear of saltwater.

Suddenly, Alerio had a moment to collect his scattered thoughts.

Fearful the constant pounding would knock him unconscious, Alerio collected coils of rope until he could roll the barrel and lash his upper body to the curved oak. With his legs acting as the ballast, Alerio Sisera rode the storm through the rest of the endless night. In the morning, clear skies greeted the sole survivor of the three-banker, Occasio's Plight.

***

Sunrise gave Alerio a direction and, even though he ached from fighting the storm, he removed the coils. After looping the rope over his shoulder, he began swimming eastward with the barrel bobbing up and down behind him.

At first, he assumed another ship from the fleet would cruise by and he'd catch a ride. But the longer he stroked, the less confidence he had in the concept. Driving away the idea of rescue wasn't just the lack of ships in his vicinity, but the wooden debris. All shaped and cut for a purpose, but now broken and splintered, the oak, pine, and cedar floated just at the surface. When four oars crossed his lane, he stopped to gather them. Shaped from young fir trees the oars gave a chilling testament to the violence of the gale. In the vast empty sea, how many oars must be afloat for him to find four.

Any hope for rescue faded when he came across two more oars. But the fir beams gave rise to a plan. He had six poles, each thirteen feet long, a barrel, and rope.

***

The barrel made up the forward center of the raft. Tied to either side, the six poles extended back to where they were lashed together. It was barely seaworthy, awkward in appearance, and had room for only one occupant. However, behind the barrel where the oars came together just before crossing near their ends, they formed a dry surface. Alerio climbed out of the water, laid on his back, and gazed at the sky.

"A loaf of bread, a chunk of pork with the edges crispy from the fire, and a large mug of fine, red vino," he announced to the sky while touching the Helios pendant. Then he added one more item to his wish list. It made him laugh because of the composition of the raft. "And a paddle."

A memory of his training as a combat rower came back to him.

"A paddle is what you use to take your sweetheart out on a pond for a lazy afternoon cruise," rowing instructor Martius informed the students. "Warships use oars."

Alerio had plenty of oars. Rolling over, he labored to a kneeling position. Then he searched the water for a piece of lumber to use as a paddle.

***

Marcus Regulus stood on the steering platform of the big transport. The forward sail snapped in the morning breeze while the giant patchwork of linen at midship bellowed with wind.

"We'll reach Qart Hadasht in four days, sir," the Greek Captain remarked.

"That's agreeable," Marcus assured him, "I'm in no rush."

Marcus turned to peer back at Pozzallo. The last time he had been at the beach, he commanded a mighty fleet and Legions prepared for an invasion. Last night, his company had been the crew of the Athenian trading vessel.

"Navy warships," the Greek said nervously.

"I don't think they'll give you any problem," Marcus remarked. "I'm a Senator of Rome."

Not long after, a five-banker glided up beside the merchantman.

"Trouble, Senior Tribune?" Marcus asked a staff officer.

"Who are you?" the Legion Tribune inquired.

"I guess I still hold the rank as no one has informed me otherwise," Marcus replied. "I am Marcus Regulus, Proconsul of the Punic Expedition."

"Sir, I hate to inform you, the men extracted from Kelibia have been lost at sea," the Senior Tribune stated. "At this time, we are searching for surviving warship and transports."

"How did this happen?" Marcus demanded. "You saved two thousand men then lost them?"

The senior staff officer dipped his chin as if sad or embarrassed. In either case, he didn't correct the Proconsul on the number of men rescued.

"Sir, at last count, we lost two-thirds of our fleet to last night's storm," the senior staff officer reported. "Our best guess is over one hundred thousand men drowned. Although most were auxiliary forces, it's still a terrible loss of life."

Marcus's knees folded and the Athenian skipper gripped his arm to steady the Proconsul.

"How? Why?" Marcus cried.

"A storm, sir," the Senior Tribune replied.

"I heard you the first time," Marcus shouted at the Legion officer. Then, when his emotions settled, he inquired. "What do you need?"

"We're asking merchantmen to be on the lookout for survivors," the Legion staff officer responded. "Consul Nobilior is offering a reward for rescuing any of our sailors or oarsmen."

"What about the rescued Legionaries?" Marcus questioned.

"Sir, they were on smaller transports. None of them had a chance."

The vessels parted and the civilian Captain released Marcus' arm.

"You asked what happened," the Athenian stated. "The fleet's commanders went for expediency instead of listening to his merchant Captains. Anyone of us can tell you, between the rising of Orion and that of Sirius in this month, bad and sudden storms come off the Punic Coast. I guess they didn't listen."

"I guess they didn't," Marcus confirmed.

Marcus Regulus was as vigilant as any of the sailors. But as he scanned the sea, his mind wandered to the five hundred Legionaries being held in Qart Hadasht. Although he had no idea how, Marcus would try his best to secure their freedom. It was the least he could do for the last of his men on the Punic Coast.

At midday, the transport sailed by the beach at Punta Secca. And while the crew was on the lookout for survivors of the fleet, they failed to spot a floating spec far out to sea.

***

The rowers' bench, at least the end section, made an adequate paddle. All morning, Alerio rowed in the direction of the rising sun. Now, with the sun high overhead, he guessed at the direction by the heat radiating on his bare head. He added a felt petasos to his wish list.

As the water passed under the raft, Alerio began to worry that he was paddling in circles. The surface of the sea looked the same in every direction and his raft didn't move fast enough to create a wake.

For a moment, he thought he saw something moving on the horizon. But it vanished, and with no way to judge perception, it could have been a bird close in, or a ship far away. He rested at high noon and napped face down on the raft. When he woke, a feeling of hopelessness washed over him. Reaching over the side, Alerio scooped up a hand full of seawater and splashed it on his face. The raft moved up and down in the swells as Battle Commander Sisera laid exhausted and defeated.

But, Alerio had things to live for and had sworn to Hektor that he would get home. Plus, Marcus Regulus should be told that the captured five hundred Legionaries had escaped Qart Hadasht. Renewed by the thoughts, he picked up the paddle, dipped it into the sea, and stroked.

For some reason, when he resumed paddling, the raft moved quicker. By late afternoon, Alerio Sisera rode the tidal flow to Sicilia, arriving at Punta Secca beach with the high tide.

Chapter 27 – Premature Funeral

Stretching out for two blocks, the funeral procession demonstrated the end of a popular man's life. Adding to his fame, two drink-mules were employed to serve the mob of mourners. Other processions around the Forum of Rome stopped to allow it to pass. At temples, other funerals waited until the grand pageant left before going in to secure the God's blessing for their departed.

"He must have been a decent man," Alerio remarked.

Colonel Sisera stood with a group of citizens who were delayed in crossing the forum by the parade. Two men looked at the dusty clothing of the traveler. While still a Battle Commander, Alerio possessed none of the trappings. The sum of his wardrobe consisted of a robe of rough wool and an old pair of sandals.

"The procession is for the Hero of Qart Hadasht," one of them said. He eyed Alerio's poor garb and decided the impoverished man needed a lesson in history. "When the five hundred Legionaries were taken prisoner at Tunis, he organized them and kept the Latians together."

"Because of him, they are healthy and alive," the other man continued. "I was at the speech when Proconsul Regulus' praised the hero."

"They say his artwork is fetching astronomical prices," a third man added.

"As well it should, being drawn by the Hero of Qart Hadasht," said someone else in the crowd.

"I've been away from the Capital for a long period," Alerio told the group. "What's the hero's name?"

"He is Centurion Lophos," the second man answered. "Born to an artistic family, young Lophos began drawing early. When the Republic needed citizens, he answered the call and went to the Punic Coast as a Legion cartographer. After being taken captive, he threw off the mantle of the humble artist, and bloomed into a powerful force for his Legionaries. That's how he was described by Marcus Regulus."

At the thought of Centurion Lophos being anything except fat and lazy, Alerio laughed.

"See here stranger," one of the men challenged. "You keep a civil tone, or I'll thrash you."

Putting his hands up as a sign of surrender, Alerio backed up.

"I am truly sorry for the memory of Centurion Lophos," he stated.

Alerio turned and walked away. There were other routes to his villa rather than crossing the forum. While hiking towards a boulevard, Alerio contemplated going to Villa Regulus and letting Marcus know he was naming the wrong man as the hero. But he wasn't dressed for a social visit.

***

From the boulevard, Alerio took a side street, being sure to stay off the road. Men on horses and wagons came from either direction making it dangerous for a pedestrian to stray from the top edge of the ditch. The pace of Rome revealed the prosperity and vibrant commerce of the Republic. Alerio puzzled on that in the face of the expense of maintaining the fleet and the yearly funding of marching Legions. Yet, he had seen growth in the Capital of the Empire as well. War, it appeared, was good for business.

After leaving the busy street, he entered a new wealthy section of the city. Household guards at bigger villas eyed him suspiciously.

"Always good to be in Rome," he whispered sarcastically.

At Villa Sisera, he banged on the gate until a man-at-arms came from the stable.

"The servant's gate is around on the side of the compound," the guard told him. He pointed in the proper direction while questioning. "Do you even have a delivery? If not, I suggest you leave for the sake of your health."

"You're new here," Alerio commented. He'd traveled so far, and now home, he faced iron bars, and a surly guard. With attitude, Alerio demanded. "Who hired you?"

"Civi Affatus. He's the…"

"I know Optio Affatus, and I know Villa Maximus," Alerio assured the household guard. "Let's try this before I lose my temper. Is Lady DeMarco at home? Or maybe Hektor Nicanor?"

"The Lady of the Villa and Medic Nicanor are in the nursery," the guard stated. "And you should leave."

At the mention of the nursery, Alerio's temper flared. This fool stood between him and his family. Somewhere in the hot anger, a civilized part of him got control and he asked.

"Is the child all right?"

***

On the same morning Alerio arrived at his villa, Marcus Regulus stepped off the Athenian transport.

"Thank you, Captain," he said.

"I trust you'll find what you came for, Master Regulus," the skipper of the merchantman offered.

"There's not much hope of that," Marcus responded. "But I thank you for the intended meaning."

Marcus strolled to the end of the dock and flagged down a carriage.

"To the amphitheater of the Special Branch," he instructed the driver.

"Yes, sir, climb in," the driver invited. "First time visiting Qart Hadasht?"

"No, but its most likely my last," Marcus told him.

As the coach climbed Byrsa Hill, Marcus Regulus didn't notice the new buildings or take in the sights of the circular military harbor, the city's dockside defensive wall, or the ships sailing on Punic Bay. Rather, he studied his hands. To his disappointment, they shook, displaying his uneasiness.

Outside the market, he climbed down. Then, he inhaled the fragrance of spices from booths in the bazaar. When he realized he was intentionally delaying the meeting, Marcus Regulus turned his back on the market and marched to the guard at the entrance.

Unlike Alerio who was challenged at the gate to his villa, the Proconsul was ushered directly into the building of the Empire's Special Branch.

***

With little on the agenda, most members skipped the morning session. This left the amphitheater occupied by the most ardent members of the Special Branch. Adding to the fierceness of the meeting, the Empire had elected a more radical Suffete to replace Paltibaal. Marcus was escorted into this den of Punic lions.

"Have you brought ships loaded with our sons?" Suffete Ahirom jeered. "And cargo holds filled with our gold? My report from the harbor seems to be lacking that information."

Marcus Regulus stopped at the center of the witness area, spun his back to the members of the Special Branch and the Suffete. He faced General Bostar.

"After I surrendered, you ordered the murder of three thousand of my Legionaries," Marcus accused. "For that I curse your name."

"Proconsul Regulus, you will address the Special Branch," Ahirom demanded.

"Certainly," Marcus acknowledged. Facing forward, he inquired. "Will you release the five hundred Legionaries you have in captivity?"

"That's impossible," Ahirom snapped.

He didn't explain that the Latians had escaped. Plus, the new Suffete was taken off guard. Marcus Regulus, during the time he was a prisoner, had been placid and agreeable. The man before him seethed with rage. But that was fine with the new Suffete. He could be just as hard.

"If we dig them up, we could produce their ashes," he lied. "They were burned alive as sacrifices."

Marcus nodded but didn't bow his head.

"Alas, I only wish I could say the same for your sons. But they are treated well, based on their service to the Republic," Marcus said. "But know this. You will never reclaim that generation. They are lost to you. I suggest, if you can, that you get busy producing more slaves for Rome."

Every member present stood and shook their fists at Marcus while yelling for his death.

"Allow me to slowly push a dagger into his heart," a member of the Special Branch begged.

The Suffete raised his arms to signal for quiet.

"Speaker of the Special Branch, I propose a leather wrap for Marcus Regulus," Ahirom directed. "Please call a vote."

Rapping the staff on the tiles drew the members' attention to the speaker.

"All those in favor of death by leather wrap," he questioned, "raise your hand."

Every arm shot into the air.

"Let it be recorded that the Special Branch has voted death for Marcus Regulus."

Marcus lifted his arms to waist level and studied his hands. They didn't shake or quiver. He would accept his fate as a General of Legions. And face death with the name Vesta, the Goddess of the Hearth, and Protector of Rome, on his lips. For what else was he but a defender of Rome himself.

"Take him out and get him dressed appropriately," Ahirom commanded.

***

Alerio Sisera let his hands drop from the bars and allowed his temper to retreat.

"Please ask Lady DeMarco to see me," he pleaded. "I'll stand back from the gate and wait."

"She doesn't like to be disturbed when she's in the nursery," the household guard stated. "And she's in there a lot."

"I promise you she'll be happy you…"

The front door opened, and Gabriella appeared in the frame.

"Merula? Hektor said I should check the front gate," she said to the household guard. "Is there something I should…"

She stopped talking and stared at the man on the other side of the gate. Then she put a fist on one hip and sashayed to the gateway.

"You've been dead for months now," she mentioned when her face almost touched the iron bars. "Everyone in Rome said as much. Everyone except for Hektor. That incorrigible boy would not allow any mention of your death in his presence. He's quite stubborn, you know."

Tears formed in her eyes and fat drops began rolling down her cheeks.

"Are you going to open the gate?" Alerio asked.

"Corporal Merula Mancini is very forceful in protecting the Sisera Villa," she told him. "He's half Latian and half

Umbrian. Hektor says he's the perfect combination of warrior and professional Legionary."

"Does that mean I have to fight him to get in?" Alerio inquired.

"Oh no man of the villa, it means you can sleep peacefully in your own bed tonight," she promised. "Corporal, please open the gate for Colonel Alerio Sisera."

"Sir, I didn't know," Merula apologized.

He pulled a key from a pouch, inserted it in the lock, and removed the chain. Before he had the gate half open, Gabriella shoved him out of the way and flew into Alerio's arms.

"You stink, man of the house," she said between kisses.

"I thought about stopping for a bath before coming home."

"We have a bath here," she reminded him.

"You do?" Alerio remarked. "Would you have a loaf of bread, a chunk of pork with the edges crispy from the fire, and a large mug of fine, red vino."

"That and much more," Gabriella promised with a wink. "But first a bath and a change of clothing. Before you go into the house, I want you clean and dressed appropriately."

Act 10

Chapter 28 – Marcia!

The soldiers prodded Marcus with their spears when he slowed and tried to scratch through the shirt.

"It's called burlap, Proconsul," Ahirom identified the rough fabric. "The Egyptians eat the flesh of the jute plant and use the fibrous part to stabilize silty soil. We found it made excellent material for a punishment garment."

Marcus Regulus rolled his shoulders and twisted his back in attempts to stop the itching.

Only forty members of the Special Branch's one hundred and four members accompanied the condemned man and the military Suffete. But they were supplemented by citizens who learned of the execution. Sipping raisin wine and talking bravely, they added to the menacing atmosphere. Most had sons, fathers, or nephews held captive in Rome. They harbored no love or sympathy for the Proconsul.

After crossing Byrsa Hill, the procession descended to rolling terrain. Olive groves and clusters of other fruit trees lined the road. Beyond the orchards, grape vineyards stretched to either side of the lane. As the land began to flatten, vegetable gardens replaced the vines. Then outside the defensive walls, the landscape leveled, and fields of wheat stretched as far as the eye could see.

"You Romans think the power of Qart Hadasht comes from our ships-of-war and sea trade," Ahirom boasted. "They help, but our strength comes from agriculture and the richness of our soil."

Marcus' throat was dry and the fibers on his bare skin felt as if tiny bugs were dining on his flesh. He stumbled and, for an instant, got a hand over his shoulder and under the garment. Before he could scratch the irritation, the butt end of a spear pushed his lower back, and he stumbled forward. To keep his balance, Marcus threw both arms out to his sides. While he remained upright, the itching continued.

"My people taught Greeks letters, and perfected planting techniques to draw more crops from the fields," Ahirom explained. He indicated a farm with a main house, a stable, and a grain storage shed. The soldiers shoved Marcus off the main road and onto a path. With the long parade following, the Suffete expounded on an Empire farming implement. "One of our inventions is the threshing board."

Two structures resembling large doors that would act nicely as gates in a defensive wall rested against the shed. Both were constructed of heavy planks. Other than the obvious weight, the threshing boards didn't appear particularly dangerous.

"What are you going to do, Suffete?" Marcus said defiantly. "Sandwich me between the boards and let your citizens walk over me. It'll take a lot of steps before I die."

"Wrap him in leather," Ahirom told a soldier. Then to Marcus, he admitted. "You're half right, Proconsul."

Two farmers pulled one of the threshing boards off the wall and carried it to an open stretch of ground. They dropped it face up and walked to a stable.

Marcus swallowed hard. Curved iron blades protruded from the board.

"We tow this device over the cut wheat," Ahirom stated. "The blades rip the kernels of wheat from the stalks, allowing us to harvest and process more grain. Ingenious, don't you think?"

Marcus grunted as his arms were pinned to the side of his body and his legs clamped together. The soldier finished wrapping his body with the sheet of goatskin then tied it in place with ropes.

While the soldier finished binding the skin, the farmers returned with a horse. The beast was backed up to the threshing board and the harness secured to a pull ring.

"We do plan to insert you between two boards," Ahirom commented. "But we won't have to walk on it. Had you brought our sons home, your visit to Qart Hadasht would have been different."

"Three thousand dead Legionaries and five hundred citizens of the Republic held in slavery would disagree with you," Marcus replied. "Rome will never submit to oath breakers."

"I did speak with General Bostar. He made no promise of safety for your men," the Suffete informed him. Then he addressed the soldiers. "Put him on the bed of blades."

Three soldiers hoisted Marcus off his feet. They carried him to the threshing board and placed his body on the iron tips, leaving his head hanging over the edge.

"Hear my prayer," Marcus cited as the blades of the second threshing board were lowered onto his body. "Vesta, give me strength to…"

One of the farmers slapped the rump of the horse. Accustomed to dragging the blades, the draft animal charged forward. Using more force than was necessary to move the threshing boards, the horse raced over the ground. With every stride, the threshing boards bounced, and the blades meshed through the goatskin, the burlap fabric, and the human skin.

A prayer to the Goddess Vesta wasn't his final word.

Before the blades ripped into his body and the Goddess Nenia took the soul from his tortured flesh, Marcus Regulus screamed his wife's name, "Marcia!"

Chapter 29 - Olivia and Tarquin

"Gabriella!" Alerio cried out. "You'll peel the flesh from my back."

"Maybe I should get a Punic girl to scrape the oil from your skin," she said.

"Why would you do that?" Alerio inquired.

"Because you've spent more time there," Gabriella answered, "than you have here with me."

Alerio turned to face his wife and took her in his arms. Before gazing into her light brown eyes with gold flakes, he caught sight of the bath water and the rinse water.

"I guess I did need a good washing," he observed.

Gabriella pushed him away and smiled.

"You'll have your home coming later," she scolded. "For now, you must dress properly and greet the members of your household."

He yawned and his stomach growled.

"Later," she informed him when he pointed down at his stomach. "For now, get dressed."

A white linen tunic rested on a bench beside a yellow wool toga.

"So formal?" he asked while dropping the tunic over his head.

"The Master of Villa Sisera is home," she advised. Taking one end of the twelve feet of fabric, she danced around Alerio while wrapping him in the toga. With a flourish, she tossed the end of the cloth over his left shoulder. "And he must appear before them as a Patrician. Not a wandering vagabond."

"Do I look magnificent, like a Consul?" Alerio beamed.

"Mostly," she said while making a clicking sound of judgement.

"Just mostly," he challenged. "What am I missing?"

"Something in your arms," Gabriella replied.

He reached for her waist, but she stepped back.

"Not me," she corrected.

Taking his hand, she led him from the bath, across the courtyard, and into the main villa. Inside, Alerio found Merula Mancini, the household guard, and five servants. Merula saluted and the staff curtsied.

"Where's Hektor?" Alerio asked when he looked beyond the last servant. "I thought he would be first in line."

But Gabriella had left the room. When she reappeared from a hallway, she cuddled a baby in her arms.

"I'd like you to meet Olivia DeMarco Carvilius Sisera," Gabriella introduced him to his daughter. "I must warn you. She's energetic and grabs everything she can reach."

Alerio pulled the chain with the Heilos pendant over his head and dangled it above the baby. Her eyes widened as the bronze caught the afternoon light. He smiled at the gold flecks in her light brown eyes.

"This I pray for you, my daughter," Alerio intoned as he rested the pendant on Olivia's belly. "May you walk, for all your days, under a gentle and nourishing sun. And may Helios shine his light into the dark shadows and chase away any evil hiding within."

Olivia reached for the medal but could only manage to slap at the bronze with her right hand. But the small motion brought a smile to her tiny face.

"Now I have almost everything I love," Alerio stated. "Well, almost everything."

"I couldn't very well bring Phobos into the villa," Gabriella said. "The horse is unmanageable."

"I was referring to Hektor," Alerio corrected.

"Yes, well, about Hektor," Gabriella whispered. Then she called down the hallway. "Hektor, come in here."

The Greek boy entered with another baby in his arms. Alerio's mouth opened forming an 'O' as he followed Hektor's progress down the hallway.

"And just who is this?" he asked while raising his eyebrows.

"We've been trying to fatten him up," Hektor said. He held out his arms to display an undersized baby boy. "He just has no taste for food, Colonel. We've been forcing him to eat."

Alerio extended a finger and placed it in the baby's right hands. For a scrawny little one, the boy exerted a tremendous amount of pressure. After prying his finger free, Alerio placed it in the boy's left hand. With just as much strength as the right hand, he gripped the finger.

"You'll stop the force feeding as of now," Alerio declared.

Hektor faded back in horror and Gabriella stepped between Alerio and his son.

"How can you be so…?"

"Silence," Alerio roared. Then softly, he said. "I was a small baby and a weak youth. But I have an advantage. I am as equally strong and coordinated in my right side as in my left. My son has the same skills. Would you please introduce him?"

Gabriella took the infant from Hektor and spun to face her husband.

"I'd like you to meet Tarquin DeMarco Carvilius Sisera," Gabriella presented the baby. "While small, he is ambidextrous and handsome, just like his father."

"Hektor, you have something for me?" Alerio questioned. The Greek boy pulled the second Helios pendant from a pouch and handed it to Alerio. "Thank you, Hektor Nicanor. You should know, I'm pleased you're here."

"As I am to be a member of your household, sir," Hektor replied.

When Alerio dangled the pendant over Tarquin, the baby lifted both small arms, attempting to grab the medallion.

"This I pray for you, my son," Alerio chanted as he rested the pendant on Tarquin's belly. "May the God Helios shine on your fields so the crops grow. And may he glare over your shoulder and into the eyes of your enemies. Blinding them to the movement of your blades."

Alerio steepled his hands and rested them on the bridge of his nose. For several heartbeats he remained motionless.

"When I was in Qart Hadasht, the thing that kept me going was getting home to everything I love," he whispered. Then he dropped his hands and asked. "Now that I'm home, can we eat? I'm starving."

Chapter 30 - The Silent Wolf

A week later, Alerio Sisera paced the floor of his adopted father's office. The walls held mementoes of Senator Maximus' battles when he was a General of Legions. But the walls displayed nothing of his accomplishments as a businessman or a legislator.

"You seemed troubled," Spurius Maximus observed.

"Tell me, Senator, have you ever carried anger from the battlefield?" Alerio asked.

"I've hurt from losing men in combat. And I've been disappointed in the failings of my officers," Spurius Maximus admitted. "But that wasn't anger. More like frustrations. Why do you ask?"

"A lot of brave men died during the expedition," Alerio told him. He rested a hand on his dagger and attempted to crush the leather and bone handle. "While some underserving men slithered unscathed from what they did on the Punic Coast."

"And you're thinking about revenge?"

"I'm considering challenging them. But I'm a father and a husband who has been gone too long and missed too much," Alerio confessed. "I'm hoping you can talk me out of it."

"Wielding real power is not visceral like sinking a blade into an opponent's chest. Or as satisfying as a financial gambit where you match your coins against his," Maximus explained. "Exercising power is secretive and delivers justice unseen by the one visiting the misery. Oh, you'll observe stress lines. But you won't be in the room when he examines the ledgers and argues with his accountant over the losses. And you won't be in his bedroom when he cries himself to sleep at night from the loss of social standing. You'll need to be happy with the inability of bold men to look others in the eyes, and seeing proud men humbled. All while not gloating or crowing about their pain. Exercising real power is releasing a silent wolf to stalk those who have trespassed against you."

"I understand," Alerio assured the Senator.

"Then I'll teach you how to use power," Maximus promised before asking. "Are there many you plan to punish?"

Alerio removed his hand from the hilt of his dagger, took a sip of watered wine, and replied, "The list, sir, is short but deserving."

The End

A note from J. Clifton Slater

Thank you for reading Tribune's Oath. I have heard authors say writing books later in a series is difficult. While I can't argue the general premise, Tribune's Oath was a story that haunted me. The story fired my imagination and as I wrote, I couldn't wait to read what happened next. Let me know if it affected you as well. Right now, read on, we have a slew of notes from this book.

Until 255 B.C., the Generals who led Legions were sitting Consuls. Each had the authority to raise two marching Legions. But during the invasion of the Punic Coast, Marcus Regulus' term as Consul expired. To grant him the authority to command the four Legions in the expedition, he was given the title of Proconsul and overall commander of the Republic forces. In today's language, it sounds normal and even later in Rome's history there were commanders in far off posts. But in 255 B.C., it was a new idea for the Senate of the Republic to cede that much power to anyone not a Consul. But they did, and they kept Marcus in command longer than was routine.

Typically, in ancient times, the fear of a General becoming too powerful was a concern for the governing body. In Carthage, the Special Branch oversaw the Punic Generals, while in Rome the Senate maintained tight control over its military leaders. We don't know why the Senate of Rome failed to send a replacement for Marcus Regulus but Roman historian *Livy*, 64 B.C. – 12 A.D. wrote, '...*the Senate did not send him (Marcus Regulus) a successor. He complained in a letter to the Senate, in which he compared his request to a piece of land that had been left by its workers.'*

Fortunately for an adventure author, the situation leaves room for conjecture. Hopefully, Tribune's Oath handled the tragedy of Marcus Regulus properly. Although, I must confess to compressing the timeline to keep the historical events in 255 B.C. Marcus may have been held for as long as five years before his release.

Something else in dispute is how Marcus Regulus met his death after returning to Carthage.

Livy simply wrote that Marcus Regulus returned to imprisonment (in Carthage) and was executed.

Consul Gaius Tuditanids, 129 B.C., mentioned the torture and death of Marcus Regulus upon his return to Carthage.

Diodorus Siculus, Greek historian 80 B.C. – 20 B.C. wrote that the torture of Regulus was invented to excuse the subsequent torturing of two Carthaginian prisoners of war by Regulus' widow Marcia. I must be a romantic guy. Because I left that piece out of the story, preferring to focus on the love between Marcus and Marcia.

Tertullian, 155 – 220 A.D. wrote that Regulus was tortured and *Augustine of Hippo*, 354 – 430 A.D., added details of a box to the nature of the torture. Seeing as Carthage invented the threshing boards, I use them as the torture device in this story.

The battles on the Punic Coast have been streamlined for this story. In historical reports, the Carthage army took to the hills and sought to defend the high ground. The terrain removed their advantage of cavalry, light infantry, and war elephants while giving the heavy infantry of the Legions fixed targets. As I reveal in this novel, the fault lay with the Punic Generals.

Locating ancient battlefields is never easy. For the Battle of Adys, I measured the 40 miles southeast of Carthage as reported in history, looking for the town. No map showed Adys or, the alternative spelling, Adis exist in that location. However, a broad plain, the preferred topographical feature for both the Carthaginian and the Roman armies, was in the area. Using 40 miles around the Bay of Tunis from the Empire's Capital and 33 miles inland from Citadel Kelibia on the coast where the Roman Legions landed, I decided on the town of Béni Khalled, Tunisia. If you follow Alerio's adventures on maps, you can locate the site and land features I used for the battle of Adys.

The location for the Battle of Tunis was simpler. The town is there, and except for locating the Medjerda River, which was call the Bagradas River in ancient times, is easily identifiable on a map.

Nonnus of Panopolis was a Greek writer from the 5th century A.D. He wrote the epic poem The Dionysiaca. In Tribune's Oath, we hear Centurion Pelle tell Alerio about the love between Semele and Zeus and the death of Semele due to the jealousy of Zeus's wife Hera. The tale, although shortened, is straight from Greek mythology.

Elephants as war beasts can backfire. Historian Cassius Dio recorded that at Beneventum, Italy in 275 B.C., a wounded elephant calf threw off its rider and went searching for its mother. The other war elephants grew turbulent and created chaos in the ranks of Pyrrhus army while looking for the calf. The Roman Legions took advantage and defeated the

Greek King, ending his invasion of the Republic. All because of a young wounded elephant.

Xanthippus, the Spartan Tail-Leader (officer in command of a phalanx), had been hired by Carthage to train their army. Although I understand the martial power of the Spartans, I couldn't uncover what he was teaching the mercenaries. Then, I looked closely at who accompanied him to the Capital of the Empire. He took 40 men of a Spartan Enomotia, which translates to a Spartan phalanx. Therefore, Xanthippus was teaching the tightly packed phalanx formation when he was overheard disparaging the Carthaginian Generals.

At his trial, Xanthippus turned a sure conviction into being hired as the supreme commander for the Qart Hadasht army. I don't know how he did it, but being a writer, I created a scene where he turned the Special Branch and made it part of the story. As the Legions were only ten miles from the city walls, the Spartan's demand for gold payment was readily accepted. However, after the victory, Carthage leadership planned to assassinate the Spartan Commander and reclaim their gold. When Xanthippus heard about the strategy, he escaped with his Enomotia and the gold to Sparta. Hopefully, I did his story justice in this book.

The use of foundation walls and footers to support buildings dates to sometime after 644 B.C. For all the modern knowledge we have of material stresses and engineering practices, ancient builders were aware of the importance of transferring loads from the superstructure to the ground. Just as Naevus, the foundation mole described.

Hybris was the Greek Goddess of insolence, hubris, violence, reckless pride, arrogance, and outrageous behavior. While her blessings were seen as things to avoid, Alerio's song turned them into characteristics needed for the fighting escape.

In 255 BC, the Republic sent a fleet to extract the Legions from the Punic Coast. It's unclear if they knew that only two thousand of the original fifteen thousand men survived the Battle of Tunis. One answer to the question was hinted at by the size of the Republic fleet. Three hundred warships and two hundred transports vessels seemed excessive for the rescue of only two thousand men. I suspect they thought there were more survivors of the expedition. After defeating the Empire fleet, the transports boarded the survivors and sailed away from the Punic Coast. Off the coast of Sicily, the fleet encountered a severe storm. One hundred thousand auxiliary troops, Legionaries, Marines, sailors, and oarsmen drowned. Only a third of the fleet returned to Ostia.

***

I appreciate emails and reading your comments. If you enjoyed *Tribune's Oath*, consider leaving a written review on Amazon. Every review helps other readers find the stories.

If you have comments e-mail me.

E-mail: GalacticCouncilRealm@gmail.com

To get the latest information about my books, visit my website. There you can sign up for the newsletter and read blogs about ancient history.

Website: www.JCliftonSlater.com

Facebook: Galactic Council Real and Clay Warrior Stories

I am J. Clifton Slater and I write military adventure both future and ancient. Until we once again step forward and take our place in a Legion's assault line, Alerio and I salute you and wish you good health and vigor. Euge! Bravo!

Other books by J. Clifton Slater

Historical Adventure – *Clay Warrior Stories series*
   #1 Clay Legionary   #2 Spilled Blood
   #3 Bloody Water   #4 Reluctant Siege
   #5 Brutal Diplomacy   #6 Fortune Reigns
   #7 Fatal Obligation   #8 Infinite Courage
   #9 Deceptive Valor   #10 Neptune's Fury
   #11 Unjust Sacrifice   #12 Muted Implications
   #13 Death Caller   #14 Rome's Tribune
   #15 Deranged Sovereignty
   #16 Uncertain Honor   #17 Tribune's Oath
   #18 Savage Birthright   #19 Abject Authority

Novels of the 2nd Punic War - *A Legion Archer series*
   #1 Journey from Exile   #2 Pity the Rebellious
   #3 Heritage of Threat   #4 A Legion Archer

Military Science Fiction - *Call Sign Warlock series*
   #1 Op File Revenge   #2 Op File Treason
   #3 Op File Sanction

Military Science Fiction – *Galactic Council Realm series*
   #1 On Station   #2 On Duty
   #3 On Guard   #4 On Point

Printed in Great Britain
by Amazon